# Previous volumes in the Spoon Knife series

*The Spoon Knife Anthology: Thoughts on Compliance, Defiance, and Resistance*
> Edited by N.I. Nicholson and Michael Scott Monje, Jr.

*Spoon Knife 2: Test Chamber*
> Edited by Dani Alexis Ryskamp and Sam Harvey

*Spoon Knife 3: Incursions*
> Edited by Nick Walker and Andrew M. Reichart

*Spoon Knife 4: A Neurodivergent Guide to Spacetime*
> Edited by B. Allen and Dora M. Raymaker with N.I. Nicholson

*Spoon Knife 5: Liminal*
> Edited by Andrew M. Reichart, Dora M. Raymaker, and Nick Walker

*Spoon Knife 6: Rest Stop*
> Edited by B. Martin Allen and J.S. Allen

# Spoon Knife 7:
# Transitions

Edited by

Nick Walker & Mike Jung

Weird Books for Weird People

*Spoon Knife 7: Transitions,* Copyright 2023 **Autonomous Press, LLC** (Fort Worth, TX, 76114).

Neuroqueer Books is an imprint of Autonomous Press that publishes fiction, poetry, memoir, and other literary work, with a focus on themes of queerness and neurodivergence.

Autonomous Press is an independent publisher focusing on works about neurodivergence, queerness, and the various ways they can intersect with each other and with other aspects of identity and lived experience. We are a partnership including writers, poets, artists, musicians, community scholars, and professors. Each partner takes on a share of the work of managing the press and production, and all of our workers are co-owners.

ISBN: 978-1-945955-40-2

Ebook ISBN: 978-1-945955-41-9

Cover art by Tim Molloy

Book design by Casandra Johns.

# Contents

**Mike Jung**

# *Prologue*

I'll launch this prologue like a tiger leaping boldly through a ring of flame: existence *is* transition. Okay, yes, others have said it before, I know - Heraclitus, for example, with his old-timey nugget of wordsmithery, "The only constant in life is change." Speaking for my own fabulously autistic self, transitional processes are far more complex and granular than a lot of people seem to think they are.

The example I've often vivisected in conversation is getting out of bed in the morning. Does one simply get out of bed? Perhaps it's more like throwing back the blankets and getting out of bed. But what if you actually lie there, resentfully contemplating some externally imposed need to get out of bed, throw back the blankets, *then* get out of bed? Maybe it's the process of assessing the splintered matrix of fluids, mineral crystals, ossified connective tissues, protesting bones, gravity-induced angles, runnels of memory (both old and new), spicules of intention, inertial drag, emotional dust devils, and all of the other, numberless murmurations of thought and feeling that constantly accompany some of us through life, determining an order in which to begin moving the necessary body parts, throwing back the covers, *then*, finally, getting out of bed.

And what if the prosaic bricks in the walls of those arbitrarily defined transitional processes are more than they appear on the surface? They may contain the dust of history, or the blood and bones of ancestors, or the vestigial remains of ancient arts that seem lost but are merely dormant. They may contain spirits; enchantments; worlds within worlds. They may also contain purely internal thoughts and feelings, which of course can comprise worlds within worlds in their own right.

How far can we push the definition of the word "transition"? Can it extend to the edge of human consciousness? To the borders of known existence? To places farther outside and deeper within ourselves than previously imagined? My answer is yes, and the stories in this collection are among the reasons why.

Welcome to Spoon Knife 7.

**Nikoline Kaiser**

# *Sprout*

It is what her father always called her. "Little Sprout." She would sprout up, they said, appearing out of nowhere like a flower suddenly blooming when midnight fell.

"We should have named you for a flower," he used to say. Jasmine, Violet, Lily, or just Flora, all of it, every flower in the world. But she was named Vera instead—like Latin for "truth," her grandmother always said. Like an actual grandmother, Vera would respond, because who had ever heard of a young girl named Vera? No one her age was named Vera, it was just her, the little grandmother in the guise of a young girl. A little sprout who should have been an ancient oak already.

The nickname became even more apt as Vera kept sprouting—kept growing and growing, until she was as tall as her father, could look him right in the eye when she was a teenager throwing a tantrum; much more satisfying than if she had to crane her neck to look at him or worse, had to get a stepladder.

She was fifteen when she met Tuuli for the first time. Tuuli with her wild, dark-brown hair and green eyes, Tuuli from Estonia who spoke in a lilting, clumsy accent that others snickered at and Vera found beautiful, beautiful, beautiful. It had been six months since Vera had sat in a movie theater, overwhelmed at a woman in a bikini and realized the reason the boys in her class didn't turn her head was not so much because they were stupid (they were), but because no boy would turn her head, ever.

She'd gone to her father first. "What if I brought home a girlfriend one day?" she'd asked, and he had lowered the book he had been reading and squinted at her over his moon-shaped glasses.

"You could bring home a tiger, so long as it made you happy," he said and went back to reading. The book looked tiny in his hands, not just because his hands were big, but because the book was small. It wasn't the answer Vera had looked for, but it was good enough.

"Oh, is there someone?" her mother asked when she went to her next, and Vera could honestly say no. Her grandmother had been hanging up the laundry outside even though the sun was refusing to come out between pillow-white clouds, when Vera went to her last.

"I knew a lesbian once," her grandmother immediately said. "She was lovely, but she looked like a man. You're not going to cut your hair, are you? It's so beautiful. Ah, if you do, get a professional to do it. You don't want it to look a mess."

It wasn't discussed again, because there wasn't much to discuss. Her father would ask about the classmates she greeted walking down the streets, girls now instead of boys. ("Is she nice?" "Yes, dad, it's just Amy, I have gym with her.") It was six months later when Vera realized the book her father had been reading, flowery and pink between his hands, had completely passed her attention by. She had been nervous when she first approached him, but now she scoured the house and couldn't find the book at all, and curiosity gnawed at her.

"What was that book you were reading?" she asked, and he gave her a look because her father was the Reader of the House, always with a book in hand, on the couch, in bed, when he cooked, when he was waiting in the doctor's office and said "half a page, I'm almost done with this chapter" to the nurse who called his name.

"Be more specific, please."

She described the book as best as she could remember, and he walked up and over to the shelf where she'd been looking an hour earlier, and there, the bright pink spine stuck out, the book with the colorful flowers.

"By Shahrnush Parsipur," he said. "*Women Without Men.* It's a very strange book. A woman starts seeing all men as headless. Another woman plants herself as a tree in the garden."

Vera took the book gingerly, as if it weighed a ton. It didn't weigh a thing, it felt like. "Why does she do that?"

"I don't remember exactly. She was sad."

Vera meant to read it, this small book her father had been holding when she'd told him a hitherto unknown secret, but the next day she met Tuuli.

•

Tuuli who wore turtle-shell glasses.

Tuuli whose hairbands broke if they weren't industrial strength steel.

Tuuli with patterned sweaters in pale colors.

Tuuli who joined the girls' basketball team even though she was tiny.

Tuuli who looked surprised the first time Vera smiled at her, but smiled back after a moment.

Tuuli who took notes in class with different colored pens, green for Biology, blue for English, black for Math.

Tuuli who wanted to be a biologist and could answer every question in their class.

Tuuli who answered freely about her ex when asked, a girl, a girl, another girl. Tuuli who defied the attempts at jokes the others made, who stared at them blankly or asked for clarification until they were stammering over their own explanations. Tuuli who asked to be paired with her in a project for Biology. Tuuli, who explained the theory to her in a way so she finally understood it. Tuuli, who didn't say 'Vera' right, but she didn't care because it sounded better coming from her mouth. Tuuli, who invited her home for dinner. Tuuli who convinced her to join the basketball team even though she was bad at sports, because she was tall. Tuuli who insisted Vera should invite her home when she heard of the vast library of books living there. Tuuli who let Vera's father talk for an hour and a half about what he was reading, before Vera dragged her away up to her room. Tuuli, who told her she didn't really care that much about it. Tuuli who just wanted an excuse.

Tuuli who kissed her.

•

It was a Thing until it wasn't. The looks from the rest of the school, the whispers behind their backs. The way some of the other girls would smile at her, strained, in the bathroom or locker-room, as if worried or just uncomfortable. As if she was now fundamentally different, an unknown and a trespasser. The boys made crude jokes until a teacher put a stop to it, and then they only made them when a teacher wouldn't hear. The novelty of it quickly fizzled out, though. Vera held Tuuli's hand when they walked home after school, and Tuuli kissed her when they were at her house or at Vera's house, and they danced together at the spring festival and another girl bumped into them and told them they were brave and wonderful, and then was whirled away by her boyfriend, grinning.

When they were seventeen the novelty had worn off for them as well, and fighting became the norm. Tuuli talked too much about basketball. Tuuli talked too much about the mink they'd dissected in school. Vera forgot to call. Vera spent too much time with Amy, who had interrupted their dance. Tuuli didn't tell her when she was upset. Vera was negative about everything to do with school. Tuuli wanted a cat when they moved in together (when). Vera wanted a dog when they did (when). Tuuli wanted to get her degree back in Estonia. Vera couldn't imagine living there, when she didn't even speak the language.

When Vera was almost eighteen, eight days to the big day, her grandmother asked: "Who is the man in the relationship?"

They were sitting together at the garden table outside, rinsing strawberries in a big bowl of water, cutting them into neat slices. It was their summer ritual, and already Vera could feel the sunlight stretching the skin of her face. She had forgotten to put on sunscreen, but now her hands were wet and sticky with the fruit, and she did not want to interrupt their annual moment. Not until her grandmother spoke, at least.

Vera nearly flipped the table over, but she managed to stay calm. "Neither of us, grandma. That's the point."

"Oh, I see. What about children then?"

"What about them?" Vera asked, biting out the words.

"Do you think you'll want them?"

"Grandma, I'm not even eighteen yet."

"Eight days," her grandmother reminded, warned her.

"I'm not going to have children as soon as I turn eighteen."

"Well, no, of course not. I just think they would be so lovely, the children you two would have."

Some of the fight left her. "Do you like Tuuli?" she asked, even though her grandmother had never given any indication that she didn't.

"I simply adore her," she answered, predictably. "Why? Do you not like her anymore?"

Vera didn't know how to answer that. "Would you... would you like it better if I didn't?"

"What in the world does that mean, girl?"

"Would you like me better if I got a boyfriend? If I was normal?"

Her grandmother looked, truly, flabbergasted. "What's that got to do with anything?"

The rest of the fight, gone. Vera wanted to curl up, but she could not move. A piece of strawberry had wormed its way under her nail, fresh red, like exposed skin. Her grandmother's hand was on her shoulder, weighing nothing, nothing at all.

"Did you think that?" she asked, and she sounded sad.

Vera shook her head lightly, not wanting to move too much. "Not really. I don't know."

"I told you I knew another lesbian. She was lovely."

"Like Tuuli?"

Her grandmother patted her head. "Like you."

·

Vera was turning eighteen and Tuuli had bought her a pair of expensive earrings she'd stopped to look at in the storefront window, and then insisted she didn't want when Tuuli offered to pay for them. That had been four months ago. She broke down crying in front of everyone, and Tuuli and her mother had to tug her away from the party-guests, who all tittered in amusement, except for those who tittered in worry.

"Did she not like them?" she heard her grandmother ask her father. "I think they would look lovely on her."

They ended up in the kitchen, her mother making noise as she made more lemonade, Tuuli holding Vera's hands, the earrings in their box on the kitchen counter.

"Did you not like them?" Tuuli asked. "What's wrong?"

Vera wiped her nose with a napkin meant for the table outside. "We fight all the time."

"Yeah, but there's been a lot. We're finishing up school, it's stressful."

"That's not an excuse."

Tuuli squeezed her hands. "It's a reason. I'm sorry, I've made you feel bad. I'm really sorry."

"I'm sorry, too," Vera said, and then. "You're leaving."

"I don't know if I'll leave yet. I've applied for some places here as well."

That soothed her, but she'd known that already. "I'm too negative about everything."

"Well, you're a pessimist. I knew that already. I'm a relentless optimist, I imagine that's annoying, too."

"You think I'm annoying?"

Another squeeze, harder. "Of course I think you're annoying, Vera."

"Oh."

Tuuli's brow furrowed. "You think I'm annoying sometimes, too, right?"

"Sometimes."

"I'm... I don't think you're annoying all the time, Vera!"

"Oh, good."

"Did you really think that's what I meant?"

Vera shrugged. "I don't know. We fight a lot."

"Because we're stressed. And because it's not new anymore. And because we're young and stupid."

"My parents don't fight as much."

"Yes, we do," her mother said, then blushed and quickly went back to her lemonade. Vera wasn't sure they needed that many pitchers of it. Her mother seemed reluctant to leave. Eavesdropper, Vera thought.

"I'm sorry," Tuuli repeated, and Vera realized she had to say it too. Had to. Wanted to.

"I'm sorry, too." She sniffed again, her nose protesting when it met the harsh surface of the napkin one more time.

"Did you not like the earrings?"

Vera reached for them. "I love them. Thank you. I'll never take them off." And she repeated. "I love them."

•

By age nineteen, they said goodbye. They had broken up three months before the date of Tuuli's return to Estonia, where she would study Biology and follow the dream she'd had since she was six years old. It didn't mean they'd acted like they were broken up, because it was difficult to stay away when you were within walking distance—and a trip to the other's house to watch a movie didn't stay platonic, nor did walks in the forests or basketball practice or parties with their friends.

In the airport Vera cried less than Tuuli, who seemed nervous about leaving her parents and the life she'd built here and hadn't slept at all the night before, but instead laid open-eyed next to Vera in her bed, the two of them shoulder to shoulder. Vera had woken every time Tuuli had shifted, and asked her if she'd slept. The answer was always no.

Vera had cried her fill in the days leading up to the departure. She'd locked herself in the bathroom until her mother demanded she get out and eat dinner or get out so she could use the bathroom for its intended purpose, which was peeing and cleanliness and not homosexual sobbing. She'd laid in her bed with her face burrowed into a pillow that smelled like Tuuli's shampoo, and her father had sat on the edge of the mattress and gently rubbed her shoulder and said, "I know it's hard, but it will be alright. A hurt heart will heal with time."

*It's okay to feel the hurt, little sprout,* he'd always said, when she was younger. *It hurts now, but it won't always. It will be okay. You will love again.*

At the airport, she hugged Tuuli so tight she thought her ribs might crack (hers and Tuuli's both), and she felt the pull deep in her stomach as she walked away, like a tether holding them together, together, together; until they were finally far enough away from each other that it snapped, leaving behind an echo-filled void of no sleep and no hunger and no thirst.

For long months, everything became less, as if the world had found itself a sepia filter and put it on like a coat. Vera woke up every day missing Tuuli, missing her wild curls and the bow of her upper lip and the sweat on her neck when they'd gone for a run. Eventually, the missing became less, too. They would call each other, until that became a *less* as well. Then less texting, less e-mails. Less and less. And less. Until it became enough, somehow. She knew Tuuli was doing well. She was happy. Vera told herself she was doing well, too, even if she felt listless and unable to decide what she wanted to do with her life.

Two days before she turned twenty, Vera became an orphan.

•

A truck had upended. There was nothing to be done. Safe driving. You can do everything right. You can only be so careful. Until it's out of your hands. And with someone else. Your life, in someone else's hands. Someone who has learned how to drive but never really learned the dangers of the road.

It was only Vera and her grandmother in the house now, though other people came by, in flocks and then in trickles. It never stopped completely, but Vera breathed a sigh of relief when the last horde of well-wishers and sorry-bearers left and she could close the door.

Tuuli called. And called again. Vera didn't pick up the phone the first many times it rang. When her grandmother complained of the noise, Vera pushed the phone towards her, and she answered it instead. Vera left the room so she didn't have to listen to her grandmother's soft voice talking to Tuuli, wouldn't have to hear the tinny, far-away version of her ex-girlfriend giving her condolences.

After, her grandmother came into her room. "She wanted to come for the funeral. I said it wasn't necessary, she should stay. Do you want me to call her back and tell her to come?"

Vera shook her head. "You did the right thing," she said. She could not fathom Tuuli being here, now. She would be too happy, she decided, to see her again. And she should not be happy now, when both her parents were gone.

Her grandmother was reluctant to leave the room, hovering by the chair Vera had huddled up in, finding words she could keep speaking so she did not have to go. "She's changed studies," she said. "She's becoming a botanist."

Perhaps that was it, what gave Vera the idea. Beneath the surprise, shock even, of learning that Tuuli was veering off the path she'd had for most of her life, was a faint recollection. The book her father had been reading, that Vera had forgotten all about.

The woman who had planted herself as a tree.

The garden became her sanctum after that. She would sit outside every moment she could get. People stopped by with food and flowers, flowers and food. Amy appeared as if conjured from nothing, with lilies and a book about grief. She came out to sit with her in the garden, both of them cross-legged on the grass.

"Are you sleeping okay?" she asked. Vera wondered if she had read that in the book, about people not sleeping well.

"I don't sleep much, but I get a little," she said. She only slept in fistfuls of naps, always outside on the grass, lying in the shade of the roof or further out in the night, under the starry sky. She only left the garden to go inside and speak with her grandmother, make sure she was eating. Vera did not eat, only pushed her food around or put bites in her mouth so her grandmother would not worry too much. She found that she did not need to eat, not anymore; her body had become a battlefield. It might grow new grass after the fighting was done, but anyone who knew, who looked at it, would see the same battlefield, as if the thing had been locked into place, timeless, immortal. Always that, before it was anything else. Vera felt she was that now, a thing that stood still that could not change no matter how much it might appear to. She would be a battlefield, forever, and battlefields did not eat.

"Are you eating?" Amy asked, as if reading her mind.

"A little," Vera lied. Tuuli had tried to call her again that day, and she had not picked up. She spent her days looking at clouds and stars, staring at the trees her mother had tended when she was still alive. There seemed to be so many of them now, a forest-line of defensive branches reaching out to hold the sky back, or perhaps to hold her there, keep her in the garden. Keep her with them.

She didn't need to eat. She stopped sleeping. She drank the glasses of water her grandmother gave her, and left the book Amy had brought on the grass next to her. The rain washed her body when it was necessary. When her clothes became too heavy and warm in the summer, she shed them: her shirt caught by her ear, and she gently extricated it. The earrings dangled against the side of her head; she had forgotten she was still wearing them. No matter, they did not bother her. They could stay. She folded her clothes neatly, put them on the grass too. If her grandmother was calling her from inside, then she could not hear her. She should come outside, Vera decided, if she wanted to talk to her. Outside where she was meant to be, among the trees. The trees—yes, she remembered the trees and the book.

Planting yourself was far easier than she might have thought. She had already grown roots sitting so long in the grass, had already felt the dirt against her skin and found that she could find nourishment deep below-ground, where the furthest waters ran their course. Vera did not know if a tree could feel grief or love or longing—if you had asked her a year ago, she might have said that they could, in their own tree-like way. It was not the way a human would feel it, she knew that for certain. A tree's first priority was to get water for its root, pump it up through the trunk and into those long fingers it called branches. It should reach the leaves, green in summer, yellow and red in autumn. It should let them fall when winter came, let the earth eat them. That would be her grief, her love, her longing, Vera decided. Tiny leaves on her reaching branches, dropping one by one, disappearing into the dirt. She could be here, in the garden, forever. There were already so many trees planted right here: why couldn't she become one, too? Shedding her leaves. Shedding all of it.

●

Vera found that seasons started becoming both more and less significant when you were a tree. Christmas did not matter. The winter-snow did, and how harsh the wind became. Before that, autumn had hit her like a sledgehammer, a deep sigh resounding from the earth below, from its very core, letting her know that now the struggle, the waiting, the enduring began. It was no longer summer. It meant reaching deeper for water. It meant holding your breath and waiting. It was hibernation—exactly what she had longed for. Here, in the deep, deep slumber of a tree waiting for spring, she could finally rest. And if people talked, if the earth tasted salt and bitter with her grandmother's tears, then what did that matter? She was a tree. The leaves were her children, her roots the steadfast way of nourishment, and that was all that she needed. She would grow taller, would grow ancient, and in decades worth of time, such a tiny amount to her, all of this would no longer matter as it had the day she had planted herself. She had done it, little sprout, she had sprouted branches and leaves and now she stayed, stayed, away from the road that goes on and on and on until it stops, suddenly, endlessly. Stops. She was not like the house, that was now fallen into disrepair: she was tall and strong.

Even as a tree, Vera sometimes wished that she still had a mouth, so she could tell her grandmother that she was alright. So she could say: see, the garden is better, is best. The garden was still beautiful. It seemed to be the one thing her grandmother did pay attention to, and Vera wished she would just plant herself, too, would grow beside her and they could Be and not have to worry about whatever it was they had worried about before. They could grow tall beside one another. How tall could she grow? She did not know. She wished to find out. She had all the time in the world and all she had to do was stand here, and let the wind rustle her and then she would sleep in the winter, wake in the spring.

It was the digging that woke her. Spring had come, but her slumber was still long, expanding for hours and breaking only when birds landed and she had a few minutes of saying hello to another creature, such a tiny one, with a small heartbeat and a curious beak. Her grandmother had planted seeds the day before, tall flowers to grow all around her, and she had been delighted, though her grandmother had seemed so sad. Why would she be digging now? Had it been the wrong seeds, the wrong kind of flowers? It was the middle of the night, why was her grandmother digging—and who was that with her?

Her feet were cold, Vera realized. Buried deep below, lapping up water, her toes and feet were freezing cold. And her arms were sore, from being held aloft for so long. She felt dizzy, fingertips tingling and knees buckling under a new weight—no, not a new weight or a heavier one, but just *her* weight, the effort of standing still for so long, the shock of being lifted, up, roots and feet and shins out of the earth. She was collapsing forward, but she did not land on the hard ground, only because someone was holding her, cradling her in their strong arms. There was her grandmother, with dirt on her hands, and holding Vera tightly was…

Tuuli.

"There you are," she said, and Vera blinked at the stars and clouds that haloed Tuuli's head. Had her eyes always been so green, even in the moonlight? And how was she here, now, right now. "I was so worried, Vera. But there you are."

And it did not matter, then, how she had come here, because she was here, now. All Vera could think to say was: "How did you know it was me?"

And Tuuli reached forward and pushed at the earring in her left ear, and it hit softly against her skin, skin she could feel again, cold and dirty and burned from the sun. Her lips were cracked and her eyes burned, and she was—she was very, very thirsty, though she thought she could remember doing nothing but drinking water for a long while. She had been sleeping, hadn't she? She had been outside, and it had been so cold. But now she was warming, slowly. They helped her up, warm presences by her side and Vera was thirsty, but she knew they were leading her to water.

**Heather Truett**

# Crazy Old Broad in the Last Trailer on Row Three

Mora has lived in at least a hundred times and places. They all had their pros and cons. Anywhere in the Middle Ages resulted in the sort of town-wide bonfires she preferred to avoid, the kind for which she always doubled as the guest of honor and the entertainment. For the last few years, she'd been holed up in a trailer park in the early nineties. She doesn't much like any time after the internet takes off, too much info too readily available. 1992 is nearly perfect, though. And the trailer park locale was inspired. No one questions the crazy old broad in the last trailer on row three. Her back door opens on a forest, or what counts as a forest in the southeast United States. No worries, she can make it any forest she likes once she's out among the trees.

Only one person enters Mora's trailer, a little girl named Tiffany. Tiffany has hair like an oil slick and skin like a fairy tale, but that's not the kind of thing people find attractive where the girl is growing up. Even among the other trailer park kids, Tiffany's considered weird. In most times and places, Mora avoided children. People get real touchy when you mess with their babies, even seemingly unwanted babies. Maybe she's getting soft, she thinks when Tiffany knocks on her door one afternoon, and she find herself inviting the girl inside.

"I heard you have kittens," Tiffany said to Mora that day, and Mora did indeed have a litter in the hall closet. After that, it was just a given that Tiffany would be at Mora's house as soon as school let out, and she'd stay until the streetlights showed their homing beacons for the trailer park kids. Then she'd wade through the thick clover that surrounded Mora's trailer and disappear in the twilight.

"Lindsay Goodman says you're a witch," Tiffany tells her one afternoon. "She says you turn children into cats, and that's why you have so many."

As if to illustrate her point, Tiffany scoops up three kittens from the floor and plops them into her lap.

Mora's in the kitchen, pouring vodka into a jar about two-thirds full of willow bark.

"You know I'm not a witch."

The girl shrugs. Mora can see her rubbing one of the kittens behind the ears, looking perfectly at home on the floral sofa Mora manifested as soon as she realized the girl would be spending time here. She hadn't needed much seating before Tiffany's arrival.

"You didn't tell this Lindsay Goodman who I am, did you?" Mora narrows her eyes.

Tiffany's head snaps up. "Course not."

No, Tiffany wouldn't tell anyone she spent her afternoons making herbal extracts and teas with a Celtic goddess whose name they wouldn't even recognize. She was a smart girl. She knew they'd just make fun of her and call her stupid. Tiffany knew they thought she was weird, and it was easier to ignore them than give them more fuel for the fire. She only told Mora what the other kids said about her when she wanted Mora to explain why those kids were wrong. It meant Mora telling stories and Tiffany loved nothing more than a good story. Mora knows the girl doesn't believe in goddesses or magic. Not really. But Tiffany goes along with Mora's stories, and Mora enjoys telling them.

"Good. Cause, if you do, I might decide I need another cat."

Tiffany laughs. "Can I be a black cat?"

Mora smiles at the joke.

All of Mora's cats are black, at least all the indoor cats, her little familiars. She knows good and well that only makes her seem all the more a witch to small children. In some times, the presence of black cats served as a deterrent, allowing her the solitary existence she usually preferred. Now she carves triskeles and Dara knots into her doorframe and no one even notices. Her sacred symbols are only decoration.

"Go on now, Tiff, the streetlights just came on."

"How do you always know that?" Tiffany asks.

Mora screws the lid on the jar of willow and sets it on the counter. It's true that she can't see the lights. The trailer's windows are shrouded in thick black and silver cloth. Add that to her stone tables and the earthy herbal smell, and Mora feels almost at home in her cave-like tin can.

"It's magic," Mora tells Tiffany. "Here, on your way, leave these on Miss Minerva's front steps." She hands the girl a few packets of loose tea and shoos her out the door. One of the big tom cats slinks along behind her. He'll make sure she gets home safe. They all take turns being Tiffany's escort.

Once Mora's back in her kitchen, heating water for her own cup of tea, she feels a slight pulling sensation in her gut. Beside her, near the table, there's a soft glow of greenish light and she smells sulfur. Then her sister appears.

"Bev," Mora says.

"Mora," Bev says.

They've agreed to use names that fit the time, regardless of how ridiculous they sound. She can't go around introducing herself as the Morrigan, and none of these modern Americans would ever look at Badb and realize it rhymes with *hive*.

"What do you want?" Mora takes two cups from the cabinet.

"Why is that girl always here?" Bev reaches for one of the cups, examining the inside like it might be dirty.

"Because I like her." Studying humanity was originally the point in all this time travel, figuring out what would become of mortal society so they could better guide it in their own time.

Bev frowns. "Well, she makes it very difficult to pop in for a visit whenever I want."

Mora takes the kettle from the stove. "Perhaps that's why I like her. Besides, you could come to the door like a normal person would. She'll just think you're another old lady."

Bev huffs at the idea. "You're the one who told a human child who we really are. It's dangerous, Mora."

Mora knows Bev would be right in most cases, but Tiffany is harmless. And the girl is so lonely. Mora knows what it is to be lonely. She takes her time preparing her tea, pouring water over the leaves and bark, humming so her chest vibrates at just the right frequency and a handful of the cats gather at her feet. She doesn't want to go back to her own time. She doesn't want to live her life on bloody battlefields, reciting poems to inspire more death, always transitioning from one shape to another, never just being herself.

"It's because you like performing," Bev says. "This little girl is your audience. You don't actually like her at all. You just like being worshiped again."

"That child doesn't worship me." Mora swirls her teacup and takes a sip. "She doesn't even believe my stories. She just likes listening to them."

Bev doesn't comment, but her face makes it clear she's not buying anything Mora's selling. "Well, you do as you like then, but I'm bored. I think it's time we move on. Maybe back to Ireland. I'm thinking 13th century."

Bev is never happy anywhere, always ready to go back, back, back. If Mora didn't keep a leash on her, they'd end up riding around on dinosaurs before the next solstice.

"I'm not going anywhere." Mora hands her sister the kettle and watches as Bev flips through the packets Mora keeps just for her visits. Bev is picky about her tea. "I've been here a year now, and no one has tried to burn me at a stake."

"No one tried to burn us in the 1950s either, but you hated it there."

"No, no burning, but the neighborhood boys were always daring each other to sneak into my yard and throw rocks at my windows or what have you." Mora grimaced.

"They don't do that here?"

"Nope. They're mostly inside playing those video games, the boys at least. Some of the girls, too. Tiffany's the only one who comes near this place."

"And you shouldn't let her. You know she will draw you out, somehow. It always happens, Mora. You can't resist. You will involve yourself somehow, and then we'll have no choice but to find a new time. Probably, I should let you. At least then we could leave."

"Look, Bev, if all you came here for is to drink my tea and whine, you may as well go on home." Mora and Bev were attached in some way even they didn't understand. It kept them from shifting times apart from one another, but at least they could have their own dwellings within their shared time. Millennia in the company of a sister could wear on anyone, no matter how much you loved her.

Bev selected a tea packet and started pouring then. She knew when her sister was done with a topic, but she couldn't help adding, "When you lose your temper and show yourself, we're going to the 13th century. I miss home." The rest of the visit was companionable, and Bev only complained twice about how Mora dried her heather blossoms.

•

The next day, after a good sleep, Mora conceded that her sister might be right. A little. The last time she let anyone into her private life had been in Pripyat in the 80s. Mora'd practically adopted that sweet girl, Tatyana, whose father worked at the power plant. The mom was dead, and the little girl was a natural with herbs. Chased by some village boys, she'd stumbled into the same clearing where Mora was picking mint. Nina, Mora's other sister, was there and she'd run the boys off while Mora made Tatyana a cup of tea back at her cottage. She, Bev, and Nina had planned to leave within the year. They knew what was coming and they never involved themselves in the big parts of history, but then there was Tatyana, and Mora thought maybe she could just save the one man, the father. Multiple times in the weeks before they were set to leave, Mora manifested in the sky over the plant, making sure the father saw her. She only succeeded in terrifying the girl, who caught Mora changing back into a woman's form after one of her displays. The local people had their own myths that should've made them see the scary dark bird giant in the sky and head for the hills, but the 80s were a modern era, and the father and his coworkers were scoffed at for their warnings. Tatyana ran away from Mora, even faster than she'd run from those boys when they first met. As the sisters were readying to leave, Nina decided to try one last time, for Mora, and she almost got all three of them stuck there, forever attached to the wasteland it became.

"You've got to learn," Bev has told her, "that we aren't that kind of deity. You were made for war and destruction, not justice and salvation."

They'd waited too long to leave Pripyat. Something inside of the three was severed in the blast. Mora and Bev shifted in and out of time until they thought they'd never land anywhere. Eventually, though, they did. Nina didn't. The gaping hole inside their beings told them she never would.

When Tiffany shows up after school the next day, Mora's
thoughts are still on Tatyana, still on Nina, so she doesn't
answer. It breaks her heart how long the girl sits on the cin-
derblock steps out front, so for the next week, Mora makes
sure she's out in the forest before the girl arrives. Even if
Tiffany were to wander into the trees to look for her, she'd
never make it to where Mora forages. She favors the ancient
groves and moors of Ireland in a time her current neighbors
would call BC. She thought of it as home, and she knew the
plants there better than anywhere.

It takes almost a month for Tiffany to stop knocking on
Mora's door, but eventually she does. Mora misses her, but
her sister pops in for regular visits and reminds her again
and again about Tatyana and all the ones before, how she did
more damage than good in the end, drew attention to their
meant-to-be-secret identities and traumatized the little girls
she supposedly cared so much about.

She never mentions Nina.

They do not talk about Nina.

Tiffany, for her part, goes to the library and checks out
books on Celtic folklore and mythology. She tries following
Mora into the woods, but when the woman vanishes behind
a tree, Tiffany settles herself to read, eating the berries Mora
taught her were safe, and accepting gifts from the crows that
take to flying overhead. One brings her a strawberry candy
wrapped in foil as she reads about the Morrigan transform-
ing into an eel to chase a man through the fjord. Another
brings her a lacy blue ribbon she ties in her hair, reading
about the Morrigan's other transformations, into a wolf, a

white cow with red ears, a young maiden, and an old woman. When the sun sets, Tiffany walks home, usually followed by one of Mora's cats.

By early fall, Tiffany convinces herself none of it is true. Mora is just an old woman, moody and not worth her time. She no longer waits for Mora to go into the woods and instead goes alone, packing peanut butter sandwiches for herself and birdseed for the crows. She abandons the heavy books with their leather binding and Celtic knot covers and instead disappears into the pages of her mother's romance novels, full of swooning ladies and broad-shouldered highlanders, duchesses and viscounts, lonely secretaries and powerful CEOs. Only occasionally is there a goddess seducing a warrior.

Mora keeps an eye, a metaphysical one, on Tiffany. She watches the girl wandering the trailer park. The black cats trail her into the woods. Crows swoop behind her, cawing at the other children as she passes. Now, instead of calling Mora a witch, people start to call Tiffany one. Mora's resolve doesn't waver until fall. She hasn't been paying attention to Tiffany so much, spending more and more time foraging, keeping up her stock and supplying the older women who live in the trailer park with tinctures and teas for their health. That October though, she's pouring tea for Bev when she senses something wrong. A crow pecks the window by her sink, and she sweeps the curtains back in time to see a man walk into the woods... the woods where she knows Tiffany has gone to read.

"Don't do it," Bev warns.

Mora flicks her inner eye in the man's direction and sees him nearing Tiffany's favorite tree, the one near the old creek bed, surrounded by a soft bed of moss.

Mora knows the man, knows which trailer is his, knows he should not be allowed anywhere near a child alone. She exits the trailer, Bev close on her heels. She knows exactly what this man is up to, and her sister's talk of "last time" means nothing to Mora in this moment.

"Nina," Bev whispers.

Mora glares. "Don't you dare."

"Nina," Bev starts again.

"Nina tried." Mora snaps. "She lost everything trying to fix this world."

"We aren't fixers." Bev reaches for Mora's arm.

"I'm a war goddess," Mora says, stomping through the trees. "And this world is always at war."

"This isn't a war," Bev protests. "This is one little girl."

"You win, Bev. After this thing is done, we can go home. Wars and worship. Fae and fomorians. We'll be just in time for Samhain."

Before Bev can respond, the sisters reach their destination.

The man is pulling Tiffany close to him, moving faster than the girl can fathom. She doesn't know what is happening, and then it isn't happening anymore. The man is pressed against a tree, Mora's hands like talons at his neck.

Tiffany screams.

"Wait," Bev says. "Just, wait, and I'll take Tiffany home."

Mora spares a glance for Bev, who is already embracing Tiffany, shielding her from the sight of what is about to happen.

"You'll actually help?" Mora asks. "You've never helped before."

"War is no place for a child," Bev replies, and then she leads Tiffany back the way they came.

Tiffany doesn't resist. She holds Bev's hand tight and walks toward the trailer park, never looking back. What she doesn't look back to see is Mora, towering taller and taller, the bony white man cowering against leaves and pine straw, a flock of darkness descending. Mora looks into the man. She sees what he's done, how broken and warped his soul has become, beyond salvation. As Bev told her, though, she is not a deity made for salvation. She is a war goddess. She is made for destruction.

Mora will leave him to the birds and let her sister have his bones. Bev can do all kinds of things with bones.

**CB Droege**

# Dust and Darkness

The dust mines were the perfect exile. Nicodemeus enjoyed the lack of chatter; the dark, narrow spaces; the glittering dust and fibers that filled his mouth and lungs with every breath and sent a tingle up and down his spine. His whole body felt stronger for the physical labor, and his mind felt stronger for the time to think and understand his place in the world. It was so different from court-life with its grand spaces, endless prat-tling small-talk, nearly constant feasting on over-rich foods, and OH! The light, so much *light* everywhere.

When the Fairy King had defeated the Lord of Light at long last, all those months ago, Nicodemeus had thought that the lands would grow darker, that the whole world would be-come like the dark and quiet halls that the rebellion had been born in. And in the weeks after the light-soul had vanished from the sky, it did and Nicodemeus rejoiced, but then the fire-orbs and illumination spells grew more frequent, espe-cially in the Fairy King's own audience chamber, until it felt like everything around Nicodemeus was even brighter than it had been when the Lord of Light had still been in power. All those years, he'd thought they were fighting against the 'Light', but now it seems the only issue most fey took with the Lord of Light was the 'Lord' part.

When the Fairy King had sent him away to the mines, he'd done it to castigate Nicodemeus. The king didn't like cynics or pessimists; he didn't like challenges to his policies, and he definitely didn't like how Nicodemeus repeatedly extinguished the lights around the palace. All the things that had made Nicodemeus a valuable ally in the rebellion, now made him a terrible advisor at court.

Of course, as Nicodemeus had been a hero of the insurrection, a great general in the war that finally freed the people from the wicked oppression of the Lord of Light, executing him would have been unpopular. Even exile could not be decided on a whim. Thus, the king had fabricated some ridiculous story that one of the royal seers had divined that Nicodemeus was an ally of the Lord of Light, and an enemy of the King's new throne.

"One day soon," the king had said in his proclamation before the court, "The Lord of Light will be reborn, as he has been a dozen times before, and if we hope, this time, to *retain* control of our kingdom, we must have unwavering, unquestionable loyalty. Any doubt is reason to be wary!" And so, Nicodemeus was sent away to toil in drudgery for the remainder of his life.

Once here though, the stout fairy had found a welcoming home. He didn't understand anymore why he'd ever bothered with politics and courtly maneuvers after the war. He'd been convinced once that it was his destiny to hold a position of greatness, but now he felt that swinging a pick underground was his true calling.

He'd had a hunk of bread and a glass of minerally water for breakfast, and it was simply wonderful. He'd walked to the mines from his tiny room in the upper barracks without greeting anyone in the street. He didn't ask after anyone's health or pretend to care about someone's distant relations. He didn't bow or scrape, and he didn't demand bowing and scraping from anyone else. He hadn't even seen his new superior, Duke Mortensen, since the day he'd arrived. That day, the round, well-adorned fairy in command of the mines had simply glanced at him, then waved him away to be shown to his new quarters and given his work clothes.

The miners walked to the mine in the faint starlight that served as their only illumination in this place, so far from the palace that it had been dark here even when The Light-soul still burned. Some said quick hellos to those they'd worked beside for years, but most just trudged in blessed silence, and Nicodemeus could *think*.

Inside the mines, he chose not to work in a group or even with a partner, like so many did, but to find a tunnel off by himself. He knew it was safer to work near other miners, but he liked when he couldn't even hear the other's picks striking stone, and he could find a world all to himself, just him and the rocks and the dust and the darkness for hours on end. If he delivered his quota of the silvery dust that kept the Fairy King in power, no one seemed to care what he did. All were equal in the mines. If only he'd known that the world he'd been fighting for was here beneath this mountain all along.

This day he had found a tunnel that looked little used, strewn as it was with cobwebs. He'd had to crawl on his belly through parts, and at one point he'd pushed through a small restrictive spell, perhaps left from some long-ago fight with the large rats that sometimes infested the tunnels, but he'd arrived at a distant vein of dust, rich and pearlescent. When he perked his ears, he could hear no other picks striking rock, no other voices or shuffling feet. He was alone.

Nicodemeus scratched at the vein of dust experimentally with his pick, wondering as he did, why no one had finished mining this place after they'd discovered it. Had the rats been too fierce here at the time? Had they uncovered another, richer vein, and forgotten about this one? Whatever the cause, he considered it a lucky find, and would not look for reasons to pass it up.

He hefted his pick, and struck, smiling as the dust flew from the face of the rock and gathered at his feet. He picked at the vein for hours, until, nearly at the end of the day, one strike caught his pick, and he could not pull it free, and he was forced to take a break from swinging.

He sat down among the piles and piles of dust around him, and took a few deep breaths, allowing his muscles to rest, and his mind to revel in the silence. Then he stood, and with a grunt, he yanked the pick free. With it came a tumbling of rocks, which made Nicodemeus fearful at first that he would become buried while out of earshot of assistance, but the rocks only fell away from a small section, revealing a narrow door in the rocks behind.

"What's this?" he croaked. They were the first words he'd spoken aloud in days. He stepped up to the door and squinted into the flickering shadows cast by the tiny candle on his helmet. The door was tall and narrow, relative to his squat form. It was set into an arched frame of black stones, nothing like the stones of this cave, or even this region of the world. The door itself was some reddish wood, gilt and filigreed with traceries of gold, and set with shimmering rubies. Nicodemeus reached out to gently run one hand along the wood grain, and to his surprise it swung inward at his slight touch, releasing a sharp, cold wind from within. A faint blue light shone through the crack.

He pushed the door the rest of the way open and stepped inside to find a cozy-looking room decorated like a royal nursery. The air inside was freezing cold, and at the center of the room, a large cushion sat upon the floor, and upon the cushion a large blue egg. This was the source of the light in the room. Nicodemeus walked into the pristine little space in shock and wonder. Along the walls, tapestries hung depicting scenes of battles and lessons in morality. In one corner was a rocking chair, in another a crib, between them, a shelf of books in a language Nicodemeus did not recognize. On the opposite wall, a shelf of toys sat below a rack of weapons and armor fitted for someone very tall.

He looked more closely at the egg. There was a raised crest upon the shell, which shone more brightly than the rest. Nicodemeus recognized it right away, the sigil of the Lord of Light. "Oh no," he breathed, and his merest breath touched upon the shell, and the chill upon it abated for the merest moment, and that was enough. A small crack appeared on the egg. It grew bigger, and more splits appeared, and in a matter of moments, the egg was breaking open. Nicodemeus stood in shock, slack jawed and mind racing. Before him, an infant lay in the remains of the egg. It made small sounds, and wiggled about, and then it opened its eyes. It looked directly at Nicodemeus, and only then did he fully comprehend: The Lord of Light was reborn again, as promised.

The foul being who had so abused the fey for generations, who enslaved and tortured his people time and time again throughout history lay, helpless and babbling, among the shards of eggshell. From this room his people's enemy would again be raised, eventually to gather a flock, and then an army, and then pull the kingdom once again into the terrible light.

Almost unthinking, he raised the pick in his hands, determined to bash the child to bits, but something stayed his swing. He couldn't bring himself to dash a child to death, no matter how terrible it may be. He lowered the pick, and turned to leave forever, but this too he could not bring himself to do, as the child would die just as surely. He'd awoken the egg before its time, and whatever caretaker the Lord of Light was meant to have in this resplendent room had not yet arrived. He could not report the thing to Duke Mortensen. He would surely be blamed for everything. He would have to... He would have to take care of the child, he realized. He would need to sneak food and water here for it, but the rest of what it needed seemed to be in this nursery. He could work the dust vein in this tunnel for years, and make sure that the child was doing well.

And then the final thought in the cascade struck him: *He would raise the Lord of Light reborn.* He could shape and guide this child in secret! The rule of the Lord of Light *would* return to the land, but this time it would be with Nicodemeus tempering the harsh light. This was his Destiny; *this was the greatness he had seen for himself since he was young.*

He would have to learn a bit about raising children. He would have to invent excuses to keep others out of this tunnel. He should probably learn to read those books upon the shelf, whatever foul language they might be in, but first: He needed to find a way to make this tiny Lord of Light not shine *quite* so brightly. It really was offensive.

**J. S. Allen**

# A Child's Stone

Yes—I have sensed your distress. The blight comes. Your roots weaken even as the blight strengthens its hold in the subsoil.

And next year I will say, "Good riddance," when the blight subsumes your seeds and your next generation is spoiled in the soil, never to grow in nice orderly rows.

Do not cry to me now. Your kind brought this fate upon itself. Your lack of vigilance permitted this fungus to fester. Now you—and your walking ancestors—must pay for your complacency.

This year your bodies will be bitter in the mouths of the walking ones. And next year, when it is you who walks with the ancestors, there will be no harvest at all. The walkers will starve, and I will say, "good riddance."

What would you have me do? Intercede with the walkers on your behalf? Warn them?

Your ancestors could have warned them last year. But they, like you, were complacent. When they passed into the bellies of the walkers, they forgot all about their plant-lives; they allowed themselves to be distracted by the pleasures of the walking-life. If only they had been warned, the walkers would have squelched this blight before you were even planted. Now it is too late.

And what, I ask, will the blight do when it is through with you? When the fields are emptied and the fungus is at its maximum, will it be sated? No, it will seek fresh ground and fresh prey here in my wood. That I cannot allow to pass.

For that reason—and that reason alone—I shall help you. I will reach out to the walkers. I will summon them to my wood with sweet perfume; my blossoms shall be irresistible. Some among them will remember the old ways and will dare to eat my fruit. Then they will see what my fruit shows to them, and in this way they will know what must be done.

•

Twer Epherum stood balanced on one leg waiting before the pump. Finally, a family came into the clearing.

The father of the family, seeing Epherum, steadied his axe-grip reflexively, but relaxed again when he saw that Epherum was only an unarmed ascetic waiting for water. Then he sneered and led his wife and children to the pump.

The woman primed the pump from her bottle, then offered a drink to Epherum. But her husband stopped her arm, saying, "He is an amanist. He is fit only to drink what others spill."

Epherum stood impassively while the children worked the pump. But when he noticed the white blossoms adorning the woman's hair, his eyes widened and he broke his silence: "Those are the petals of the torka."

"Yes," said the woman. "Our torka tree has bloomed again, its first bloom in twenty years."

"You speak to my wife?" demanded the man.

"Please," said Epherum, "where does this torka grow?"

"In the wood beyond the ruin," said the woman, pointing.

After the family was gone, one of the children lingered in the clearing and threw a stone at Epherum. Without lifting his gaze, Epherum caught the stone in one strong hand. The child fled.

Epherum lay on his belly and lapped up the spilled water before rising and walking where the woman had pointed. He passed through the ruin, a temple of old. From the temple he could see the fields of the farmers stretching for miles.

He followed the scent of the torka tree and found it blossoming in the shade of a cliff-side hollow. Men were in the tree cutting its vines and passing them down to groups of women who stripped off the blossoms and put them in buckets.

When the women saw Epherum, they stopped their gossiping and called to the men. The men in the tree waved their machetes. "This is our torka tree. We better not see you around again."

Epherum looked up at the single cluster of fruit at the pinnacle of the tree. Three elongated, yellow fruits sprouted toward the sky.

"Go on, get out of here," shouted the men. So Epherum backed away and returned to the woods.

When Epherum was gone, the men said to one other, "He will be back. That old amanist wants our fruit. He will make a poison out of it and have his revenge against us." So they decided to keep watch all night.

But the guards fell asleep. Unchallenged, Epherum slinked from the wood and silently climbed the torka tree. He broke one fruit from the cluster and wrapped it in a leaf before descending the tree and disappearing again into the night.

Epherum hid himself in a cave while he prepared the tor-ka fruit as he was taught. Careful not to touch the meat of the fruit with his bare skin, he peeled and mashed it between two stones and left the pulp to bake in the morning sun.

In the afternoon, Epherum returned to the cave, having prepared himself to partake of the fruit. He placed a small amount under his tongue and waited. An hour later he was writhing on the dirt floor while the sun bore down on him through the mouth of the cave. Spasms gripped his body, his teeth gnashed, his eyes rolled back.

But an hour later, Epherum rose again, covered in sweat, breathing like a dying beast. He cast his gaze about, seeing as if for the first time. Then he turned to the remaining fruit pulp and covered his lips and tongue with it.

The remainder of that day and the whole of the night, Epherum was visited by visions. In his visions he saw the coming harvest ruined by blight, a hidden blight which attacked through the roots. He saw two years of mass starvation after the following year's crop failed to bear. He also saw what must be done to avert these things: The current crop must be overturned and burned in the field; all supplies in all granaries must be burned; all grain-ships must send their cargo overboard; the people must go hungry this year, relying on chicken and game and what nuts they can gather; the governor must arrange for fish to be imported from the coast; and in the following year, the fields must be left fallow; the farmers must turn to secondary crops grown in secondary fields. Only in the third year may corn from foreign places be seeded in the field again. Failure in any of these areas would result in the blight expanding its scope, spreading to other regions, and possibly leading to the downfall of Sarta itself.

The next day when Epherum emerged from the cave, he was very thirsty. So he went to wait by the water pump. He waited a long time. Finally, a child came; it was the same one who had cast a stone at him before. The child asked him, "If you are thirsty, why don't you use the pump?"

Epherum answered, "I am an amanist. I follow the old ways. I must always try to do no harm."

"But who is harmed by taking water?"

"You are harmed," said Epherum. "Water I take will not be there for you tomorrow."

The child went away, but returned shortly to throw a stone, this time hitting Epherum in the head.

A few minutes later the father appeared. He pointed his axe at Epherum and said, "You again! You are not welcome here. You should be ashamed, intimidating small children. This is not your well, this is our well."

Another man, hearing the commotion, ran into the clearing with a machete in hand. When he saw Epherum, he shouted, "You are the one who stole the fruit of the torka. Now you are caught skulking about the water supply?"

Two more men with machetes came into the clearing, and the first man said, "I caught this one trying to poison the water supply."

The men descended upon Epherum with kicks and blows. Epherum, weak from his vision and woozy from the child's stone, fell easily.

"Admit it," shouted the men, "you stole the fruit."

"I took only one," said Epherum, between blows. "Not enough to kill a man."

"But enough for a child?" demanded the father of the child.

Soon a rowdy crowd assembled. Epherum regained his feet and cried, "I poisoned no one. I ate the fruit myself."

"Impossible," said the leader of the men. "Whoever eats torka will die."

Epherum spoke so the crowd could hear. "No: I ate the torka in the manner of the old ways, and a great vision was bestowed upon me."

The leader guffawed in his face. "And what vision did you see?"

"I saw your future ..."

Everyone stood quietly to hear what Epherum would say. He looked at the assembled for a long moment. Finally, he declared, "I saw great prosperity, victory in war, and the blessing of the gods!"

The crowd cheered and lifted Epherum onto their shoulders. A great party ensued.

**Luigi Coppola**

# *I built a tower of all my fears*

I built a tower of all my fears: syringes,
spiders, people touching my neck, intimacy,
failure, being found out, being made a fool,
mispronouncing an Italian item on a menu,
someone seeing the sweat mark my arse crack
left on the chair when I stand up, the crazy person
sitting next to me on the bus, the person on the bus
that I sit next to thinking that I'm the crazy person,
love, lost love, aging, taxes, death—all of this and more;
oh, and waiting for the tower to fall.

**Carmen Peters**

# *Preservation*

It took two weeks for Cynthia to smell the ghost.

She swiveled her head to find the source, dislodging a frizzy curl from her bun in the process.

"Does it smell off here?" asked Cynthia.

Josephine had made herself at home on the loveseat, her whole attention soaked up by the notebook in her hands.

Cynthia repeated her question.

Josephine's eyes remained glued to the page, but she asked for clarification.

"The smell," pressed Cynthia. "Like mothballs, or bad lemons or something. I thought I got a whiff when we first moved in, but now I'm sure of it."

Josephine shrugged. She chewed on the end of her quill and snuck a glance upwards, as if expecting to catch the scent floating past the bookshelves. Then she sank back into her poetry, and the scratching of her quill again dominated the living room.

Cynthia took a few more test sniffs, wrinkled her nose, and decided to crack open a window. She went over to one facing the garden, and wiggled the frame until it slid up with a soft pop. Warm, salty air blew through the garden and into the cottage, filling the house with thick sea-breeze.

Cynthia grimaced and adjusted her shorts, perpetually vigilant in case something came untucked. Not that anyone would see except Josephine, but a lifetime of paranoia was hard to escape from. She eyed the soft sun wrapped in wooly clouds, its rays casting the coastline with the amber lines of evening. The sight was beautiful, practically an oil painting, and Cynthia should have been enjoying her first full day in the new house. And she was, really, but there were a couple niggling details that kept getting in the way. The stucco was flaking off more than they originally thought, the garden suffered from a particularly invasive kind of weed, and now, there was this smell.

Cynthia sighed. All sorts of unexpected problems came up when you moved, let alone across the country, and she needed to adjust her expectations. Perfection would never come, but if she had a bit more patience, soon she and Josephine would be happy.

They had unearthed the house on one of their late-night listing digs, and as soon as they saw the profile Cynthia knew it was the one. The opening picture showed a witchy cottage painted mint green with red trim, its pointed roof curving rakishly down on one side. It reminded Cynthia of a tomato with a bad haircut, but she and Josephine had quickly fallen for its quirky charm. An inquiry, phone call, and virtual tour later, the couple had made a lowball offer, and to their surprise, it was accepted the next day. A week later they found themselves packing up and moving across the country.

Since then, Cynthia had managed to secure a job with a marketing firm in the nearby city, and Josephine seemed pleased, swearing that the cottage was already feeding her poetry. Everything was aligning as well as could be expected, but what Cynthia relished most was feeling like she could breathe again. Before, at the old place, the stasis had grown unbearable.

•

Yet when all is dark and still, Cynthia lays in bed unable to fall sleep. She can't escape the notion that the house is waiting for something, its breath held tight in its stucco walls and its hardwood floors and its limestone basement.

She needs to be awake when it gasps for air.

•

Two weeks into her new job, Cynthia came home to find Josephine set up on the kitchen island, mason jars scattered over the tabletop. Empty brown plastic bags littered the floor like discarded cicada shells, and a breeze from an open window had pulled a few into the living room. Josephine didn't seem to notice; all of her attention was focused on the thick tome in her hands. Cynthia's eyes narrowed when she spotted the price sticker still pasted onto the spine of the book. Just what she needed, another spending spree.

Josephine must have finally sensed Cynthia's presence because she looked up, her cheek cherry-red where she had been resting her palm. She gave a small, distant smile, and inquired about work.

"Fine, ended up having 'The Talk' with my boss," said Cynthia, dropping her purse by the sink.

Josephine's eyes widened from behind their cat-eye frames. Cynthia was originally supposed to wait until after her trial period was over.

"I know, I know, we had a plan," pre-empted Cynthia, "but she seemed like someone who would take it well and I wanted to get it over with. It gets to be too much if I keep it to myself. You know how it is."

Josephine knew.

Cynthia leaned against the kitchen counter, letting her eyes follow one of the plastic bags drifting in lazy circles on the living room floor.

Josephine asked her something.

"Huh?" said Cynthia, still watching the bag. It had continued to circle and was now floating a bit off the ground. It whirled up higher and higher, until suddenly it got sucked out the window, into the garden.

Josephine asked again.

"Oh sorry. Yeah, for the most part. Afterwards, I decided to rip the Band-Aid all the way off and made an announcement to the whole team, and *that* got me some looks. But it was the right thing for me, I think, and by the end of the day no one seemed to care."

Josephine gave a relieved smile, the dimples on both sides of her mouth pushing into her cheeks. Sometimes Cynthia resented how much that softened her up.

Cynthia freed her hair from its bun, shaking it down past her shoulders the way Josephine liked, doing some softening up of her own. She gestured at the book and jars.

"So... what's with all this?"

Josephine declared they were for canning, her eyes lighting up the way they did whenever she discovered a new "thing."

Cynthia dreaded these "things," as such interests tended to strain the bank account. Plus, if Josephine was getting absorbed by a new hobby, it meant that the poetry wasn't going well, which meant large gaps where Cynthia was the sole bread-winner.

Josephine asked Cynthia if she had heard about pickled watermelon rinds.

"Why on earth would anyone want to preserve rinds? To gnaw on like a rat?"

Josephine huffed, saying they were full of vitamin C. Besides, weren't they trying to save money? Waste not, want not.

Cynthia bit her cheek, resisting the urge to point out that buying a recipe book and dozens of mason jars and ingredients was in fact *not* saving money. Instead she walked over and began rubbing Josephine's shoulders.

"Hmmm, that's a good point, babe," Cynthia murmured. "Look at this rural dyke, learning all these life skills. So *industrious.*"

Josephine purred and leaned into Cynthia's touch.

"Actually, Josie, I've got a question now that you have all this knowledge. What actually prevents things from spoiling? Always seemed like magic to me."

Josephine clicked her heels together, practically vibrating with excitement. She flipped back to an earlier chapter and began rattling off detailed instructions. Cynthia tried to listen, to be the supportive partner, but she kept getting distracted by the smell.

That awful sour stench had never left, and each day it lurked in a different corner of the house, just on the edge of perception. Now it was stronger than ever, and the canning book now stank of it too. Cynthia licked the inside of her mouth. She breathed the smell in, and it coated her tongue in a bitter tang of lime peel and soap. Surely Josie would mention it soon.

•

But Josephine never notices, so Cynthia says nothing. Instead she listens to her wife enumerate every step of canning, the musk of the room nestling deep into her mouth.

It makes her eyes water.

•

"So get this, I come home at lunch—had to pick up some files for my next appointment—and I find Brian squatting down by the daffodils. But he's not just *looking* at them. His whole head is in the bush, like an ostrich in sand or something. It's utterly ridiculous, but Brian's so absorbed with whatever the hell he's doing that it curves back around and becomes kind of charming. So anyway, I cough and he springs up, face beet-red like when I caught him watching pay-per-view porn. I ask him what he was doing, and you know what he tells me? He tells me that he was *sniffing* the daffodils, as if that wasn't damn obvious. So I ask him why he was sniffing them *like that* and he gets even more embarrassed and he says that he never noticed it before, but they remind him of me. So I get real quiet for a moment—shocking I know—and then I tell him

'Brian honey, there's no way you love my scent that much. If so, you'd spend more time in the bush between my legs!'"

Mary guffawed at her own punchline, and Josephine laughed along, and the two clinked their glasses together. Cynthia gave a small smile.

The three of them were sitting on Josephine and Cynthia's back porch, having mimosas and finger sandwiches. It was a lifted patio of dark wood that overlooked the burgeoning garden, the body of the cottage acting as a shield from the strong winds of the coast. Josephine had been spending more and more time out here. She called it her happy place.

Mary swiveled in her seat, her attention gliding from Josephine to Cynthia.

"Speaking of flowers, it looks like you two are developing quite the green thumb. Where do you get the time to do all of this?"

Mary spoke with a polished New English accent and had an elven jawline, a feature that Cynthia found herself increasingly obsessed with as the conversation wore on. Still, there was something about Mary that was chipped, a bit rough around the edges, like fine china that had been shattered and glued back together.

It made Cynthia uneasy, but Josephine loved neighbors like Mary. She considered them great inspiration, and so Cynthia often found herself entertaining guests that she wished she could sweep off the porch.

"Josie gets all the credit for the garden," said Cynthia. "She's started canning fruits and veggies, so the next logical step was to grow everything herself." She grabbed Josephine's hand, and was relieved when her wife squeezed back.

Mary smiled. "Now that's dedication."

The woman leaned forward, ready to pounce.

"But I suppose any writer worth their salt jumps into things with both feet. With all these new hobbies, god, not to mention the poetry, I'm sure life's never a drag."

The comment seemed innocuous, but Cynthia wondered if it was a dig. Josephine, as usual, was completely oblivious to the undertones. Instead she spent the next few minutes waxing on about soil quality and tomatoes, and ended by declaring that none of it would be possible without the support of her partner. She squeezed Cynthia's hand tighter.

"The sacrifices we make for love," said Mary, taking a bite out of her sandwich. "I wish my Brian was half as dedicated as you are, Cynthia. It would sure make my life a hell of a lot easier."

Mary leaned back and looked up at the clouds, and Cynthia wondered if she had been mistaken about the woman's intentions. The three of them continued drinking while Josephine prodded Mary for information about the town's history, the previous inhabitants of the house, and the latest drama downtown. It fascinated Cynthia how Josephine could turn random material this way and that, separating and melting ideas until they were spit out as a few lines of verse that some mid-tier magazine would purchase for a week's worth of groceries. She wondered what parts of their marriage made it into Josephine's work.

Mary poured herself another mimosa, her porcelain gaze roving for a new target. She settled on the house. "So, a new home on the rocky coast, away from the hustle and bustle. It's been what, two months now? You both settling in?"

"Of course," said Cynthia, unthinking. "What's not to love?"

Josephine mentioned that the garden had been so therapeutic.

"I can't help but notice that the extra bedroom upstairs isn't in use," said Mary. She winked. "Planning a little family expansion?"

Cynthia chose her words carefully. "We've considered it."

"It would be nice to get some kids running around here," said Mary. "Area's aging up as families get priced out. I'd volunteer myself, but Brian can't have children, and fortunately that's not a deal breaker for us."

Josephine said it wasn't for them either.

"That's good, less pressure," said Mary. "But—and pardon my curiosity—if you did decide to have kids, how would you go about it? Obviously there is adoption, but if you went the biological route, have you thought about who would carry the baby?"

Cynthia gathered herself. This wasn't the first time she had disclosed, and it wouldn't be the last. "Only Josie can have a baby, so there isn't much of a choice."

Mary gave a sad titter. "I'm sorry to hear that, dear. Even if you don't want kids, it's hard to be infertile."

"Fertility isn't even on the menu. Unless medicine makes some big strides in the next few years, I'm stuck providing the other half of the puzzle."

Mary looked confused, and then color rose in her cheeks as she realized what Cynthia was implying. "I'm so sorry, I didn't know. For what it's worth, I would have never guessed."

"No worries," lied Cynthia. "Just another part of being me."

She took an extra-large swig of her mimosa.

Josephine said nothing. Her attention was riveted on her newly-bought cucumber plant. The first of its flowers had started to bloom.

•

After Mary leaves, Josephine does the dishes and Cynthia wipes down the table and chairs. She uses soapy water, and then resorts to bleach, but no matter how hard she scrubs, Mary's seat still stinks of bad citrus.

•

As the summer waned, Josephine spent more of her time visiting Mary, and Cynthia pretended she was okay with it. If Josephine texted and said she would be gone for a couple hours after Cynthia got off work, Cynthia would take walks and photograph the changing season, making sure to avoid going anywhere near Mary's place.

But mostly she cleaned.

She'd crack open all the windows and turn on all the fans, and then mop the place top to bottom. She'd polish the furniture, dust the cabinets, and scrub the claw-foot tub until it gleamed. She'd use Q-tips to clean any cracks she couldn't fit a rag in, and when she couldn't think of anything else she could do, she'd start all over again.

And when Cynthia would finally rest, airing herself with pruned, bleach-irritated hands, the smell would remain, clutching at her like a needy child, pulling at a memory she couldn't place. And it was winning. She didn't go into the basement because Josephine stored the finished jars there, and she tended to avoid the garden. The air in those places felt stale.

After one such long afternoon of cleaning, Cynthia was shaving in the shower and trying not to think of the last time she had enjoyed her career. She was just getting to the hard-to-reach parts behind her knees when Josephine walked into the bathroom. It was so sudden that Cynthia dropped her razor, the clang of metal on ceramic making her wince.

"You scared the shit out of me," said Cynthia. "Next time warn a girl first."

Josephine apologized, saying she was looking for her reading glasses.

"Try inside the mirror. I think I saw them when I was getting the moisturizer."

Josephine nodded, or at least that's what it appeared she did through the blurry filter of the shower curtain. Without another word she opened the mirror above the sink, popped out the glasses, and dipped out the door, shutting it behind her.

Cynthia finished shaving, and had switched to conditioning her hair when Josephine re-entered the bathroom. She walked back over to the sink and opened one of its cabinets.

Cynthia had been chewing on something and decided this was as good of a time as any to share it.

"So I've been doing some thinking about that spare room," she said, keeping her tone casual. "Why don't we turn it into your writing den? Having a private space might help kick-start some ideas, you know?"

Josephine pushed her hand deep into the cabinet, rattling its contents about.

Cynthia frowned. "It doesn't have to be permanent, of course, but I thought it would be a good compromise. We haven't *quite* run out the clock. There's still time to think about the future."

That's what Cynthia always called it: "the future." If she didn't outright name it, maybe Josephine would find it less daunting.

Josephine didn't respond. She had stopped searching the cabinet, and was now staring into the mirror, stock still.

"Hello? An acknowledgement would be nice."

Josephine lifted one finger and began writing in the condensation of the mirror. The sound should have been a dull squeak, but instead it was a sort of chiming clink. Was Josephine wearing something on her fingers? Cynthia felt a flush of irritation at continuing to be ignored, but then dread flooded her.

How did she know *for certain* this was Josephine?

Cynthia swallowed, gathering the will to peel back the curtain.

The shape that might have been Josephine stopped writing. Then it left the room.

Cynthia turned off the water and tried tapping back into her earlier frustration. She was being ridiculous, how could it be anyone but her wife? Josie just had her head wrapped around some big idea, and it was taking all her attention. Wouldn't have been the first time.

Feeling rooted back in reality, Cynthia stepped out of the tub. She looked at the closed door and blinked.

Josephine had shut it on her first exit, and Cynthia should have heard it open when her wife returned. She looked towards the mirror but the writing had faded into mist, if it had ever existed at all. She flicked on the vent and immediately retched. The smell was back and worse than ever. Was it circulating through the ducts?

After getting dressed Cynthia walked outside to find her wife sitting on the patio, glasses on and canning book in hand. Josephine looked up from the accursed thing, her eyebrows knotted in concern.

She said Cynthia looked like she'd seen a ghost.

•

Later Cynthia has a nightmare, or something she believes is one. She is in bed and everything is quiet, so quiet that she can hear the house shifting. She feels woozy, and the spit in her throat tastes like bad tequila. The flavor brushes against something from her past, but she can't grab ahold of it, and then it's gone.

There's someone else in the bed, but she knows better than to pull back the covers. Instead, Cynthia gets up to go look for her wife. As she does her foot kicks something, causing it to roll into the wall with a clink. She looks down.

It is a mason jar: vacuum-sealed so the brine doesn't leak. Even in the darkness Cynthia can make out the pickles floating within, their slices phosphorescent.

A trail of such jars leads towards the bedroom door, which is cracked open. Cynthia follows the jars into the hallway, past the living room, past the bathroom, letting their fairy-lights guide her. They wind all the way to the sliding glass door, and there they end. But Cynthia doesn't need their guidance anymore, for beyond the door is the garden.

Outside the quietness has grown heavy, the black sky's immeasurable weight slowly descending upon the house. In the garden, her naked body entwined with cucumber vines, is Mary. Her skin glistens like fresh-washed vegetables, and she reclines in sensual serenity: an Aphrodite born of fibrous, green flesh.

Her eyes are closed, and when she speaks to Cynthia her mouth stays still. "I see you've emerged from the house. Are you ready?"

"Where's Josephine?"

"You know where she is, Cynthia. She's underground, soaking her wishes in little glass jars."

"Get away from my house."

Mary laughs without moving her lips. "It's not your house and it never will be. You can't claim it."

"Why not?"

"Because you haven't laid in the garden."

Mary's eyelids open, and inside are two perfect, blinding-ly yellow daffodils.

Cynthia wakes with a start. Light trickles through the blinds, and she hears the faint trill of birds outside. There are no mason jars on the floor, and Josephine is sound asleep, where she belongs.

The only remnant of the dream is her tongue, still numb from the taste of brine.

•

Cynthia moved a few of her wife's offspring from the kitchen table to make room for her bowl of tomato soup. The infernal things were conquering all the free space in the house, so Cynthia had bunched herself up in the corner, ready for her personal Alamo.

Josephine was at Mary's again, and had texted Cynthia a few hours ago to say that the two of them were going out to the bar for food and drinks, and that she would be back before ten.

Cynthia couldn't wrap her head around it. Going out to dinner, when there was a metric ton of canned food in the cottage? What happened to being economical?

She grunted in disgust, and then hated how masculine that made her sound, and then hated how insecure it made her feel. She shoved her bowl away, appetite gone, and stared at the basement door.

She had cleaned the house top to bottom four times this week, but she had avoided the basement for months. Most of Josephine's obsession was squirreled away down there, and whenever Cynthia passed by, the acrid odor of lemonade vomit made her gag.

But the *poet* didn't have a verse to say about any of it. Where was all the flowery prose? Where were Josie's stanzas of decay and secret glances and endless fucking processions of mason jars?

Cynthia stood up, gripping the back of the chair for balance. She had been having a little bar night of her own since leaving work, and the whiskey was making her fuzzy. But mostly she felt petty, and she was done being intimidated by the basement.

She stumbled over to the door and opened it.

It was dark, and the light was at the bottom of the stairs. Cynthia covered her nose with her shirt and breathed through her mouth, but it did little to dilute the smell. She paused.

That elusive memory had come back to her.

•

*Once as a boy she develops an awful canker sore, so her mother presses a fingertip of white powder into Cynthia's gums. Her mother calls it alum, and says it is a preservative that also dries out infection. The barky tartness creeps into Cynthia's saliva, trickling down her esophagus every time she swallows, slowly pickling her.*

•

Cynthia scrubbed her tongue with her fingers until she heaved spittle. She half-stumbled down the basement stairs, kicking jars left and right until she reached the bottom, where she tugged the lightbulb cord.

An amber glow illuminated dunes of canned goods. Cynthia figured there must have been a thousand. The jars near the back looked packed with food, but the newer ones held different things. In one was a vial of nail polish, in another a pair of sunglasses, and in a third was Josephine's quill. Cynthia sank to her knees and picked up one close to her.

Dull-green liquid sloshed within, protecting a little triangle of paper. Cynthia popped the lid and fished the scrap out.

On one side was half an image of a pot stuffed with blanched vegetables, and Cynthia realized it had come from the canning book. She flipped the paper over. Written in permanent marker was the fragment "SPARE ROOM."

Cynthia's heart skipped a beat. She put down the container and found another one holding part of the canning book, and then another and another.

"PEACE OF MIND"

"DISTRACTION"

"LETTING GO"

Cynthia dropped the fourth jar, gasping for air.

She glanced up at the top of the basement steps, where Josephine stood.

Or at least it could be, but the drinking and tears had made everything blurry.

Josephine asked Cynthia what she was doing.

"I needed to know. I'm tired of being scared."

Josephine asked Cynthia why she was scared.

"I quit my job."

Josephine asked Cynthia why she had quit her job.

"I saw it stretching out before me, forever. I saw us on loop. Something had to give."

Josephine began to clink and rattle down the stairs, so

Cynthia shut her eyes, and

•

she opens them into darkness. Her mouth reeks of alum. Josephine is under the covers next to her.

Cynthia clutches at her pounding head, struggling to remember how she has gotten up from the basement. Her memories are compressed dough.

The curtains twitch in the breeze, and through the open window Cynthia can hear voices. She slides out of bed, still drunk, and peeks outside.

A person crouches in the garden, their back towards Cynthia. They are chatting with someone below them that Cynthia can't see. Then the crouching person laughs, and with a start Cynthia realizes it is Josephine.

The Josephine outside turns in the direction of the bedroom window. Cynthia ducks down, her heart vibrating against her ribs.

The person in the bed moves.

Cynthia crawls back onto the mattress, to the lump growing under the surface. With one shaky hand she grabs the corner of the comforter and pulls.

In the bed is Josephine, but it also isn't. It has her panties, and her hair, but its skin is smooth glass. Gelatinous liquid oozes under its surface, and there appears to be little else inside the glass wife. At least until Cynthia looks at the stomach.

A creature floats in the syrup, its limbs dead stalks, its skin vivisected with wrinkles. It might be sleeping or it might be dead, but its eyelids have not endured the preservation, and so it stares at Cynthia with irises the color of daffodils.

The glass wife grabs Cynthia by the arm, pulling her down until Cynthia's face presses against the ice-cold, translucent abdomen.

"He's got your eyes," says the glass wife.

Cynthia pushes away, clawing at the burgeoning belly, at Josephine. She falls off the bed, and keeps falling, through the floorboards and the dirt of the garden and the rotting, heaving basement. There doesn't appear to be a bottom.

●

Josephine told Cynthia that Mary had a family emergency so she couldn't send them off, but she relayed her heartfelt goodbyes.

"I bet she's sad *one* of us is leaving," said Cynthia.

Josephine asked her to be kind, and Cynthia rolled her eyes but didn't press it.

She was, after all, in a good mood. They had found a place in Oregon about a month ago, still near the coast, much to Josephine's delight. Cynthia had already accepted an apprenticeship with a photography studio, and their cottage hadn't been on the market for more than a week before being snapped up, for more money than they had bought it to boot.

As they drove away, Josephine mentioned that she had gotten a new idea for a poem. And not just one poem either: a whole anthology. They discussed it for some time, and even at this nascent stage Cynthia could tell it was one of the good ones. There wouldn't be any of Josephine's "things" for a while.

The remains of the canning book, which Cynthia had found half-buried in the garden, were not discussed. Josephine hadn't said anything about the book, and that was good enough for Cynthia.

Cynthia kissed her wife on the forehead, loving the way she smelled.

"Josie, I think this is the start of a beautiful new chapter," she whispered.

Josephine smiled, reaching one hand into her pocket to caress a little satchel of white powder.

•

She thinks so, too.

**Taylor Rae**

# How Space Fell in Love with Time

I imagine them in a café, just like this one.

Maybe Space sat there, pouring a cream-nebula into his coffee, watching Time from across the room. Maybe Time looked like you, your face so pink and nervous, as he tuned the newborn universe's first guitar.

You sit on a makeshift stage, backgrounded by the shop's front windows. The street behind you is dark, snowy. There's only a couple dozen people here. Just a tiny café in a nowhere town. Your first coffee shop show.

Your eyes flash to mine. I know you too well. Anxiety tightens your shoulders, but you wink at me and say, "Evening, everybody," into the microphone.

And when you start playing—God, and *singing*—the whole place hushes. It feels like even the street is listening, the snow, the growing night.

I think of Space, holding the words on his tongue. Maybe Space and Time were roommates, just bros, and Space dug black holes in his heart because he'd rather have late nights playing video games with his best friend than nothing at all.

Maybe even Space is terrified of being alone.

I know I'm wrong. I know it's all prions and proto-particles, but I want that primordial heat.

After the show, we smoke cigarettes in the parking lot. I stand weak-kneed, like Space on the night of the big bang: risking chaos, risking everything.

But I lean forward. I pluck your cigarette from your lips.

I dare to make a universe with you.

**Emily Jon Tobias**

# *Vida*

To tell you about Vida, I have to go back to when I'm fifteen and all I want is a good fight. To when I don't know nothing—*nada*—about how love works. When el amor solamente means bad things are coming. I love Mami. Then she dies with a needle in her arm. Y Papi? He's shot dead on the streets of East L.A. before I'm out of diapers. I don't remember him, but I guess I got a little bit of his love left over on me after all. A brand that never goes away. See, before he died, Mami let him name me. He said I'd turn out just like the coyote, just like him. Wild. They say Papi was a smart man on the streets. Not smart enough to stay alive, I say. He was smart about naming me, though. Name's Wiley. Es verdad, suits me just fine.

When Mami dies after Papi dies, I get shoved off to Abuela for a few years. I still got my Abuela's ring, the thing she gave me at her bedside days before she died. To remember her by, she said. I wear the ring on my left hand on the finger that means you're attached. Or committed. I can't remember which.

Abuela doesn't want me at first, I can tell. Hardly says much between her missing front teeth. But then she starts to cook for me. Pozole and pastor. Chiles roasted right on the burner of the gas stove. Comida in big pots and pans like she's feeding an army, but it's only us two. And tortillas. Not those kind you get at El Mercadito in the package. The real ones. And not in some tortilla press, neither. No, she mashes the masa by hand.

Until the cancer.

At the end, she only eats plain chicken, no skin. Any smells in our apartment make her sicker. One time, I try to make her favorite—café con leche. I even run a cinnamon stick along her cheese grater for more flavor on the top. Then I carry it to her, wobbling on a tray. She pukes in the trash bin next to her bed. After that, no more cooking. No more smells of chiles and chocolate. All aromas are banned. Her body turns into a tiny peanut in its shell with all that loose wrinkled skin.

I'm the one who finds her one day, head slumped. Dead in a straight-backed chair. She made it all the way from her bed to the TV room to die. I remember wondering which telenovela was worth all that extra energy just to up and die for. I do not cry. I just wonder.

When Abuela dies after the others, I get put in the system. I'm on my way to Vida. Strange details stick out when love's coming your way but she's not here yet. Things that, after someone's come and gone, you'll want to savor—sweet and sour—like tamarindo on your tongue. Really, you don't get to choose how things look in your head. Memories are like my street art—once it's tagged, the colors stand, good *and* bad, splattered across the mind like a crime. Mi Vida? She's all the colors in one. My mural.

•

The house had cracked paint. Yellow—mustard, more like, with the way the sun beats down. Sucks all the shine out. East L.A. sun makes for angry summers. You can see the heat come off black tar gone soft on the street like oil in a fryer. Everyone's a badass in August, and everyone wants a fight. People get all riled up when it's that hot. Me? Not yet. I just wanted to get the shit over with. The introductions and whatnot. I know how it goes, a new foster home. I been in the system long enough to have the lowdown on how fitting in with families takes time. You got to remember the small things that make up a family's memory. You got to let them see you cry—at least once, I've learned—to get them to like you. I never stay long enough. For me, crying doesn't come easy.

So, I'm on the porch smoking. The foster parents seem to know they can't stop us from smoking. Most teens in the system smoke. Passes the time waiting for the next move. There's always another move. I do a French inhale. Some kid from a home way back taught me that. I got my hat pulled down low on my forehead. Flat-billed L.A. Dodgers like Papi wore, they say.

That time, my caseworker took me herself. Said it was no trouble, she had the time. I stand on the porch watching her from behind. She's searching for her briefcase in the car. (*Stay here, Wiley. Don't move. Damn kids. Always causing trouble.*) She's got her whole body shoved into the back seat moving things around. Her skirt rides up and I can see the top part of her pantyhose where the girdle starts. She's a big woman—Ms. B. That's what the kids call her. Says, This way it's easier to remember, Wiley. Just one letter. She reminds me of my Abuela—her size.

I put my smoke out before Ms. B gets back from her car. (*Put that cigarette out! Make things easy on yourself for once, Wiley. No one wants a kid who smokes.*) Ms. B and me stand at the door with her briefcase. Her size seems to make her sweat more than most. Also, she seems nervous. I know she wants me placed without trouble this time. It's gotta be at least ninety-five degrees, and that kind of heat don't help things. Her hands slip. She drops her pen at my feet. Says she wants me to really feel safe and at home with these nice folks. She tugs at the elastic waist on her skirt. Says to act right and everything would be fine, she says, she says, This time might be different, Wiley, be a good girl. You're almost an adult now. Act your age. I stop listening after the nice folks part. Plus, remember, I'm only fifteen.

I think to myself, Just say it, woman, say what you want to say: Do not lie; do not steal; do not shout, FUCK YOU, LADY to the foster mother; do not scream, GO SUCK A COCK to the foster father; do not rage or hit other kids (*You East L.A. kids are no joke, Wiley. I know you're angry.*); do not tag the bedroom walls with Sharpie; do not tag the outside gate with spray paint; do not run away; do not stay; do not waste my mother-fucking time. I know what she *wants* to say: Do not be your real damaged self. What she means is, Hide. Instead, she sweats. And lies.

There's grass there. Greener than at most homes. I think there are tomatoes growing. They have hot peppers in old plastic paint buckets. Red and yellow and orange. My Abuela ate Hungarian hots raw, right off the stem. Said they were hotter than any habanero. She'd sweat and snort. Wipe her forehead with her sleeve then use the cuff to blow her nose. The water would run and run and run from her forehead like a busted faucet. Never complained, just took the heat. Never bitched about the cancer, neither. No one might have guessed she was dying except that she couldn't wear the wig in summer. Too hot. She was tough. I think she loved me. Until she died. Then she was just ... dead. Not so tough, after all.

I act nice to Ms. B. I try to show the caseworkers respect. (*Show me some respect, goddamnit. No wonder they don't want you.*) I don't know why. No point, really. She got so many kids, soon she won't remember my name. They might give me someone new next time. I don't want someone new. Ms. B's okay. (*Tuck your shirt in, Wiley. And pull your pants up. You've got to look more presentable. I want them to like you. You know how many cases I got right now? Too many. I need this one to stick.*) I bend down to grab her pen. Holding the thing out for her, I notice the porch is clean, swept. Next plot over is an empty lot where another house should have been, but no house, just brown grass and trash. There's a rusted out metal barrel with a grate on top off to the corner of the lot. On its side, someone tagged *QUE TENGAS UN BUEN DÍA* with a little devil to the side. I wonder what it might be like to choose how a day feels. The devil makes me smile. The front yard here is completely fenced in.

I stay quiet, of course. I am no idiota. In a way, I want them to like me too this time. See, I'm feeling tired of being shuffled around like a domino. Also, Ms. B and me, we have a relationship now like she's my mama but her only duty is to make sure we go our separate ways. Somehow, I want to do right by her. I'm gonna do Ms. B a solid, so I take my hat off. I never take this hat off. I tuck it under my armpit. Ms. B rolls her eyes, snatches her pen from my hand. (*Take that hat off, Wiley. You look like a little boy. The fosters want to know what kind of girl they're getting.*) Then, she faces the door. Pen. Click. Click. I look at my feet, hands down my pockets. She rings the bell, again. We stand on a mat that says, *Home Sweet Home* in curly letters. The *Sweet* part is larger than the letters spelling *Home*. I let my backpack slide from my shoulder to the ground. We wait.

Ms. B's back always gets straighter when the foster parents open the door. (*Stand up, girl. They're coming.*) This one is a tall man with a big gut. He's dressed nice enough—button shirt, decent pants. He wears a leather belt. A wide metal buckle is front and center with an American flag painted into the steel grooves like a banner. He rubs his fingers along the front of the buckle, then tucks his thumbs into his pockets. One of his buttons is undone where the shirt tucked into his waist.

This the new one?

Yes, sir, Ms. B says.

Wiley, right?

That's right, she says.

Nice to meet you, I say, eyes down. (*You need to learn some manners, Wiley.*)

Well, let's get on with it, then, he says.

He moves aside, opens the door wide, propped by his foot. Ms. B touches my back with her sweaty palm to nudge me in. I lean back into her for a moment. When I bend forward to pick up my backpack, my hat falls to the ground. I grab it fast. Something about the father makes me not want to wear it. Instead, I bend the bill and stuff the hat down the side of my backpack. I slide both arms into the straps and tighten. Then, I tuck my hair behind my ears. I have to try hard to straighten up.

When I'm inside, he locks the deadbolt behind us. I turn to look for Ms. B. Through the small glass window of the front door, I see her again from behind. She's untucking her blouse from her skirt. She walks faster, stalls at the gate, already fumbling for her car keys in her purse. I hear the beep when she unlocks her car and closes the gate behind her. Then, she glances one last time toward the house. She shakes her head, checks the gate again. To make sure it shut. Sometimes I wonder who waits for her at her own home. Through the small pane of glass, I know she can't see me anymore.

•

The thing about new homes—you can tell a lot of what you need to know in the first five minutes. I can tell right away there's no mother here. But I don't ask questions about that. (*Don't ask so many questions next time. No one wants a nosy child.*) The shades are drawn across the windows of the front room. There's one brown couch, two wooden chairs, a big screen TV on a black stand. On the coffee table, a cigar sits in an ashtray on top of a couple men's magazines. The TIME Magazine has Donald Trump on the cover. The whole place smells like burnt popcorn and Budweiser. I look at the walls.

The only thing hanging is one framed photo. In the middle, it's the foster father, younger, with his arms around two other men in uniform. One has a big gun strapped across his chest. In the background, there's only desert sand. Above the photo, a wooden cross. There's no green anywhere in this place. No fake plants in the room, no real ones either. No flowers, no doilies or coasters, no paintings, no clutter. No color to anything at all. The man's in charge.

This is my room, got it? he says.

Yes, sir. (ESTÚPIDO.)

You ain't allowed to laze around in here, got it?

Yes, sir. (CHINGATUMADRE.)

And in this house, there ain't no woman to clean up after you, got it?

Yes, sir. (HIJO DE PUTA.)

So you're gonna have to clean up your own mess, got it?

Yes, sir. (*Each family has their own rules, Wiley. You're going to have to learn to fit in and adapt to differences.*) How many kids live here? I ask.

With you, makes three. I'm on the light side with fosters right now.

I stretch my neck to look past him down the hallway toward the back of the house. There's a kitchen back there. A couple other rooms, too. Doors are shut. I can't get a feel except that I'm not allowed back there.

My room's upstairs then? I ask.

Kids' rooms are all upstairs.

I follow him up with my backpack held tight. He still has his work boots on. On the lower stair beneath him, I see mud caked in the trenches of the boots. A small sheathed fixed blade hangs on his belt. He's a lumberjack of a man—gruff, this one. Still resembles the soldier in his photo but rougher and wider with more chinks in his skin.

He takes me through the hallway with his thumbs hooked on his belt like he's a guard checking on the inmates. On that side, I got Santos. Santos Ramirez. He hasn't been here long, he says, tapping the door with his knuckle. He points ahead. You're at the end of the hall. You share with Vida.

She another foster? I ask.

Sure is, he says. He gets quiet, sort of sucks himself in. Then I hear him whisper her name, Vida Arenas Lopez, and way under his breath, Sweet little thing. I notice the color change in his face—red to pale—when I look at him after he says it. He's tense, tight in the mouth, like a kid caught cussing in church.

Vida, I say. Then, *Vida, Vida, Vida* ... and I don't know why I sing out like that, but I do, I say her name over and over, I do. I haven't even met her yet, but I want him to know our names don't belong to him. Since then, I've learned that un-fit love can make you do unreasonable things even before you put a face to it.

Finally, he cuts in, snaps, Get yourself situated. We eat at 6:00PM, sharp. You miss dinner, fend for yourself. That's how it works around here, got it?

Yes, sir, I say. When his back's turned, I give him a one-fin-ger salute.

In my room, I toss my bag on the top bunk. New kids al-ways take the top. I take a breath. It's like the first gasp a newborn takes in the world after the womb. And you're all alone for that one moment. Until you're not. I know there's a girl in the room behind me because I smell her. I see colors when I smell her. Pinks and reds splattered wild on some white wall like spray paint from the can. I already know her name: *Vida, Vida, Vida.*

You can have the bottom, she says behind me.

I can take the top, I say. No problem.

I'm used to sleeping up there.

Whatever you say.

I feel safe sleeping closer to the stars, she says.

I pull my hat down. You been in this home long? I ask.

A few months.

How is it here?

She shrugs, turns away from me. De miedo, pero, it's okay, she says. I wonder what she's afraid of. Kids like us learn how to box and bury fear like a body.

What's your name?

Vida, she says, hushed.

She reaches her hand toward me like a shake, but somehow I come from underneath with my arm, so her hand lands in mine like a ball to a glove, palms cradled, face up. I don't mean to touch her like that. I don't mean to like it when I do. But I do.

I'm Wiley, I say and close my hand around hers just a bit.

Silly name for a chola, she says. How'd you get a name like that?

The coyote.

You wild?

Maybe I am.

Should I be scared of you little Wiley? she laughs.

Cuidada, I say. Careful.

(*If you keep acting like a wild animal, Wiley, no family will take you.*)

Pues, you might be tough, but I think it's pretty, your name. The way she says my name, how her tongue rolls around—*W-I-L-E-Y*—the word seems safe in her mouth. Like somehow, she'd caught me, too.

•

When I meet her, Vida's seventeen, almost old enough to get out. You can tell by how she tiptoes around the yellow house, bending herself around things, like she's trying to disappear ahead of time. Como un fantasma, like a ghost. Some would say I was too young to fall for her. Tal vez, maybe, pero yo sabía. I know how I feel. Lo siento todo. I feel *everything* after so long of feeling nothing at all.

I'm in the yellow house for weeks and still, I can't sleep. I hate the pinche place. Especially at night. I hate being up- stairs with no AC in summer heat, and there's a burning smell in my nose, but no fire. Summer cicadas buzz on hay- wire, and I can hear the fiesta of roaches in cracks of the walls like tiny tap dancers. I got a can of spray paint in my backpack. Always do. I imagine lighting the whole room on fire with my art. Light it up with flames and demons and ev- ery vulgar word I know.

I'm on my bottom bunk. She's on top. I got my arm crooked behind my head, elbow in the air, watching the coils of her mattress worm when she moves her body. I know Vida's awake, tambien. When she can't sleep, she sings. At first, I hate her for it. I hate how she can stay so calm lying there in the dark. For me, the sleeplessness makes me angry like having my hands tied behind my back in a fight. I want to scream, break free. But not Vida. She just sings and waits.

One night, I'm listening. I know she's still awake, but barely, because she's humming, no words. What's that song? I ask. She tells me it's, Oh! Susanna, and then she keeps singing, so soft, like some kind of lullaby and I recognize the tune—not the words, no—the sound, somehow deep, way down, in my bones. I feel her voice in my toes. I don't remember falling asleep, but I do. The girl can sing.

I don't know if it's the song that makes me dream or Vida's voice. That night, I see them all there. All the ghosts. Mami with the needle hanging out her arm. Abuela—bald— wig in her hand. Even my Papi's there, I think that's him. He's got the Dodgers hat tucked under his armpit, and the gun that killed him in his hand. Then, it's him there, the foster father, el señor, he's got his belt in his hand. He buckles the metal American flag around Vida's waist and tightens, and he's yanking her toward him like she's leashed. When he shuts the door, he puts his finger to his lips, Shhhh, he whispers, Shush. I wake. They're gone. The ghosts. I'm sweating. I jump. Bang my head on the top bunk. It's already morning.

You okay, wild Wiley? Vida leans down from her bed above.

Bien, bien. I'm fine, I say.

You were crying in your sleep.

Fuck that. Was not.

Okay, okay, Vida laughs. Guess what?

¿Qué?

Today's my birthday.

No mames wey.

Sí. I'm eighteen.

Holy shit.

I'm going to get out of here.

When?

As soon as I can, she says, and lifts her mattress. I almost have enough.

I don't know where she got that money. No importa. All that matters to me is how she *trusts* me. I don't know why she trusts me. And that don't matter neither. I feel valuable, like when Abuela let me use her kitchen knife for the first time—bonded by the risk we share. Like finally I have someone who wants my loyalty. That's the thing with young love. More heart, less investigation.

•

It's a Saturday. Vida's eighteenth. I remember because the foster father's gone and we don't have school. Santos is still in his room when Vida and me tiptoe downstairs. She wants una fiesta, she says, in the empty house. For her birthday. In foster care, privacy is like pinning the tail on the donkey. You only win it when you're not looking.

I'm standing aside from her, watching. I got my arms crossed at my chest, one leg hooked over the other, leaning against the doorframe. My hat's pulled low. She's rummaging through the kitchen searching for booze, flinging cabinet doors open, one after the other, yanking on drawers, and I'm just standing there wondering what this puta's gonna find in some junk drawer that can fuck us up. I smile. She's rushing for no good reason. We know he'll be gone for the day. His agenda's penciled in on a calendar. Says right there, he'll be busy until 5:00. El señor is strict about time being in the military, so I think we're in the clear.

Finally, she finds a bottle in the back under the sink with the cleaners. Cazadores. Cheap tequila but at least it's something. Then, she finds a couple limes rolling around the back of the crisper drawer in the fridge. Grabs a knife from the drawer. Cuts around the brown parts to make slices. She grabs the salt and says, Tú y yo. You and me, Wiley. On the porch. Ahoríta.

I look at her then. Holding the bottle in one hand, limes in the palm of her other, juice running down her arm. Suddenly, I think of Mami before all the drugs, before the leaving and the dying, before all this. I mean I actually feel her rhythm in the room way down in my gut. I see her in Vida's bang—so pretty like Mami used to be. Mami loved to dance. She'd play the radio and when Santana came on, she'd move and sing— *oye como va, mi ritmo, bueno pa' gozar*—she'd spread her body around the room, moving her hips, sucking on limes against her lips after shots from a tiny glass. Mami y yo, I'm so little, happy, she dances with me, *Baila conmigo mi chiquitita, te amo mucho, muchisimo*, she says and takes my tiny fingers in her hand held high so I can twirl under her arm and spin. She catches me and won't let me go. And I can't believe it, how much of Mami I feel when I see Vida.

What do you say, wild Wiley? Vida says, holding the bottle out.

My shoulders roll down my back from up near my ears. My chest opens. She's so bright, brighter than the graffiti in my mind. She's blood-red jewels and pink roses, orange shades of fire and flames, yes, she is, she is. She's the boldest red in her face, at the rounds of each cheek. But there is more. I stall. I stare at her body's surface like right before I tag a wall. She's the white light of a blank canvas *behind* the paint, she has the softness of diamond shine and the warmth of gold. *Pura Vida.*

Claro que sí, I say. It's on.

We're on the porch smoking and taking shots. When Santos comes downstairs, we invite him. It's a celebration, we say. ¡Feliz cumpleaños, Vida! No te preocupes, el señor is gone till 5:00! we say. We lick the backs of our hands, sprinkle salt for each other. Vida pours. We clink glasses, take the shot, lick the salt, suck the lime, and again. I sit next to Vida on the bench. We're so close, her arms rests along my thigh. It's got to be almost a hundred degrees. Booze helps us forget about the heat.

You guys want to play a game? Santos asks.

Sure, Vida says.

Birthday girl goes first, he says.

I stay quiet watching Santos. He's leaning against the porch railing. I see him eyeing one of the buckets that el señor grows peppers in. A small orange habanero hangs from its stem. I know that the small bright ones are usually the hottest. I look at Vida. She doesn't seem to know what's coming. But I do, I do.

Vida, truth or dare? Santos says.

Dare, she answers, fast.

Santos leans over and plucks the pepper, smiling wide. The pepper's dangling off its stem when he hands it off to Vida. Cometelo, he says, the whole thing.

That girl, just when I think she might be soft. She doesn't even bat an eye when she snatches the thing from Santos and pops it in her mouth. I watch her the whole time. She keeps her eyes on Santos. Chews twice or three times. Then swallows. She swipes her hands together, opens her empty mouth wide at him, and says, Bueno? Que mas? like what else you got for me, chico.

I stare, can't get my gaze off her. When Vida's eyes start to water from the sting, I see Abuela clear as day, tough as nails, chomping on her Hungarian hots, wiping the sweat from her face. They're bigger than life to me—both of them—and strong—fuerte, fuerte, fuerte—in color, como el fuego, blazing like fire. I don't know if it's the tequila that's got me, but oh—mi corazón—my heart pumps me full of feelings I've never had before. Seeing Vida. Remembering mi familia. I'm bursting.

Santos looks stunned when Vida stays quiet with el chile in her mouth. Suddenly, she gasps, and spits, and we all break out laughing like hyenas, hopping up and down like little conejitos.

Your turn, Wiley, says Santos. Truth or dare?

Dare, I say. Bring it on, puto.

I *dare* you to kiss Vida. En la boca.

My heart stops. I mean it actually stops beating. When it starts up again, I feel the thing bulge in my chest and plummet to my toes.

No way, Santos, I say. Not going to happen. I'm looking down when I say it, and I feel my face red and burnt up like el diablo. I shake my head fast. My hands tingle. Even my ears are hot. My stomach sloshes with tequila like a washing machine.

Está todo bien, wild Wiley, Vida says.

What? Are you serious?

Let's just do it.

I shove my hands down my pockets. I've never kissed anyone, much less una chica bonita, the prettiest girl I've ever seen with hips as round as her lips, big brown eyes, and the kind of hair that's made for a doll, like black silk. Vida gets up from the bench, stands to my front. Then, she reaches out to me, holding out her hands to help me up.

I don't think about doing it. I just do. I kiss her. Un beso. One time. Right then, it starts to drizzle. You see, I remember the rain—I will always remember the rain—because in L.A., summer is like the Mojave, and it just never did. Rain. I remember thinking about my mama with the needle in her arm, hoping that she felt like this—the one kiss—right before she died. One kiss. On the jawbone, accidentally, at its angle, just beneath her ear. Our lips only graze one another's. But I want her. My sister. My *pinche* sister. Mi amor? My lifer. I go red. How could I? Mi Vida. Then, just like that, it's over. I pull back some. She's still close when she whispers, Tranquila amor, tranquila. Then she says, Tienes que salir de aquí. Ir a correr. Run far away from him.

¿Qué dijo? I say, and step away from her. What did you say?

Vida releases my hands. That's when I see him standing there under the frame of the front door. Our foster father. I bite my tongue. He must've parked in the alley behind the house, come in through the back door. He's early.

What the fuck is this? he says. You all think you can have a party in MY home?

Santos says, It's Vida's birthday, then backs away. I watch Vida when her body buckles, collapsing into the bench. It seems to me she's trying to fold herself up into a thing too small for him to notice. Suddenly, she's so small, tan pequeña, and somehow I know that he's coming for her. That this is not the first time he's had her.

I take my hat off and set it gently on Vida's lap. I turn toward him. I stand taller than I know I am, feet wide, arms crossed at my chest. Then, I move my body to shield hers, directly between them. I block him from getting to her. Sitting behind me, her knees touch the backs of my calves. The father stomps. One boot. Two boots. Slats bend where wood is rot. He's closer to me. The Cazadores bottle wobbles on the porch when he steps. He grabs the bottle. Hurls it over the fence into the empty lot next door. He hits the rusted-out metal barrel square on the mark where the little devil's tagged. Glass shatters. Vida flinches.

You, he says to Vida, you're coming with me. Get up.

He tries to shove me aside to get to her. I puff my chest. No, I say. Don't touch her.

Move aside, girl.

You're not taking her.

He pushes his hands down on my shoulders as if he's trying to drown me. Pressing, hard, to sit me down. I lock my
knees. I go nowhere. I squeeze myself tighter, arms around
my chest.

No, I say, No.

He's yelling now, Move your ass, you freak of a girl. I feel
spit on my face, he's so close.

No, I yell. No!

Finally, he gets a good grip on my shoulder. I see that
blade he wears hanging off his belt. He shoves me. Hard. I
fall to the side. I grab for the knife as I fall. I miss. His belt
breaks from my grab. I'm on the ground, his broken belt beside my head. I lie flat, long, so he has to step over me to
get to her. He picks up the belt. Finds the knife alongside
the bench. When he steps over me, I see between his legs
from the ground. Then, he's in front of her. Looking down on
her. He threads the belt through each loop, secures the knife,
never taking his eyes off her.

Vida does not resist when he drags her off the porch, into
his house, by her hair. Instead, she flexes her body into him
like a dancer on a pole. I stay flat on my back. My neck still
burns from the hot pepper where Vida's lips touched my
skin. When they're finally gone, I do it. Un poquito, just a
little bit, I cry.

•

It's late. I'm lying face up on my bunk, one hand over my
heart, waiting for her, in the dark. I got the bill of my hat
pulled low. My eyes are wide open, though, gaze pinned to

the bottom of Vida's bunk from below, as if I might miss her getting back unless I keep looking.

Finally, I hear the door open. I don't know if I should pretend to be asleep or say something. But then, she's there, next to me, in my bed. She nudges me away. Move over, she whispers. I shimmy toward the wall. She turns her backside toward me, fitting her edges perfectly up against the angles of my front. Then, she lifts my arm and wraps it around her waist, tucks my hand under her hip, as if she's buckling herself into a car seat. Her chin is tucked into her chest when I hear her quiet sobs.

I don't ask questions. I don't need to. She trembles when I touch the bruise on her face. I feel what he's done to her in my own bones when she cowers as I cover her with my sweatshirt, tensing her belly when I situate my arm. Lying with her, I wish I was prettier than her so it can be me who has to take it from him. So I could've saved her. But she is so damn pretty. Too small and too pretty. I'm not the one he wants.

Suddenly, I prop myself up. I want to take you somewhere, I say.

Where? she says, still crying.

Get up.

Wiley, it's late.

Vamonos.

We'll get caught.

He won't hear us leave. Andale.

Promise?

Promise, I said, I said.

Lo prometo, I say, I say.

I promise.

We're standing on the tracks. Her two feet on one railway track, mine on another, facing one another. We're in the train tunnel. Abandoned tracks. My surprise for her. Our sounds vibrate, echoing like they'll never end. Sounds that are colors of the underground, colors of all the unknowns come to tag their names, to tell somebody (*no one can hear you*), anybody (*keep your voices down*), that they exist (*you are invisible*). A million tags in neons overlaying the others, each one scrubbed, ghosted to make space for the next, for another, to rise. When I hug her into me, I see HOPE in green, graffitied on the tunnel's curve behind her. I could sit her down inside the O, I think, I think, She'd be safe there, inside HOPE. Instead, I hold her. I whisper into her shoulder.

How long has he been hurting you? I ask.

The whole time.

Did you try to tell someone?

No. I been in worse homes.

My caseworker, Ms. B. I can call her.

I just have to get enough money to get out.

You don't have to keep taking that shit from him. El cabrón, I say.

I'm eighteen now. I can leave as soon as I have enough, she says. I think about her stash under the mattress. Seems to me it's not nearly enough to get herself out of there. Then she says, You know, he's not going to let you stay in the house, Wiley. After what you did.

Lo sé. I know. I know. We could leave here, together, I say. Tu y yo.

She's quiet then. I look toward the open end of the tunnel behind her. I'm certain she can see the other end, wide and free, beyond me. Two ways to get out. We're in the middle, on the tracks. Safe from the rain when it begins to fall. Drops are like footsteps—like the pitter-patter of ghosts—on the ground above our heads. She pulls away from me, gently.

She sits on the side of the tracks, her back rounded against the tunnel. Her elbows are on her knees, head hanging down. The air is thick from the heat in the tunnel, wet from the rain outside. I walk to her. There's an angel behind her painted on the tunnel wall, all white, outlined in black. It's kneeling, hands together at the chest in prayer. The angel is perfect. I look down on Vida. She's perfect. She's crying. I look away. Up. No face. The painted angel has no head.

I take her hands to pull her up. I guide her to the middle of the tracks to show her the angel. Then, in my backpack, I find the can. Gloss Banner Red. She watches while I tag her name in big bold letters—VIDA—across the blank spot where the angel's head would be. I hold her hand. We face her name.

Everyone I've ever loved has died, or left me, I say, I say, I don't want to leave you, I say.

If you stay, it will get worse for me.

But I love you, I LOVE YOU, I think, I think, *Te amo, mi Vida*, I do not say. I think about my mama, then. My mama died with a needle in her arm. That's what they say. They say. Say. (*Say nothing, Wiley. Act right. Maybe this will be the one where you stay.*) Abuela told me once that Mami said I came out her womb frowning with a full head of tight black curls. Didn't make a peep. Not a cry, not one sound at all. She said Mami loved me. I look at Vida. I think about how, before her, the only love I've ever known was that of ghosts.

Back then, I wore it on my pointer finger. Abuela's ring. In the light at one of the tunnel's ends, I take it off. I slip the ring into Vida's hand, close her palm around it.

Use this to get out of here, I say. It's worth something.

Walking back, she sings to me, Oh! Susanna so softly, the only sound against cicadas and stars and I hum along to hide my crying. At the house, she drops my hand to unlock the gate, then closes it tight behind her. I say, Happy birthday, I say, I said, I will never forget. Lo prometo.

•

I'm on the porch smoking. Ms. B's on her way. Only took her one week to place me in another home after el señor made the call. (*I knew you'd ruin this, Wiley. What did I tell you?*)

During my last week in the yellow house, Vida's eyes tell me to go by how she looks *past* me, how she already has her shoes on when he comes for her again, how she stays standing, rounded in her body, hands down her pockets, waiting for him. She doesn't say a word. Doesn't stall or shift. He doesn't have to call on her either; she's already walking toward him.

The last time I see her, she slips the ring off her pinky—the gold band I'd given her when we were safe on the tracks. She sets the ring on the small table beside our bunks. I never told her how long I'd worn it, since before the system, before all this. I'd worn it on a chain around my neck as a kid—from home to home—until I was old enough for it to fit a finger. By the time the door shuts behind her, the ring is still teetering.

I close my eyes, still have the burn of Vida's lips on my skin. Us two. After one kiss. My bottom bunk. Me wrapped around her from behind. Blowing across those welts in hand-prints on her cheeks. Que se siente bien, she said, feels good, feel so good. I leaned into her forehead, her tears wetting my chin, our hands—four into one—gripped together between us at our chests.

Maybe, I should've left the ring for her. I didn't. Pero, en-tiendeme por favor—you have to understand—I couldn't. Instead, I put it around my own finger. So I could remember she was no fantasma. Vida is here, see, she's around my fin-ger, real as gold.

I put my smoke out, tip my hat back. I nod toward Ms. B as she's rushing up the porch toward me. Next house is in Long Beach. I wonder what color it will be. In my mind it's blue. I imagine what I'll say to the next girl I share a room with—I should say, I will take the top bunk. No hay prob-lema. I like to sleep closer to the stars. I wonder if she will ever have been loved or left before. I wonder, should I warn her?—¡Cuidada! Beware!—love can get made in these color-ful houses. Then disappear. Faceless, like a ghost.

**Dani Alexis Ryskamp**

# *Ghostlight*

*March 2020*
*March 2021*
*March 2022*

The ghostlight
is not lit
to chase the ghosts away.

It is lit to keep them company.
Ghosts, too, need friends:
they struggle with social distancing

made worse by rumors of their deaths.
It's not that no one cares
when you're a ghost; only

that you rank too highly on Maslow's hierarchy to rate
when the schools close, the shops.
*In sancti spiritu*, when the breath

in the lungs
fails,
so too does the breath in the soul.

But those of us who breathe?
We light the ghostlight,
place it on the stage and seal the doors;

we play our roles in hospitals, at home,
as the bodies stack like cordwood. Ghosts are patient:
ghosts are kind: ghosts forbear our neglect. They wait

in the wings as the breathless world
contracts: *Survive,*
they whisper. *Loves, survive.*

**Dani Alexis Ryskamp**

# *Faceless*

This
is what it means
to suffer from pareidolia:

to see faces
in the mist
of what used to be a city,

to see people
where there are no people,
to see life where there is no life,

to see hope
where there is
no hope.

**Dani Alexis Ryskamp**

# *Anechoic*

Grief is an affair of the heart
break. No one says this. No one tells you how
to proceed with a heart, your
heart, shattered—beating? How to
read the facile texts, the cards [without
him], *thinking of you.* No one says you have to live.

But you do. Have to live,
I mean; the body persists, the heart
beats on, the little shit, without
regard to your howling, *how*
*such pain, and live? How*
*to stop?* no stop. one stop. His. your

pain but not its cause is real (your
"real" here "material"; you live
in spacetime, sentient, sensible to
sense a senseless heart
less interplay of entropy, atrophy: a human, how
ling down the centuries of sense, without

a within, which the living locate without:
go out, get out, speak out, as if your
grief is noise? or silence, as if how

you bear grief speaks to suffering, which, if not live,
allows a life to live without a heart
that beats aware of where it's going to.)

One time we were two, to
gether one, ten years; without
one warning, our one heart
collapsed; my half staggers, your
half stills. *Survive* won't rhyme with *live*.
(Trust me. I know. I know now how

to rhyme (survive) alive). why? how
our wedlock passes tense, to
wards away to live
with and you without.
I see it in my sleep: your
center, all of me, my heart your heart.

A widow lives. I cannot tell you how,
even as my heart rends from one to
two. one. your. mine. we. he. without.

**Dean Gloster**

# *Proof of the Existence of Dog*

Because of logic, fourteen-year-old Carrie Marten knew—absolutely—that her perfect furry best friend for life was somewhere close. She would, she promised herself, find and adopt that dog this weekend, while her parents were out of town.

A solid plan. Grownups were like rivers: They were all headed downhill, and—while they made babbling noises at everything and sometimes even briefly split to go around islands—they generally followed the path of least resistance. Like anyone who's seen prior mistakes, Carrie knew it was more difficult to undo things than to do them.

Seize the initiative. Create a new, paws-on-the-ground normal, hard to undo.

*Who will take care of the dog?* I've been taking care of him for five whole days already, she'd answer.

*What about shedding?* I found a hair dog that doesn't shed, she'd say—a poodle or adorable doodle-dog hybrid.

*Honey, things are uncertain right now, and it's not fair to—* That's right. It's not fair to make me give up this dog, who's so adorable.

Logic dictated that would be true, but—of course—Carrie hadn't just left things to chance.

Six months earlier, she'd started her dog-walking business, taking neighbors' dogs every afternoon to the fenced dog park, carrying treats and getting to know the different dogs and their personalities.

Three months ago, she'd started volunteering at the Berkeley animal shelter, caring for the dogs there. And this month she had told everyone at the shelter to be on the lookout for a non-shedding dog she could adopt.

Now everything was coming together, with the precision of a heist movie scheme: Mom and Dad had declared a temporary truce to take Carrie's older sister Zoe on a tour of possible colleges all the way across the country, on the East Coast. Mom's sister, cool Aunt Martha, was supposed to supervise Carrie, but had sprained her knee at Aikido and was supposed to stay off stairs—like the ones up to Carrie's house. And last night, the volunteer coordinator at the animal shelter had texted Carrie with the exciting news that they expected to have a labradoodle available for adoption this morning.

•

Which is what brought Carrie to her best friend Mia's apartment before 7:20 in the morning on a Saturday.

"I don't need your advice," Carrie explained, at Mia's shiny little kitchen table, keeping her voice low so it wouldn't wake Mia's mom. "It's complicated, getting a dog while your parents are out of town. I need your moral support. And for you to come along, so I'm not doing it alone."

There was a long pause while Mia crinkled her forehead. "I am happy to support your morals. Also, it's interesting to see the wreckage when your ideas collide with the real world. It's like art."

Carrie crossed her arms. "Calling it 'wreckage' isn't being supportive."

"I said 'art.' Totally supportive. Plus, if this collision triggers the end of the universe, I want to be at the point of impact, not just waiting while everything unravels."

Carrie sighed. Back to Mia's obsession with vacuum decay and the end of the universe. "It's not the end of the world. I just want a dog."

"Does this dog-getting involve actual crimes?" Mia asked.

A long pause. Technically, the part where she was going to have Rick, the homeless guy, impersonate her dad at the animal shelter was pretty sketchy. "Nothing we can't get expunged from your record. Long before graduate school."

One side of Mia's mouth curled into an uncertain *I don't know about this* expression.

Carrie let out a long, sighing breath. "If—at some point, without warning—the universe does end, then before that I should at least have a dog. Plus, this will be an adventure together. Please?"

"I'm in," Mia said. "You have a plan?"

Of course. Carrie always had a plan. She outlined it.

•

"Any progress solving vacuum decay?" Carrie asked out of politeness, while they were walking on Solano Avenue for the plan's next phase. It was a beautiful Berkeley morning, sunny but still cool enough to be walking a newly adopted long-haired dog. She'd worried that Rick might not be at the corner outside the Starbucks. But there he was, standing in his usual spot, two blocks ahead. Somehow, though, seeing him didn't make the worry in her stomach go away. It felt like a live goldfish was wriggling inside her.

Mia shook her head. "Right now, the math is a little beyond me."

"Mmn." Carrie made a sympathetic noise. The math was also currently beyond all the physicists on earth. Mia was part of an email list where they discussed research and theories and exotic equations, none of them knowing she was only fourteen.

According to physicists, the whole universe was in a Higgs energy field, which had something to do with Higgs Boson particles that give everything mass, so gravity can hold things together.

Vacuum decay theory was also important, it turned out, because scientists weren't sure what kind of Higgs energy field we were in: We might be in a stable universe, like sitting in the flat bottom of a valley floor. But probably instead the entire universe was just in a false vacuum state, like on a cliff ledge above the valley floor. Everything could be jostled out of it. Some random high energy event could bump part of the universe down to a true vacuum state, causing a bubble that expanded at the speed of light, unraveling everything. All planets, stars, particles, and life.

Even dogs.

Which, Carrie thought, was a serious design flaw.

"How are things at home?" Mia asked.

"Quiet, with Mom and Dad gone." No yelling about Dad's girlfriend. Although, in fairness, the yelling had stopped weeks ago. It had been mostly awkward, cold silence in the last month. Dad had moved out of Mom and Dad's bedroom, all the way down the hall to sleep on a foldout bed in his office.

"Is your dad still—?"

"Yeah." Carrie said quickly, to cut off whatever exact unpleasant shape the question was going to take. Dad was still dating the 23-year-old assistant from his former job. He was supposed to start a new job in a week—for lots less money—after the college tour trip. And now, in response, Mom had two dating apps on her phone.

Mom and Dad were, though, sharing a hotel room on the trip to look at colleges for Zoe, even if it had two beds. Mom had said, before they left, that they were "rekindling the romance," but she had rolled her eyes up at the ceiling when she'd said it, so there was about a 99% chance she was just being sarcastic.

"How do you know Rick's going to help?" Mia helpfully changed the subject. They were less than half a block away now.

Partly because of the Ontological Argument for the Existence of Dog, but it was a little early in the adventure to get into all that. "He's my friend," Carrie said. "I always buy his Street Sheets." That was the homeless paper Rick sold, with poems in it about having no money.

"That makes you his *customer*," Mia corrected. "Not his friend."

"We're *also* friends. Sort of. We talk a bunch." They did. Rick was basic grown-up old like her dad, but even more wrinkled from being outside in the sun. Unlike most grownups, though, he wasn't in a hurry on his way to Somewhere Important, and he actually listened when she talked.

"Hmph," Mia said. "This will be good."

There were several tables along the sidewalk outside Starbucks, two of them unoccupied, and Mia slid into one of the chairs about ten feet away from Rick. "I'm going to sit, and rest my legs while you two talk," she said. "Conversations with neurotypicals are exhausting."

Carrie frowned at her. That wasn't being completely supportive, but it was as close as she was going to get. Mia fluttered a *go on* gesture at her with both hands.

Carrie turned toward Rick with what she hoped was a winning smile. "Rick. I need your help. And I have a plan to re-vitalize your acting career."

He raised an eyebrow. "Re-vitalize?" His shirt and jeans were clean, and he was shaved. Totally presentable for a fake dad.

She nodded. "Resurrect. Renew. Reinvent. I need your help to get a dog."

"This is me." He raised both eyebrows. "Re-acting confused."

She explained the plan, and Rick's role in playing her dad. They'd take a quick walk to the animal shelter. They'd meet the dog, agree to adopt, and sign the papers. From her dog-walking profits, she had $120 to pay the adoption fee, and she'd pay Rick $147 for the acting job. (When she'd looked online for advice about paying for services, one piece of advice was to start with a fixed odd number, so it didn't sound negotiable.)

"Carrie." He ran a hand through his thinning hair. "That's probably illegal."

"You think?" Mia said from the nearby table. She was furiously thumb-typing on her phone, probably looking up crimes on Google.

"What happens when your actual dad comes home?"

"I'll be fully in love with the dog by then, and he won't take her away from me." Besides, Dad felt guilty about the 23-year-old. It was time to get some leverage out of that.

He sighed. "I run my life to *not* have $147 at one time. I'm in recovery."

She hadn't thought of that. "I can pay you in installments."

"You're right about the crime thing," Mia announced, looking at her phone. "False personation. Fraud. Obtaining property on false pretenses."

Carrie scowled at her. This wasn't helping. "Dogs are *dogs*. They're not *property*." Dogs were basically four-legged repositories of tail-wagging joy and unconditional love. Not things.

Rick leaned back. "I don't want trouble with police."

"We won't get in troub—"

"Do you know why my tent, my stuff—the whole encampment of us, really—is down at the Ashby onramp to the freeway? Where it's windy? Loud all night? Trucks going by?"

Carrie blinked at him. She had no idea. That was kind of a weird place to sleep.

"Because it's not police jurisdiction. It's Caltrans. Who—mostly—gives us warning before they clear us out. The police don't. They just take our stuff. I can't get involved in this."

"You can," Carrie said more accurately. "I just haven't explained it well enough for you to want to. We're *friends*. And this is really important to me."

"I know." He kept his voice gentle, the way you talk to nervous dogs without spooking them. "But friends don't ask friends to do things that get them arrested and go to jail and make them lose all their stuff."

"Oh." Carrie said.

"You're smart," Rick went on. "You'll find another way. I'm honored you thought of me first for this role. But as a fully retired actor, I must decline."

Carrie, of course, also had a plan B.

•

Five minutes later, she finished forging her dad's signature on the dog adoption papers, a pretty good impression of his bold scrawl.

"I don't get how this is going to work," Mia said, looking at her phone again. "The web site says 'all family members' must meet the dog before the adoption, and must all be there in person."

"All rules have reasonable exceptions," Carrie said. "Like when people were sick, they did Zoom. My parents are practically separated, if you consider the closed door to Dad's office. And I'm a volunteer. With dog skills. Not a weird stranger."

"How do they know your *family* isn't a bunch of weird strangers?"

Carrie took a deep breath and deliberately didn't say, *Who got obsessed this year by physics and the possibility of the surprise end of the universe?* "I'll vouch for them. Besides, in the application, I'm pretending that I live with just my dad." The key in dealing with adults was to be fierce. Relentless. To wear them out with your focus and determination, while they had lots of other things to think about and were already tired from the years of unreasonable compromises they'd made.

"Not entirely accurate." Behind her large frame glasses, Mia's eyes were dark. "You seem weirdly confident this will work."

"Yes." Carrie took a deep breath, before explaining the ontological proof of the existence of dog. "It's because dogs are known as man's best friend."

"I thought *I* was your best friend," Mia said.

"You are!" Carrie hoped that would never change. "Dogs are the best *non-human* friends. And," she went on, "evolutionary scientists call dogs the 'perfect' hunting companions for humans, because we have great eyesight and walk upright, but dogs hear better and their sense of smell is a hundred times better than ours."

"So...?"

"So, if a dog is our best non-human friend and perfect companion, they must exist and be nearby enough to meet and adopt." Carrie held out both arms in a *ta-da* gesture, like a stage magician showing off at the end of a magic trick.

Mia was looking at her blankly.

"Implied in the definitions," Carrie went on. "Cause if they were imaginary or far away, they wouldn't be best. Or perfect."

"That's not, like, a mathematical proof." Mia frowned. "It's just defining a word a certain way."

"The ontological argument has been around since the *eleventh century*," Carrie sputtered, unable to keep the outrage out of her voice. "And never been decisively refuted."

"People were arguing about getting dogs in the eleventh century?"

Carrie nodded. Parents were probably unreasonable even back then. "Originally, the argument was about the existence of a Supreme Being." Carrie waved that away with the sweep of a hand. "But 'God' is just 'dog' spelled backwards."

"If," Mia said, "you're only talking about the word. And ignore other definitions. Just so you can claim that definition shapes reality."

"The one thing I've learned from vacuum decay," Carrie said, "is that it's important to beat reality into a useful shape." Like that little notch that provided a metastable place for the whole universe to rest, short of annihilation. "I don't like it when we disagree," Carrie said. "This is supposed to be our adventure together."

She tried to explain it in a way that Mia would understand. "Dogs are like Higgs bosons. They change things around them." She looked down. "Maybe they help hold everything together."

Mia sighed. "It will be interesting to see the art this idea's collision with reality creates."

Things did *not* go ideally at the shelter. Shannon Washington was on duty, which was sort of good, because she really liked Carrie, but sort of bad, because Shannon was thorough and less worn down than most grownups.

There was a steady, regular bass note of a big dog barking, which periodically set others off yapping and baying. The faint whiff of dog pee over freshly hosed concrete wafted, which didn't bother Carrie, but Mia wrinkled her nose.

The dog's name was Scruffin, a small, ten-month old poodle mix of some kind with light brown hair. Scruffin mostly shivered and tried to shrink into the corner of her cage, until Carrie coaxed her into her arms with treats, but she kept shivering, even while Carrie fed and petted her.

"I think she was neglected," Shannon said. The tight set of her lips announced what she thought of humans who got dogs and then neglected them. "Seems a little traumatized. I'll let you get acquainted."

Along with cleaning cages, a big part of Carrie's volunteer job at the shelter was holding the nervous dogs, and she was good at it, getting right down on the ground with them and comforting with gentle strokes.

After almost ten minutes, when Scruffin was *still* shivering and cowering, a teensy voice inside Carrie questioned whether Scruffin was the perfect dog predicted by the ontological proof. *No,* she told herself. *The timing is too perfect. I'm going to find a dog this weekend, and she's here. Besides, I can help her feel finally loved and taken care of, which would make having her even more perfect.*

Mia mostly just stood and watched. A couple of times, Carrie gave Mia treats to offer Scruffin, who wouldn't approach her and instead kept shivering in Carrie's lap.

*Maybe having a nervous dog who needs to be calmed will give me purpose,* Carrie thought. Like Mia had purpose, trying to find math that would establish that we were actually in a stable universe. If Mia succeeded, then physicists everywhere could breathe a sigh of relief and go back to confusing their graduate students, instead of worrying that the entire universe might unravel during a long faculty meeting.

When Shannon checked in with them the first time, Scruffin had finally calmed down and even stretched her neck to let Carrie scratch behind her ears.

"Wow," Shannon said. "You're a magician. No one else has gotten her to stop shaking."

Carrie beamed. This was totally going to work out.

"I'll be back," Shannon said, "after I update our website on available adoptions."

Yikes. That would include Scruffin. Carrie had gotten here just in time, first thing in the morning, which was critical. Hair dogs that didn't shed—poodles and doodles—were in huge demand. Even kids who were allergic to dogs wouldn't get all weepy and sneezy with one around.

Her phone dinged. The text was a dog-walking request for Bo, a sweet Husky mix who got along well with all dogs and who especially liked small ones.

That would be a chance for Scruffin to hang out with another dog. Socializing was important for young dogs, so the timing for this morning was great. *Yes,* she texted back. *I'll be there by 11 to walk him.* That would leave her plenty of time to finish adopting Scruffin, and they could walk by Bo's house on the way back home from the shelter. For good measure, Carrie sent a group text to her parents and Aunt Martha. *Hanging out with Mia. Then going to walk Bo.* The way to deal with grownups was to bombard them with texts about your every activity, so they felt like they were all over that checking-up-on gig. Especially important when you were secretly adopting a furry forever best friend.

Except there was a hiccup in the adoption plan.

"Scruffin is wonderful," Carrie announced when Shannon came back a second time. "We'll take her."

"Great." Shannon smiled. "Just have your family come by this morning to meet her, and—"

"Actually, it's just me and my dad," Carrie said. "My parents are splitting up." In the sense they'd split their bedroom into two different parts of the house, although Carrie had the sinking feeling an even bigger divide was coming.

Shannon wrinkled her eyebrows. "What about your sister?"

Right. Carrie had mentioned her sister when volunteering.

"Headed off to college." In a year and a half, anyway.

"Hmmn," Shannon said. It was not a *that sounds right* sound, it was an *Oh, I have concerns.* "So, when your dad comes in today—"

"Well. Dad is out of town. Basically, a work emergency. But he signed all the paperwork in advance, if I could get a non-shedding dog, and I know you make exceptions, because some family members just did Zoom..."

"Then let's set up a Zoom call or Facetime now with your dad, so he can meet Scruffin on video, and we can see that he's on board—."

"Work." Carrie said. "Emergency." She tried to keep her voice from rising an octave, only partly successfully. "We can't. But he's on board. He signed." She waved the carefully filled-in canine adoption agreement.

"Everyone in the family has to meet the new member."

A long silence stretched while they looked at each other. In her lap, Scruffin started to shiver again.

Shannon lowered her voice. "Carrie, I know you want a dog. Desperately. But it wouldn't be fair to Scruffin if she went home with you and then had to come back to us. She needs to feel safe, that it's her forever home, where she ends up."

"But if I have to wait, someone *else* will take her."

●

"That went well," Mia said, deadpan, half an hour later while they were walking Bo to the Albany dog park. "No one got arrested for forgery, or fired as a volunteer, and we weren't even pelted with dog droppings."

"Mmmmph." It had gone terribly, but she did appreciate that Mia had volunteered to hang out with her all morning, so she wasn't wrestling with failure and loneliness alone. "Leave it," Carrie ordered Bo, as he strained to go meet a little pug across the street a woman was walking the other way. Carrie felt a pang. Scruffin was missing out on hanging out with Bo, who loved all dogs, and missing out having a new doggie friend. Although by now Scruffin was probably getting adopted by a whole family. That thought caused a different pang.

Mia's phone dinged. "Oh good." Mia thumbed through what were probably emails. "More answers to my Higgs boson questions."

"How do you get experts to answer you?" Like, important questions—*What holds the universe together?* and *How can I get a dog today?* and *How do I keep my family from flying apart?*

"I have a system." Mia's voice was serious, and maybe a little proud. "After I ask the question, I go on a different email account to answer it with something plausible but definitely wrong." Mia tilted her head and looked thoughtful. "Busy people won't stop to answer something, but they jump in to correct some other nimrod. To prove they're smarter. Plus— their answer is thoughtful and complete, because they don't want the other physicists to jump in and stomp all over it, like they just did to the other guy's."

"Oh. Cool." That *was* cool. And smart. Carrie wished she was getting expert advice on how to hold important things together.

"Have you heard anything from Lillian?" Mia asked.

"No." Since first grade, Lillian and Mia and Carrie had been three best friends who did everything together. But six months ago, Lillian's dad took a new job, and their whole family had moved—all the way to freaking Montana, where wild animals wandered around on the roads, animals so huge that parents could wreck their car if they ran into one. Carrie worried sometimes that Lillian had been the glue that held the three of them together as friends, and now she was gone. "She didn't answer my last text." Or the one before that.

"Now she has her own horse," Mia said. "It's probably not safe to text and ride. Or maybe she lost her phone again. She's done *that* before."

That was a nice, loyal way to put it. But the truth was, Lillian had literally moved on. After eight years of being besties.

And in the fall, Carrie and Mia would start high school, and things would change. She snuck a glance at Mia. For all Carrie knew, Berkeley High came with small, roving packs of higher math nerds who would burst into the hallway from morning Latin class to sweep Mia away into passionate discussions of polynomials, and Mia would never be close friends with her again.

"Hey." Mia pointed ahead. "Is that dog lost? He doesn't have a collar."

•

A small black-and-white cute wriggling mop of a dog was waiting at the gate to get into the fenced dog park, its back low and submissive, but its tail wagging. His little head was swiveling, as if anxious to see an owner or friend. He didn't have a collar, which was weird, but the fur on his neck was pushed down, as if there'd been one there until recently.

He looked like a Bernedoodle, a cute cross between a Bernese and a miniature poodle. "Hey, Bernie!" Carrie called him over. That just seemed like it would be his name.

And he reacted as if it really was. He perked up and romped over, his tail wagging. His little pink tongue was hanging out, maybe a little dry. Bo greeted him, doggy sniff fashion. Carrie pulled out the little plastic bowl from her backpack, and poured water into it from her water bottle. Bernie lapped it up furiously, as if way overdue for a drink. After that, he wolfed down the treats she offered him.

"So, is he lost?" Mia asked again.

Bernie tilted his head. Along with the black and white, he had adorable lighter brown markings above his eyes, so he looked cheerfully eyebrow-raising amazed at whatever was happening to him.

Carrie shrugged and pulled the leash and collar out of her backpack that she'd planned to use with Scruffin. "Can I put this on you, little guy?" He had no objection, so she put the collar and leash on him. Bo nosed him with another friendly nudge, even though little Bernie had been getting almost all the treats. "Let's see if someone knows who you belong with."

•

Besides Bernie and Bo, there were only seven dogs in the dog park, so while Mia threw a tennis ball for Bo to fetch, with Bernie running alongside, Carrie went from each little group of humans to the next, asking if they knew anything about Bernie or had heard about a recent lost dog. One man crinkled his eyebrows and said he thought he'd seen Bernie there a couple of times before, but weeks ago. The woman he was with nodded.

An older teenage girl with a light-colored Labrador said, "I heard there was a woman who lost her dog here. While she was on the phone." She rolled her eyes, making it clear of what she thought about anyone so absorbed in a phone conversation that they didn't notice their dog leaving when someone opened the gate.

After running with Bo, Bernie finally flopped down onto the grass, next to Carrie, panting. She ran a hand over his back.

Could he have been abandoned? He'd been missing his collar, and if you were going to dump a dog, the fenced dog park was the perfect place for it. He'd be busy playing, while his old owner just left, and was gone before he could follow out the closed gate the next time it opened.

"I'll bring him home with me," Carrie said to Mia, when she stopped by, "after we drop off Bo. We could look online for lost dog announcements."

Mia raised an eyebrow. "I have to get home. I can't dog sit, and don't you have a call with your mom?"

Bernie rolled over so Carrie could rub his belly, which she did. "I have a feeling it's all going to work out."

•

"Are you *sure* everything's okay?" Mom's voice was small and definitely worried, coming out of the phone as Carrie paced in the living room.

Because Mom was a medical researcher, looking at myste-rious diseases all day that kill you suddenly, she was a little paranoid about Bad Things Happening.

"Everything is fine, Mom. Better than fine. Tell Dad I even have an idea that will help my dog-walking business." She slid a treat to Bernie through the gap between the wall and the almost-closed glass-paneled sliding door to the kitchen, where he was. Dad had been so into her dog-walking business that he even had business cards printed for her. If Bernie really was abandoned, when she was asked about her canine experience she wouldn't have to explain that she didn't even have her own dog.

"Are you obsessing about getting a dog again?"

"I don't have obsessions." Carrie frowned. That was Mia. Who only had one obsession, singular, the end of the universe through vacuum decay. "I have areas of focus."

Bernie barked.

"Do you have a dog there?"

"Cocoa," Carrie said. Cocoa was a King Charles springer spaniel who lived down the block. Carrie sometimes dog sat her, in addition to walking.

"Doesn't sound like Cocoa's bark," Mom said.

"Yeah." Carrie paced over to the sliding door to the kitchen, looked through at Bernie, and slid two more treats through the narrow gap. "Cocoa really doesn't seem herself today." She changed the topic quickly. "How does Zoe like Brown?" That was the name of a university, about 3000 miles away from Berkeley, in a ridiculously small state named Rhode Island, which wasn't even an island.

"She *loves* Brown."

"Hmmn," Carrie said. "Will that really go with more color-ful degrees, like art history and theoretical physics?"

Mom didn't laugh. "Honey, we're going to support her whatever decision she makes."

"It's so far away."

"I know." There was sympathy in Mom's voice, then a long silence.

"So how are things going with, uh, you and Dad?"

Her mom sighed. Not a happy sigh. "The same. He's off on a long call now."

A long, long pause.

"Hey, honey," Mom's voice went on, with an artificial *everything's fine* cheeriness. "Your sis wants to say hi."

Zoe got on the phone, excited about—of all things—Brown, including its *amazing* rec center for students. Carrie briefly imagined that Zoe was talking about a "wreck" center. Maybe Mom and Dad's marriage could spend time there.

It was several minutes before there was a break in the glowing descriptions of Brown.

"So, uh," Carrie asked into that brief silence, "any sign Mom and Dad are 'rekindling the romance'?" That was hard to say even in an ironic tone of voice.

"No. Dad's on the phone with the girlfriend now. Ugh." There was a long pause. Zoe sighed, loud through the phone. "Today Dad said he wants you and me to meet him and Anya for lunch. That we'd 'like' her." Another pause. "You know, because we have so much in common with her, her being closer to our ages than to Mom's."

A punch in the stomach.

Carrie completely did *not* want to meet Anya. If she never met Anya, she could pretend Anya—and Dad supposedly "falling in love" with a 23-year-old assistant from work—wasn't real. She sat down so suddenly that she basically crumpled. On the other side of the glass door, Bernie looked worried and whined softly. He wagged his tail, but kept his back low and scratched at the door, kind of a *let me in to comfort you.*

"So, I'm going with a big no," Zoe went on, her voice far away, "on the romance front."

Dad was apparently still on the phone with Anya, the assistant girlfriend, so Carrie said, "Tell him I'll text goodnight," before she signed off.

•

*Ding.* Twenty minutes later, while Carrie was petting Bernie, a text arrived from Aunt Martha, inviting her over to eat dinner. *Veggie spiced rice. Your favorite.* Aunt Martha and her partner lived just blocks away. But dinner would also mean hanging out and questions like, "how was your day," and leaving poor Bernie alone for at least an hour in Carrie's strange new house.

*I'm having dinner with Mia,* Carrie texted. *Bean burritos from Cactus.*

*She can come too,* Martha shot back.

*We're kind of discussing intense friend stuff,* Carrie thumb-typed. *And weird astrophysics.* That was the key. Make it sound both difficult and boring. *Maybe tomorrow night?* By then, Bernie would be more settled in the house, and she could leave him for a quick dinner at Aunt Martha's.

*Tomorrow would be great. But also tonight if you change your mind.*

The house felt less lonely with Bernie in it. An hour later, as it got dark, she took him for a long walk through the neighborhood, all the way back to the fenced dog park, where he stood for several long minutes, sniffing and then staring into the empty dimness, as if waiting to see his prior owners suddenly appear. He made a whining sound of doggie sadness, and she scratched him behind his ears.

When she got back home with him, something was off. Even from the bottom of the stairs, the lights inside her house were bright, blazing. Carrie was almost completely sure she hadn't left them on.

*A burglar?*

Carrie dialed 91 on her phone, so it was only one digit from 911, but didn't hit the call button. Maybe she *had* left the lights on? Bernie picked up on her mood and seemed on alert, right by her side. Having a dog was good, even a small one. Burglars were afraid of dogs.

Carrie crept up the front stairs, dog leash in one hand, her phone in the other, with her thumb poised over the screen. When she got near the top she peered in the window, to see eyes staring back at her.

It was worse than a burglar.

It was Aunt Martha.

●

"How did you get up the stairs?" Carrie asked her, once inside. Bernie, tail wagging, was enthusiastically greeting Aunt Martha.

Aunt Martha had on a black hinged knee brace, over maroon yoga pants. "I limped. Your mom seemed to think you had a dog here." She bent down and petted Bernie.

"Uhhhh...."

"Mmmp." Aunt Martha raised a hand. "No need to tell fibs. I know you want a dog."

Carrie explained about finding Bernie near the dog park and him not having a collar or name tag and dog license, and her theory that he might be abandoned. And that if he was abandoned instead of just lost, this might be the perfect home for him. If Mom and Dad would let her keep him.

For someone related by blood to Carrie's mom, Aunt Martha was almost ridiculously cool. In addition to the whole Aikido throwing-around-two-attackers-at-once, she was an artist and taught art at Oakland School for the Arts. Maybe she would be on Carrie's side. "Could you help?" Carrie asked.

"First," Aunt Martha said. "You have to tell your mom and dad about the dog."

"I hinted." In the sense that Bernie was overheard.

Martha raised an eyebrow.

"I know," Carrie said. "I'm working up to it. I need to pitch it in exactly the right way." She looked down. "They have to say yes. Look at him."

"He is, objectively speaking, adorable." Aunt Martha scratched Bernie behind the ears. "A Bernedoodle?"

Carrie nodded.

Aunt Martha sighed. "Honey, Bernedoodles don't get dumped or lost. They cost thousands of dollars. Have you tried to find the owners?"

"We looked on NextDoor. And Mia posted that we found him." In the silence that followed, even Carrie felt like it sounded inadequate.

Along with Aikido, Aunt Martha's alarming habits included talking about deep stuff and telling the truth, so Carrie changed the subject to the most difficult question she could think of. "Are Mom and Dad going to get a divorce?"

"I think so." Martha sighed. "Probably."

Carrie frowned and sat on the couch. "That means it's even *more* important to have a dog." Dogs were especially good when you were lonely and sad.

"Things are in flux, honey." Martha sat down next to her and put an arm around her. "Your mom and dad might have to sell this house if they don't live together anymore. You might not have lots of space for a dog."

Sell the house. More things changing. This whole situation with Dad and Anya was an ick sandwich, with ick bread, slathered with ick, around layers and layers of ick. With extra ick. "Bernie's small," Carrie said. Yet another reason he was perfect. "He can adapt to some new place, especially since he isn't even used to this house. Unlike me."

Aunt Martha didn't say anything.

"And if everything else is changing," Carrie went on, "my dog could stay the same—dogs just totally love you."

"You have the rest of your life to get a dog." Her voice was sympathetic.

The sympathy didn't help. Grownups put off important and fun things until they forget the concept entirely.

"My friend Mia thinks the universe could end at any moment." All the possibilities instantly shrinking to none.

"That must make her fun to hang out with." Martha said. But then she looked thoughtful. "Although that does make you live in the moment."

Carrie's phone dinged. This conversation with Aunt Martha was going so badly, Carrie checked her phone, to give herself a break.

Mia had texted a picture.

Of a "Lost Dog" flyer.

With pictures of a Bernedoodle.

Named Bernie.

•

"It was taped on the light pole practically right in front of our apartment," Mia said an hour later, sitting across the table in Carrie's kitchen. She'd walked over. "They're, like, all over."

After Mia had arrived, Aunt Martha had left, with a goodbye wave and a final *follow through with returning the lost dog, Honey*.

There was a $250 reward for Bernie's return. Which was ridiculous, because you shouldn't charge for returning someone's dog to them. Seeing it full sized, the picture on the poster looked even more like Bernie, with identical markings and even his cute little pink tongue sticking out. In another of the pictures on the poster, Bernie was sitting up, on a couch next to a boy in a wheelchair. A boy about Carrie's age.

"Please tell me," Mia said into the silence, "you're not thinking about stealing a dog from a boy in a wheelchair."

"My mom says we all sometimes have bad thoughts," Carrie said primly. "The important thing is not to act on them."

Of course, when Mom said that she was probably thinking about Dad and the 23-year-old assistant.

Mia looked at the poster more closely. "Stealing a dog from a *really cute* boy in a wheelchair."

There was a phone number and an address on the poster. The address was less than a mile away, in the Berkeley hills, up past the Marin Avenue circle. She sighed. She took several selfies with Bernie, and selected the one where he looked at her most adoringly.

Along with the picture she typed:

*I think I found your dog, Bernie, missing his collar. He's delightful. No reward necessary. I can bring him to your address at 9 in the morning, if he turns out to be your dog. Text me if you get this, if that's okay.*

•

That would be Sunday morning, when most people would be around. But maybe the owners were wheelchair guy's clueless parents and they'd listed a landline phone number, so they wouldn't even get the text.

But her phone dinged in less than a minute.

*YES!!! THANK YOU!*

Less than another minute.

*Ding.*

*We can come get him now, and spare you the trouble. We— and especially our son Julian—will be so relieved.*

Carrie sighed. *No trouble,* she typed. *My parents are out of town and wouldn't want me meeting people at night. But in the morning I'll text you when I'm on my way.* She'd get one night, anyway, hanging out with Bernie.

Four minutes later, her phone went *Ding. Ding. Ding. Ding. Ding. Ding...*

Texts from another number.

*Thank you thank you thank you thank you thank you thank you. See you in the morning. How is Bernie?—Julian.* With half a dozen sweet pictures of Bernie, ranging from now to when he was a puppy. In two of the pictures, there was a boy— presumably Julian, the same boy who was on the poster in a wheelchair. He was definitely cute. In one, he was in the wheelchair, petting Bernie. But in another, he was running, in a soccer uniform with a soccer ball, while Bernie chased him. He was wearing a Mavericks jersey, which was the competitive club league traveling team. He must be *way* good at soccer. Did he have some kind of sports injury?

Carrie took two more pictures of Bernie and texted them back, along with another of the selfies she'd taken with Bernie. The one where she looked the best.

*Bernie is great. And very charming. See you in the morning.*

●

"Thank you *so* much!" Julian said the next day, between wriggling snuggles with Bernie, who'd climbed into his lap. Julian's mom had shown Carrie and Bernie into the house and to the living room, where Julian was waiting in his wheelchair. His left leg was missing from just above the knee.

Carrie felt awkward just standing there, and she didn't want to loom over him, so she sat on the couch.

"I was afraid Bernie was lost for good," he went on. "Did he do okay with you?"

Carrie launched into a discussion of how she found Bernie and had fed him and petted him, and how he was overnight. "You're going to need to get him a new collar, though."

"He's a little escape artist," Julian said affectionately. He rubbed Bernie's belly. "Mom was distracted, on the phone. Probably fighting with the insurance company over this." He waved an arm to take in his leg, or maybe his whole body. "Bernie left the dog park with another dog, when someone opened the gate."

Julian was wearing a baseball cap, but the cute curly hair from the pictures he'd texted wasn't poking out from under it. He had a super-short buzz cut instead. "I don't know what I'd do without this little guy."

*He's lonely.* The realization hit her so suddenly, but she knew it was true.

"It's harder for me to get him out for enough exercise now." He rubbed Bernie's head affectionately.

"Oh." Carrie said. "I can do that. I'm a dogwalker. Like, professionally." She dug out one of the business cards that her dad made up for her and passed it to him. His hand brushed hers when he took it, and her fingers tingled afterward. "I charge, but for Bernie, I wouldn't have to, always. He was sort of family, for a day, anyway."

She looked down. "I don't have a dog. For a couple of hours, I had this fantasy that Bernie was abandoned, and I could adopt him, while my parents were out of town." She explained about the plan, and how it wasn't totally realistic. That her parents still probably needed to be worked on and softened up over time. "Still, I had this idea. That when they came back, they'd let me keep him."

Bernie wagged his tail.

"Because—" Carrie waved a hand at Bernie. "—totally adorable."

"Yeah." Julian laughed. "My parents aren't really dog people. But he won them over. Partly, anyway." Then he looked more serious. "That might be good. The dog walking. My parents can't really keep up. And I don't get out as much," he went on. "I don't exactly get to soccer practice anymore."

The picture he'd included in his texts the night before looked recent, when he'd been wearing a Mavericks jersey and had two legs.

"How long?" She asked. Involuntarily, she glanced at the space where his leg ended. "Since you, uh, stopped going to soccer practice."

"Four weeks." His voice was matter-of-fact.

How could you go from playing competitive soccer to missing your leg? "What happened?"

"Cancer." He frowned. "I thought I just had a sore leg, after a game. But it didn't get better. And when they looked at it, they found...something bad. Two days later, surgery. *Bzzzzt.* Bone saw city."

"Wow."

"Yeah," he said. "Kind of freaks everybody out. Like, on the soccer team. Who doesn't sometimes have a sore leg?"

He looked over at the TV, with its dark, blank screen staring back at them. There were a couple of game controllers next to it. "When we weren't practicing, the guys used to come over to play FIFA world cup soccer. But—" He shrugged. "—I've somehow lost interest in that."

There was a long silence.

"It's really aggressive." He was looking past Bernie, at the wall or something in the distance behind it.

For a moment, Carrie didn't know what he was talking about. Her confusion must have shown in her face.

"The cancer," he went on.

"So," she said, "not some kind of blood cancer?" Carrie's mom had mentioned that most of those were fixable, for kids.

"Nah. Tumors."

"Oh." Tumors. Plural. Her mom had said most hard cell cancers, in kids, were really, really bad. "My mom's a medical researcher."

Their eyes met and there was an electric moment of connection. *Then you know.*

"Yeah," he said. "Maybe they didn't get it all."

After a long moment, Carrie was the first to look down. "I'm really sorry." *He's like the universe with vacuum decay.* Maybe he was stable and would be totally fine. But maybe instead he'd completely unravel.

"And my parents." He looked at Bernie. "They're not really great with dogs." He rubbed his eyebrow, like he was brushing the hair out of his eyes, but had remembered at the last second that he didn't have hair there. They were great eyes, brown pools of intense feeling. Almost as pretty as a dog's eyes.

Bernie came over to her, and Carrie scratched him behind the ears, the way he liked.

She should probably get going instead of hanging out during long awkward silences thinking about cancer and death and the end of things. But she kept sitting. She knew about lonely. And about everything changing too fast.

"We could dog share," he said quietly.

"What?"

"Dog share." He said it like it was a thing. "You know, like a timeshare, but with Bernie, not a weird-smelling vacation condo with a pool." He smiled, tentative.

"For real?"

He nodded.

"I could come almost every day," she said, the words coming fast. "To walk him. You could come in your wheelchair. And when I took him on longer walks, I could tell you how he did at the dog park, and what dogs he met. And could train him with treats. I mean—he's good with recall, but he could be even better."

"And if I have to do overnights at the hospital again," Julian said, "Bernie could stay with you."

"Totally. Any time."

He looked relieved. His smile was broad now, like the sun coming out from behind a cloud. "That would be perfect."

**Holly Schofield**

# Grin and Bear It

"In what alternate universe is this considered coffee?" I asked the cafeteria worker wiping the nearby table. She just smiled and shrugged, probably used to the criticisms and odd phrasings of us folks from the physics department on the floor above. I adjusted a bra strap. Why the professor from the arts faculty had wanted to meet at this greasiest of diners instead of Beanzers down the street was hard to fathom.

I set the execrable coffee on the interactive tabletop and drummed my fingers.

And this must be her, striding through the morning sun across the checkerboard floor. In a crowd of care-nothing-about-clothing physicists, her handwoven multicolored poncho stood right out.

I gave a brief nod as she wended her way toward me. Hopefully, this wouldn't take long. My current physics experiment was waiting for me back at the lab. I was trying to disprove a particular set of pre-selection and post-selection quantum paradoxes, burning up my computer with calculations between banging my head on the wall. After too many nights on the too-short cot in my lab, I probably should have showered in the gym before this appointment but, really, I couldn't be bothered. I'd never met this person, or anyone from her department for that matter, and I probably never would again.

She stopped at my table. "Tina?"

"You must be Sophie." I said, trying not to be surly. "Nice poncho."

"It's my roommate's. Bit of a stereotype, innit?" Her English accent drew a glance from the people at the next table. Long black hair fell over her forehead as she scooched out of the garment and laid it over her chair back. At least her rumpled T-shirt and faded jeans were more in keeping with a harried professor. And if she wasn't harried, working at the University of Eastern Alberta, she wasn't pulling her weight, even in the Arts department. The university President's "voluntary" cross-disciplinary, academic, culture-building exercise that was requiring us to meet today was a time-consuming exercise in futility and almost as frustrating as my lab work. We shook hands and yet more of my time was wasted as she flagged down the disinterested waitress and ordered a cup of the terrible coffee.

"President Wilson has a lot to answer for," I said.

"President Wilson is a stupid sod. He couldn't find a rabbit hole in Watership Down." She tightened the elastic on her ponytail, thanked the waitress, sipped her coffee and winced. "Sorry for suggesting we meet here. If I'd known the coffee was this abysmal, I would have suggested Beanzers, but I didn't want to keep you from your work any longer than I had to. And I'm in a great hurry—I have a wedding to plan. I'm spread so thin, you can probably see right through me."

I nodded again and forbade myself to check the clock in the table display.

She drew out her phone. "I brought the list of tasks we're supposed to be doing. I mean, the list of 'cross-pollination techniques'. It's made *me* rather cross, I must tell you." She sent the checklist to the tabletop where it flickered at us feebly.

At least we were on the same page with the value of Prez Wilson's exercise. "As long as we can finish inside of an hour. Like I said in my text message, you show me what art you've developed and I'll say if it reflects my current project, we check off all the boxes, and then we can both get back to work."

I could already guess what she knew about quantum mechanics. Laypeople always thought Schrodinger's cat was all there was to it—and either the cat was there or it wasn't. Whatever pathetic thing she'd crafted, even if it was a paper-mâché kitty in a box, I'd approve it. Partly to get the hell out of here and partly—I tried not to stare—because of her pretty green eyes.

She swiped open an app on her phone. Her fingernails were tattered and paint-stained. A ring glinted on her third finger. It figured. The first person to remotely interest me since Alyx left and she was about to be married.

After a moment, the app chimed, the table flickered and then a large orange-and-white cat appeared, hovering above the checklist. I scooted my chair back a bit so I could focus on the low-res image. "This table's electronics are rubbish," Sophie said. "Rest assured my program renders it substantially better than this."

"Uh huh," I said, trying not to groan. Sophie was cute but that was clearly all she had going for her. "Schrodinger's cat isn't quite what I'm working—"

"Oh, no. It's a Cheshire cat. You see, I read your article in the IJQM."

"You did? Wow!" I doubted even any of my peers had read my article in the International Journal of Quantum Mechanics, except for maybe the obsessive Simon at MIT.

"Sure. Now, let me tell you about it in layperson's terms. We can call that the 'interconnectedness' portion of the checklist." She ticked off the box with a bold stroke of a finger. "You put a cat, or an electron, in one of two boxes. The electron, or the cat, ends up with the animal in one box and the purring in another." She touched her phone again. The cat hologram crouched, its eyes gleamed neon green. Then, the speakers at the empty table next to us gave a burst of static followed by a low rumble like the trucks out on Fourth Street. "Magic, innit? Well, with a decent equalizer, it is."

All of sudden my day was getting better. Magical, even. Someone cute who could program a holo that well? And actually *got* what I was interested in? Sophie's ponytail swung in the sunlight as she gestured. Was I even ready for another relationship?

Sophie was still looking at me, head tilted.

I mentally blew out the candle flame that had been Alyx and hastily found some words. "It's not *quite* like that, but then most things in quantum physics aren't."

"Ah, that satisfies the 'technical evaluation' component." Another swift checkmark. "Just a few more boxes remaining." That silky swing of the ponytail again. And, was that a wink? I wasn't sure. She leaned forward, smiling. A definite wink and then: "What do you think 'robust interaction' could possibly mean?"

*It means I want you in bed at my apartment*, I thought to myself and looked anywhere but at her and the ring on her finger. "Um, how about you make the cat do something and I put it into physics-speak?"

Her fingers tapped her phone, and the cat slowly disappeared, leaving only its grin behind. "Curiouser and curiouser," she said with a low chuckle.

I cleared my throat and sipped the awful coffee, trying to pretend I was talking to a class of first-years, not a new love interest. "In a Mach—Zehnder interferometer, the cat itself is located in one beam path, while its grin is located in the other. It's simple, really—"

"I'm sure it is, Tina, to you. It makes *me* dreadfully puzzled. All I know is that my confusion is separate from your words, across the space and time of this table," she said with a sly grin.

"That's not what it—" I broke off. That was *exactly* what it meant.

She tapped the phone again. The cat's grin widened until it stretched over to the next table and into a student's bowl of pudding (or perhaps it was pea soup). The student spooned in mouthful after mouthful, intent on some equations, tapping her table impatiently to turn pages, oblivious. That had been me the past eight years.

In fact, maybe that *was* me now. Maybe this was all a dream that would slip away. Alyx had left to pursue her career overseas, and now I'd met Sophie after she was engaged, too late on the space/time continuum.

I rubbed my eyes. The neutrons waiting for me in the lab suddenly seemed much less important.

"Are you all right? You want to go?" Sophie touched my hand. "I'll just check off the rest of the boxes in a random sequence and we can say goodbye then." Precise flicks of her hand and the cat disappeared, the form was filled, and a copy sent to my email. "Our little secret." She stood and picked up her poncho, suddenly brisk.

"Yes. Nice meeting you," I mumbled. "Hope your wedding day goes well."

"Oh, it's not *my* wedding, it's my roommate's. I'm just helping her plan it. Checklists, spreadsheets, and the flowers. I'm good with arrangements of all sorts," she said from the depths of the massive poncho. She pulled her head free and saw my eyes on the ring on her hand. "That? That's just a bauble from London that a friend gave me. I'm dyslexic so I wear it on my left hand for an inside joke—one just between me and me."

"Oh," I said, faintly. "Can you bring the Cheshire cat back for a second?"

She obliged and the mangy beast hunkered over the table-top. I covered her hand with mine, meeting her eyes for the first time. "Want to get a couple of lattes at Beanzers? They make a nice smoked butterscotch." I kept my hand there so she'd separate the meaning from the action.

"That'd be lovely." She smiled and reached for her phone to close the cat app.

"Can I?" I took it from her and changed some settings. "There. That's better."

We strolled out together into autumn leaves fluttering on the sidewalk.

I took Sophie's hand in mine and glanced back at the duplicate cat's grin I'd set hovering over the table. The toothy smile would sit there until the university computers scrubbed it at sunset.

I was suddenly sure my own grin was going to last longer.

**Alicia K. Anderson**

# Don't Eat the Canapes

How did you hear about me? Oh, yeah. That.

Well, if you're looking for a god, always check paradoxes first. That's where they live. If you find something pretending to be a god, it will live somewhere normal like a cloudy mansion or a shoe. Those pretender gods aren't comfortable anywhere near a paradox, and if you can nudge them close enough to one, it's fun to watch them squirm and warp and become real gods for a change.

No, no. I'm not a god. But I'm more comfortable leaning up against a paradox than I am wandering in Saturn's rings or shopping malls.

Why? If I can hear my own heartbeat and the sound of your chewing gum suctioned to your molars and that man's nose-whistling sinus problems all at the same time, then I experience the interiority of me, and you, and him. If I can hear the girls laughing like little songbirds and the dog itching his shoulder again, then I understand the exteriority of all of us, as well.

Because I can hear all those things at once, inside and outside, and itching dog and chewing gum, I let it all wash over me and lean against the paradox of public intimacies. Private displays.

Without a paradox to steady me, the noises become overpowering, and I close my eyes to make the world quieter.

Since I hang out in their neighborhoods so often, sometimes the gods invite me in for tea. Some gods make better tea than others. A few even offer snacks. I don't really recommend eating any of the snacks. They upset my stomach with too much metaphor.

And some of the snacks come with catches—especially those of the gods of the dead. If you're going to visit a paradox about death, you probably ought to know the rules. The death paradoxes are quiet and dark, though, and I can relax the best in the quiet and the dark. I just don't eat anything when they invite me in.

What's that? Oh, because most death paradoxes are also life paradoxes, duh. That's their nature. You can't have one without the other, and they coexist somewhere and everywhere.

The frustrating thing about that is that the death and life sorts of gods also always have the best smelling food. Fresh baked bread, juicy pomegranates, homemade tamales, you just don't see that kind of stuff back at home. But those cornhusk wrapped nuggets of deliciousness include a catch. You can't eat the food belonging to the life and death gods, or it keeps you trapped in their world. Even the demoted gods that are just fairies still have those rules.

Look, don't underestimate fairies. Don't get me started.

Yeah, yeah, I know you just asked me for directions. But you're not listening. If you want to fold space like it's warm towels right out of the dryer, you're going to need a god. And you're not looking in the right places. That beardy guy over there with the eyebrows does *not* know how to fold space. I promise you. He might be able to fold time, but come on, even I can do that.

Fine. I will take you. But you can't eat anything. And let me do the haggling. Gods are sort of literal and tricky, and they like to play lawyer when making deals. You want to do the—

There's no need to be impatient. I told you I could bend time, didn't I? Sit down on that bench. Yes, you travel there by sitting down. (Have you ever even touched a paradox before?) Now sit. Close your eyes. No, I'm not going to pick your pockets.

Well, if you set her as the guard she won't be able to come with us. She has to sit down and close her eyes, too. And I don't recommend menacing anyone with a gun like that where we're going.

Look, I'm sitting too. Three birds in a row. Tweetle-dee-deet.

No, I'm not turning you into birds. (Though now that you mention it...)

Breathe. Just breathe. You are holding your breath, miss. I can hear it. You, sir, are very close to a panic attack. Just breathe. It's not hard. In and out. Like ocean waves. Just....

*I didn't know you had friends, Little Listener.*

Did you hear that? Feels like a voice in your head but it shakes your skull from the inside out?

Well, we found a god for you. Open your eyes and look—but don't stop breathing.

Miss, don't point that gun at a god. Yeah, this isn't the greatest of neighborhoods. Good / Evil are still well-maintained, but accidentally-on-purpose is really looking ragged. You, my adventurous ones, have found a trickster. Tricksters like people like you. But much like kittens, they are not recommended for beginners.

*Greetings, Travelers.*

Whoa! Your voice in my ears is way different from the voice in my head. In my ears it has screaming behind it. Is that me screaming? Oh. No, it's him. Cut it out, guy. This is what you came here for.

So, yeah, these two want to fold space. They have a mission or something. There's a big deal happening in the bowl of the little dipper.

*What's in it for me?*

Look, screaming isn't helping your barter here, man. What have you brought to trade with the gods? What do you mean? You came here looking for gods with nothing to offer? Shit. I might have a little cone of incense in my pocket or something, but that—

*I would accept blood.*

Very kind of you to offer, sir. Now, um, miss. I believe your companion has fainted. Look, he's all white and pasty. Yes, you can get off the bench to help him, it was just a focus. We're already here.

Well, when he said he'd accept blood that meant one of us would have to bleed in his honor to pay him. Yes, actually bleed. I don't know. Couple pints? I'm sure he has a basin around here that could give you the idea. No?

Me? Ha, well, my blood wouldn't work. That would get *me* to the little dipper not you. And frankly, I went to a party there once and it wasn't all it's cracked up to be.

*The canapes were nice.*

Were they? I was a little afraid to try them, they had poetry all over them.

*huh. Maybe that's why the band died early.*

Oh, what's that, miss? Oh, your friend. You want to go *back?* Back where? Back where you found me? That's impossible. We folded time to get here. We are already back. And if we fold forward to get *then*, well, your friend will never wake up. Why not?

*These people really don't understand paradoxes.*

Or gods, frankly.

**Dora M Raymaker**

# My Father's Skin

The Receiving Room smells of antiseptic and false roses. The sort of scent that says, "We are very clean here." And also, "We are slightly pathetic." Luna's Sector Q Nursery has four such Receiving Rooms, tight enough to induce anxiety and prevent lingering but not so off-putting as to preclude business. That business being the purchase of Operators like me.

All of the other Operators have been here since birth, but my father sent me here four years ago, when I was twelve. He told me it was because my tutors had not succeeded in making me normal. I thought he would have purchased me back by now. In what way have I not succeeded in becoming normal? I am indistinguishable, in every way.

Is there some additional test I need to pass? Or have I already failed?

"Jordis? Are you paying attention? This is your future." Nursery Mother's voice crawls caustic over my skin. To my synesthetic senses it sounds like being rubbed in rust.

I suppress the urge to scratch my arms with a snippet of motor programming and engage an algorithm to heighten the appearance of even more rapt attention. My face beams and Nursery Mother's shoulders relax. *This is your future?* No. My future is to take over my father's business. This—this is my last chance of getting out of the Nursery the easy way.

Well, I am starved for a challenge after these boring, stuck-sitting-on-my-hands past four years.

And, while I would rather use diplomacy than violence, violence is just fine too.

Anything to stop all this waiting around. Wondering when I've done enough for my father to take me home or if a corporation will sponsor me or if my father's enemies will kill me in my sleep. Whatever is going to happen, it must be today; tomorrow is my birthday.

"The *problem*"—the Buyer from Felicity-Ko whines the word—"isn't with Jordis' aptitude. Her competency exams are impressive and her promotional footage more so. The problem is that she is Jordis *Ansari*."

When I was a child, I thought people talked about me like I wasn't in the room because of my age. Now I know it's because I'm a genetic-defective k-syndrome mutant with defects in communication, sensory processing, and motor planning. Not that anyone can tell.

"Well, we, ah—" Nursery Mother stumbles over her omission of my lineage.

I adjust my body into a posture of low-threat, eyes lowered. "Should Felicity-Ko sponsor me," I lie, "I assure you my allegiance will be with your corporation, not with my father."

The lie lands easily because the neurotranslator attached to the computer in my brain runs a million subroutines to match my private language of flavor and sensation into the flat words normals use. Then it runs a million-million more subroutines to stimulate my neural pathways into moving throat, face, breath, tongue into speech-sounds to form those words aloud, along with the appropriate nonverbal accompaniments—ones I've chosen, not ones I actually feel. This occurs without perceptible delay. My vocal and facial affect is flawless. Normal. Indistinguishable from my non-afflicted peers.

"Oh, I'm sure the poor dear is too simple to play Black Market games herself." The Buyer pats my hand, utterly conned but not yet convinced to take me. "Unfortunately, Ray Ansari could still get to us through her."

*My father's not who you have to worry about,* I think. But then, she knows that. That's the real source of her worry, which is why any confidence game of reassurances, no matter how successful, will likely fail. Who on Luna doesn't know Earth's moon runs in uneasy truce between chartered corporations like Felicity-Ko and Madame X's Luna Black Market? Enemy of my House.

So why am I still here? Why hasn't my father taken me home? I've learned all of my lessons. I've played all of the right games. My record is immaculate. My promotional materials simply ooze with how amazingly normal I appear. There is nothing left in this Nursery to conquer!

"Jordis' father has no interest in her, I assure you," Nursery Mother says. "He signed the same mandatory disowning papers as anyone turning over a K-syndrome child."

The Felicity-Ko Buyer rises, straightening the creases in her slacks.

I record the gesture to integrate into my own behaviors. My coding specialty is body hacks. I have quite a collection of physical nuances I've observed from others, from these kinds of casual tics to how my father kills a man with his bare hands. It is these trivial, unconscious gestures that signal normal body language and make me so indistinguishable from my peers. That, and how well I can read human nature when no one expects me to. Not that it's seeming to matter.

"You are aware," Nursery Mother flusters, "that Jordis' age and undesirability mean she'll be sent to a Farm. We can't keep them more than a year past major, and her birthday is tomorrow. It would be such a waste of a Class Fifteen with her aptitudes. You're the last Buyer we have on the books for her. I can lower the sponsorship fee even more, I'm even willing to take a large deficit for the Nursery—"

"For Signal's sake! Ray Ansari leads the second largest crime syndicate in inhabited space and I'm offended, frankly, that you think you can pawn her off on us. Just because we're a small corporation doesn't mean we're socially retarded like the things you foster here. There are other Nurseries on Luna. And some animals—" her eyes flick over me as normals' often do, like I'm an infection—"Well, it's just safer for everyone to put them down."

Nursery Mother opens her mouth but runs out of sufficient caring before words emerge. Sure, the failure will hurt her quota, but otherwise it doesn't matter to her if I'm sponsored by a corp or stripped of my tech and sent to a Farm. And I don't think I'm one of the ones they'll keep alive for repetitive labor. I'm a double threat. A defective who can manipulate large-scale quantum computers with her mind and the daughter of organized crime. No one wants that. Except my father. Why hasn't he taken me back? That was the point of banishing me to Luna, wasn't it? So I could get a full education in how to act normal, beyond what my tutors on Europa could give? That's what he said.

I want more than anything to taste the brine of Europa on my lips. I want to contribute to the family business, which isn't nearly so terrible as outsiders think it is. I had already started proving myself. I had taken the initiative to fix the Smith problem. I had organized Raj and the others, and we'd made the collection. After that, there was no way the Smiths would ever steal from my father again. I know my father was pleased by the outcome—he praised Raj for it all up and down the Europa torus, even though Raj told him quite plainly it had been my idea and none of it would have happened without my skills. But my father told me I wasn't normal enough and sent me to this Nursery the very next day. Was it because I got blood on Nana's carpet? No one had ever cared about such things before.

What more do I have to do? Am I failing some test by not convincing the Buyer to take me?

"No one needs to know who I am," I say, keeping my eyes and shoulders in the low-threat position.

"What?" She stares at me.

Nursery Mother stabs her eyes my way. I'm not supposed to take any initiative in these meetings; I'm the goods, not the negotiator. But what can it hurt when it's my last-ever chance?

"You could take advantage of my skills without incurring my father's notice—or anyone else's—if..." I trail off, pretending like I am struggling for my thoughts. I need to appear normal, and normal people don't generate complex, sharp-witted cons on the fly when they are supposed to be socially defective. Sometimes the hardest part of acting normal isn't pretending I can do things that I can't, like speak, but pretending I *can't* do things that I actually can. My entire time in this Nursery has been an exercise in holding back!

"If," I pretend like I've finally put the pieces together, "we send my citizen ID number to the Farm but give me a new one and send that one off with you... I'm just a collection of numbers in a system, aren't I? And if I'd come here as an infant, like most Operators do, the Nursery would have assigned me a new citizen ID number to prevent my family from being stigmatized by the birth. It's only because I was so old that you used my birth one."

I bite my lip as though unsure of my next point, even though I'd already absorbed enough corporate law to be a lawyer before my banishment. "I think... I think the law isn't entirely specific in this regard. I know how to keep a low profile. No one here knows who I really am, right, Nursery Mother? I don't brag. You've seen how discreet I am in my promotional materials. I can make a successful sponsorship."

Nursery Mother is horrified that I'm speaking out like a person, but her expression shifts subtly toward complicity as I tack that last sentence on. She doesn't need this as badly as I do, but she does need to maintain that quota. "We would be willing to consider any and all options," Nursery Mother says, trying to look at both me and the Buyer at once.

The Buyer half-laughs, and my heart sinks without being surprised. "Amusing, for sure. But still, no." She almost looks at me. "I'm sorry Jordis' talents will go to waste, and I know this is not a good outcome for the Nursery. But the risk to Felicity-Ko, even with attempts at obfuscating Jordis' lineage, is just too high." The Buyer's face sets into a final "no" position.

Well, at least it's definitive. I dislike protracted rejections, when a Buyer makes polite noises like they will sponsor me only to decline hours or days later as soon as they don't have to look anyone in the eyes. I can't afford to wait this time.

The Buyer stands. Nursery Mother stands. I stand. They shake hands. The corporate sigil of Felicity-Ko flashes, a tiny metal pin, on the webbing of the Buyer's thumb. I duck to keep the blue of the equipment beneath the skin of my forehead in shadow. The "O" of an unsponsored Operator shines on my thumb, a mark of disgrace at my age. I should be wearing the peacock-feather pin of the Argus Hotel and Casino on Europa.

I suspend my motor programming so that I don't reach out and crush the Buyer's neck. I know I'm mad at myself, not at her, for not meeting the challenge of the moment.

I leave the dim light and thick carpets of the Receiving Room for the bright lights and hard, echoing surfaces of the Nursery. They say this will help us desensitize and refine our sensory programming to improve function. But I didn't grow up in a Nursery like the other Operators, and soft beds and the delight of light breaking in rainbow swords from crystal goblets in no way impeded the efficacy of my sensory programming.

I behave perfectly normal; why has no one taken me home to Europa? My father could even sponsor me directly. It's not illegal to sponsor your own children.

It doesn't matter. What matters is I failed to be sponsored, no one has come to take me home, and at midnight I turn seventeen. I'll be stripped of my tech and taken to a Farm some time tomorrow.

If only I had access to the informationsphere I'd know exactly when. But here in the Nursery I've been hobbled against transmitting or receiving for anything other than my lessons. I can't even access the local news feeds unless someone turns the jammers off.

For most Operators that would be the limiting factor of any escape plan. They think first of an information solution. Hack this or obscure that signal or search that database there. I don't blame them. It's not like anyone who grows up in a Nursery knows a world exists beyond programming tasks and structured, off-time activities.

But I know—because I am Jordis Ansari, heir to an empire who did not grow up in a Nursery—that there are infinite ways to get any job done.

Like providing two years of free fucks to the Nursery janitor in order to obtain the Luna Sector Q maintenance maps, a sharp knife, and a few hours of privacy after he puts the security camera in my room on a loop so we can do it.

I follow Nursery Mother to my room, gentle-blinking so as not to spill the water in my eyes. I don't even know why I'm crying. Frustration maybe. Disappointment. Maybe my father just wants to see how I get myself out of a worst-case scenario. Maybe this is the final test.

But, no, the stories of tests and rescue I've been telling myself since I was twelve are childish and bare now that I'm completely out of time and far too old for them. There never was any final test. My father didn't send me here to become more normal, but because I never would be normal. I have perfect recall. *"No amount of tutors can ever make you normal."* That's what he said before he sent me away. He never meant anything more than that. I was just too socially stupid to realize it when I was twelve and then, well, after that I had to survive this awful place somehow. It was as good a lie as any.

I wipe the corners of my face with the back of my hand—a gesture normals use.

The door to my room closes as Nursery Mother leaves in disappointed silence.

The pearl of Europa, glowing from the poster on my wall, is even more luminous through tears.

I reach out a finger and touch it.

All I want is to touch Europa's waters again. To roam through the majesty of the Argus Hotel and Casino and know that it is all mine. All I want is to be normal enough to pass as my father's non-defective offspring and take my rightful place as heir. I don't even care about my father anymore; I just want to go home.

And then I scoff at myself.

Four years in this Nursery has almost made me as pathetic as everyone here wants me to be. I was an Ansari before this place made me an Operator. It's not like I'm going to just go belly up.

I look at the camera, watching me weep. No janitor will loop it for me this time. The Nursery will know what I'm up to and they will come for me immediately.

But that's better than waiting for tomorrow. And the nearest security station is ten meters away.

I snap my programming to full-bore motor-sensory multi-threading as I've rehearsed a thousand thousand times over—

My room: a desk, a dresser, a sensorcam in the ceiling's top, left corner. The sharp, blue shadows of the everbulb cast strong as I reach beneath the bed, to the box spring slit. Fingers finding the knife, the bandaging.

I push the bed aside.

At the baseboard, I have worked the screws in the ductwork loose. It's been a few months since my last janitor tryst, which is the last time I tried to fit. I've grown since then. Who knew I would end up so tall? Calculations tell me I will still fit, but it will be tight.

It's a good thing I'm out of options now and not six months from now.

I hear security move toward me in the hall. Unusual activity detected in my room.

I initiate a programmatic override for anti-self-harm instincts—the sort of thing I'm not supposed to be able to do but, well, bio-hacks are my specialty. I carve the O-shaped pin out of the webbing of my thumb so no one can track me.

I'm a blank now. A rone Operator. Something so dangerous authorities are instructed to kill it on sight.

I lick my lips, imagining the taste of Europa's brine. I like being something so dangerous.

I bandage my wound and trigger endorphin-simulators to suppress the pain. My hands do not shake at all.

There's audible movement in the hall now and my time here is up. I can only hope whoever is coming for me is larger than I am.

And that I am not, now, larger than this ductwork.

Sure, they can track where the duct leads, but I have many paths I can take after that.

All large-scale habitats on unterraformed orbitals have intricate environmental systems. My Europa City, a free-floating ring around Europa's rocky core, is designed to keep ocean out and pressurized atmosphere in; most of its inner workings are only accessible to small machines.

But Luna—Four hundred years ago, Luna was something quite other than the suburb of Earth that it is today. As the first non-terrestrial habitation, it's riddled with tunnels built for miners—and smugglers. Sector Q is old and ugly as anywhere gets on Luna, and it's filled with human-sized passageways. If I can just squirm my way to them. Of course, there is the problem that in Sector Q they are human-sized passageways belonging to *Madame X*, but one problem at a time.

I've made my way down the hole, yes, but my shoulders are squished and I don't dare take a deep breath for fear of realizing there's no room for it.

In my mind, I pull up the janitor's maps I'd glimpsed. One

glimpse is all it takes to record a visual and toss it up later into an augreal overlay.

The pitch-black duct renders visible through the alternate sight of the augreal. I'd hoped to do this next part face first, but I'm too big to turn around so I angle my feet into the crook at the bottom, ignoring the sensation of warm air flowing up my slacks to tickle the hairs on my legs. As soon as I can, I bend at the waist and slide through.

The floor squeaks above me. They've pulled out the bed and found my escape route.

I shimmy through the tightness.

Behind and above, muffled shouts, voices, and a loud bang shudder through the ductwork, but I can't care about what any of it might mean now.

All focus goes into my body.

A dark time later the air current changes and I know I've almost reached the junction.

The shiny interior of the duct renders through the augreal as light spills from the grille ahead.

Turning and positioning to escape would have been easier a few months ago, but I can't think about that now.

All of my thinking goes into my motor and neural programming.

There are more things a human body can do than a human mind will allow. There are self-harm breakers and pain feedbacks, neural hard-wirings and fight-or-flight instincts—

But I have a large-scale quantum processor in symbiosis with my brain; I have billions of nanowires tipped with swarm-intelligent weak AIs burrowed into my nervous system.

People are right to hate and fear Operators and keep us from realizing our full potentials because look what I can do—

I spin in the tightness, ignoring the snap-pop as a shoulder dislocates, ignoring all pain-overrides to smash into the grill with my feet in a space with insufficient room to build a momentum.

SMASH

If it hurts, I don't feel it. But I need more.

Trigger adrenaline surge NOW.

SMASH

The metal whines and bends.

SMASH

again

SMASH

The grille gives and clatters to the floor.

I drop the two meters barely conscious in the adrenaline flow and immediately trigger programming to relax the dislocated arm. I can't linger here—it's the one sure place I'd end up outside the duct—but I need the use of both arms.

I lean against the wall below the vent, eyes on the dented grille a little way off, and breathe until my elevated heart rate slows. I will need to run soon, but I can't think about that now. I have to relax. Quiet mind. Engage parasympathetic nervous system. Increase acetylcholine production.

Push and twitch—the dislocated joint slides back in place.

There is probably a fair amount of pain associated with this, but I haven't let up on the code that triggers endorphins.

I look around the room as I shove myself back toward a heightened adrenal state. I don't need to use as much programming now; the raw reality of the situation is enough. I'm deep in enemy territory. My pathway is easy to trace. I'm on a clock. I can't regulate my hormones indefinitely. At some point my metabolism will reach its limits and I'll collapse. But for now—for now I still have a lot to work with. I'm sixteen and very fit, after all.

I smile. After four years of restraint at the Nursery, that felt wonderful.

No, it's not something normal people can do, but no one ever has to know.

I examine the augreal maps, overlaid on my physical sight. There is a camera in the room, in the corner, focused on the door not the vent. But the angle is wide enough to have seen me.

Which means Madame X has seen me.

I don't bother smashing the camera. Any damage is done, and time spent now will just slow me down. With a few quick hops to make sure I didn't miss any significant injuries, I am gone.

I enter the twisting passageways of Luna Sector Q and pick a random direction, assessing next steps.

I wear soft clothing, in the luminous violet-blue associated with Operators. It's the color of the processor beneath the skin of my forehead, which I cannot hide. My soft shoes are meant for shuffling around the Nursery, not for kicking out metal grilles, and already one has split at the seam. Blood seeps through the bandage on my hand where I carved out my identification. Perhaps I went too deep. All these things must change.

I need to find people but not too many people.

I alter my sensory programming, enhancing the frequencies of human voices, foot falls, breaths.

To the augreal overlay I add a visual of the soundscape, splitting my attention three-way between my current location on the map, the sound visualizer, and the path out of X's immediate territory. I'm not sure what to do after that, but if I can find a place that's safe to stop and think for a moment, I will meet the challenge. Plans slot satisfyingly into place, adapting and shifting to realize needs, resources, targets.

From the augreal, at the next fork, I choose the branch that brings me deeper into Madame X's territory.

Madame X—the enemy of my House. She is what keeps my father from claiming the Sol system as his own. Someone by the name of "Madame X" has ruled the Luna Black for over two hundred and fifty years, though even with modern medtech one-eighty is humanity's upper limit. So Madame X must be a title not a person, even though the management style, the long game that started even before the moon had artificial gravity, the ability of the Luna Black to operate within and outside the law, within and beyond corporate structures, to transgress every boundary there is—it is so specific. There is too much continuity to the Luna syndicate's history. I saw Madame X at a conference once, as I peeked around the curtain, and her holograph was eldritch. Like something inanimate that almost—but not quite—passes for alive.

Before my exile I learned much about her operations from listening to my father and his captains, but nothing about *her*. That makes for a dangerous enemy. But an exciting one.

If I could bring home information on her, gathered here in her territory, it would be of great value. It would be the kind of proving that would grant someone a Captain role, even young and otherwise untried. It would be exceptional, but not outside of the realm of what a normal person could do.

I follow my map, dodging both too many people-sounds and areas labeled things like "to Sector Q Market." My route is defensive to avoid anyone finding me, and that displeases me. I would prefer the upper hand. But my route is also strategic. And around the next bend, according to the dual-overlaid map, I see what I need.

It's a risk—a corridor piled with crates and chattering people, corporate pins in the shape of tiny "Xs" glittering on the webbing of their thumbs.

But it's not *too much* of a risk as long as I don't step out into it dressed as I am now. And that's about to change as a single person passes where I hide—

I catch them with their guard down—after all, it's safe territory here—and I catch them with the near-preternatural speed of adrenal-amped reflexes and the truly preternatural accuracy of my programming.

Before they process what's happened, I push them against the wall and dig my knife point underneath their—his— clothes aimed at a kidney. I lean in, long and low, like we're making out—just in case anyone comes by. "What's your name?" I whisper in his ear.

"Liu-li," he gasps and, "who the fuck are you?" He squirms just enough to test if I know how to use the knife and then stills.

"Your new boss," I whisper back. I flick my head to make sure he sees the blue across my forehead; step back just enough so that he can see the Nursery uniform. "And don't try to com for help; I will know you've done it and I've got nothing to lose." I lie about my ability to access information-space and remind him viscerally of the knife.

He swallows and nods. I'm not sure if he's afraid of the knife or of my Operator status, but either works.

I steer Liu-li back the way I came, with the knife hidden in the folds of his cloak so it looks like we're chums.

When I get to an unmonitored storage closet, I push him inside, stand with my back to the door, and make it clear the situation with the knife hasn't changed just because it's no longer pressing into his flesh. My hands shake with the strain of running so many programs at once and the flow of adrenaline, but my voice is steady as I say, "Strip."

He glares at me, the kind of look that makes it clear I've made an enemy for life. Undressed I can see he's just a boy, really, even younger than me. His clothes fall a bit short on my long bones, but they're soft, silent, and easy to move in. The shoes are a little too wide and a little too short but better than the torn Nursery slippers. Based on the clothes I peg Liu-li for, perhaps, a sneak-thief.

He puts on my cast-offs while I dress, without any prompts or cares from me; it's chilly in here. Then I smile and say, "Thank you," as I smash him hard enough in just the right place on his head to keep him out for a while.

I turn out the light in the closet and allow myself three and a half minutes of darkness without any programming to silence my shaking hands.

Then I reach into the pockets of Liu-li's cloak.

I recognize the object immediately. It's a security key. The kind meant to unlock a specific physical location, rectangular and notched, not any sort of global pass. Shutting the door, I pull it out in the light of the hall. It has a huge "3C" on it. I pull up the hood of the cloak so no one can see the blue of my forehead, point myself in Liu-li's original direction, and flow into the busy hallway.

Now all of my motor programming goes into moving like those around me. I add a little bit of a soft pad, a sneak-thief's pad, a duck and nod. I keep my hands in my pockets so no one can see the wound bleeding through, or the absence of corporate identification. Nearly indistinguishable from normal? Ha! I *am* indistinguishable as I initiate algorithms to shift my physical nuances and blend.

And I use my map and my eyes to search for anything marked "3C."

Eventually I find a strange, narrow door erected to fit in the irregular space of the tunnel. It has old mine markings, and if the paint weren't so worn, they might have read "3C." The lock responds to the key in my hand by clicking open as I approach, but that door's not the payload. Just the foreplay.

The large metal blast door beyond, framed by raw lunar rock in a space more cave than corridor, has a small slot at the height of a handle.

I slide the security key in.

Woosh—

It's a treasure chamber inside.

Well, not actually, not the kind with chests spilling gold and goblets—though an oddly large volume of paintings and artwork fill the space. No, this is a crew drop-point, and my father has many like it scattered throughout Galilean space. It's where crews drop off things for each other—a kind of internal post or exchange.

Since Liu-li's pockets were empty besides the key, he must have been meaning to pick something up. In here there will be secrets the Galilean Black can exploit. And I have perfect recall through the computer in my brain. All I need to do is keep my senses open.

I enter the large, rough-carved cavern and make for the slots along the far wall, stacked with digipages and smaller containers. Blackmail materials? Information about politicians on the make?

I drop Liu-li's security key back into my pocket and take three breaths to enjoy the pleasure as I pick up what's clearly a blackmail dossier on the CEO of Felicity-Ko.

I don't scan everything.

I don't have that much time, and even if Liu-li's clothing protects me at a glance, it doesn't protect me from a closer inspection or swipe with an ID reader.

But I scan enough. And then a little more.

Time to get out. To get to a public coms terminal and send a small taste of what I've found back home on one of my father's encrypted channels the same way that a normal person would. A taste with promises of the rest—but only after someone has picked me up. And then, finally, I will be home.

The door opens and a crew enters. It's a generic-looking bunch—two rookies, not much older than me, two bored-looking up-and-comers, and a grizzled veteran who seems irritated about being stuck with the others. They're not carrying anything. Maybe what they have to drop is small, in a pocket. More likely they're there for a pick-up.

I keep my head down, forehead covered over by the hood, and nod, slinking past them with my hands in my pockets, fingers curled around the handle of my knife.

They nod back, as an up-and-comer and a rookie pass me.

As I step past the second rookie, she grabs my arm.

Program switch: full-bore motor-sensory multi-threading fighting-mode—ON.

Adrenaline boost, killing routines, sensory acuity, just like I practiced in my room in my purchased moments of security camera looping, with my hair flying behind me as I danced, proud and competent, alone—

Rookie 2 lacks time to register surprise as my palm slams into her throat. Her windpipe crunches and she's down.

There are two behind me now—Rookie 1 and Come-upper 1.

Two in front—Come-upper 2 and Veteran.

No time to duck, cover, crouch behind the large cargo areas or that pile of antiques, or to make use of anything weapon-like in the room; I'm too outnumbered and my advantage is all in precision and speed and control of my reflexes, so I'll just keep flying—

Come-upper 1 gets a full-force crotch-full of heel while I spin-and-land before Rookie 1, my knife tasting that kidney

Liu-li's cooperation denied it earlier.

I spin back, finishing Rookie 2 along the way with my blade in his neck.

Next set of trajectories plotted, I face Come-upper 2 and Veteran.

To hear the click-and-whirl as a set of implanted pistols with nasty blades on the ends pop out of Veteran's forearms.

All my calculations go moot.

No time to duck or hide, all I can do is abort and throw my hands into surrender or be shot.

If he's got those things wired right—and I must assume he has—he'll be just as fast as I am.

Veteran grins, showing teeth so needlessly yellow he must stain them for the intimidation factor. "That's a good girl, Ansari, settle down."

I start to spit on him but Come-upper 1 smashes me across the mouth. She catches me by the wrist before I can fall and yanks and digs into the flesh until my knife clatters to the ground. Pain makes its way through the best of my endorphin numbing as she tugs the injured shoulder.

Dizziness hits then, nausea, and my knees drop me to the ground. Too much adrenaline push. Stress chemical saturation. Too much...

I would have won the fight if it wasn't for the implanted guns.

I would have...

Two more of X's people enter and take me from the room.

They lead me to a lift. They take me down, down, down. For a long time we go down. My mouth hurts; my hand bleeds; my ankle swells monstrously inside Liu-li's ill-fitting shoe. I ache everywhere because while I can program muscles and joints to move in ways no human body is meant to move, I can't program them to repair the resulting damage. My hands shake and sparkles cloud my vision.

So many threads of consciousness running so many programs. I can't keep holding them all. My father is right. The Nursery is right. I am a worthless k-dromer. Feeble. Not normal. Because the fact is that none of my indistinguishability from normal is because my tutors or the teachers in the Nursery made me normal, but because they taught me how to fake it. Nothing of what I just accomplished is because I am normal. Worse—the parts of the failed escape I most enjoyed were the ones that most indulged my defects.

That's what my father meant when he sent me away saying, *"No amount of tutors can ever make you normal."*

The problem isn't how I act.

It's what I am.

I should make a wrong move so X's people will kill me.

Except, even though that's how I should be thinking right now, how I've been taught to think, I don't feel it at all.

How many floors have we gone? And are we going down or up? There are no numbers or visible controls in the smooth, gray interior of the lift.

The lift opens without sound to a sheet-metal hallway drenched in activity.

X-shaped pins flash on hands. Awareness of the throbbing where I cut out my corporate pin begins, along with the pain in my shoulder, foot, and everywhere else as my body's ability to produce endorphins reaches its limit. We're deep as it gets into Madame X's territory, deep like the heart of my father's hotel. But no one has killed me yet. Likely they are saving me to extract secrets of their own.

X's people lead me to a room with black walls and white light. Guards in body armor hulk over a heavy wooden door, bare hands flashing with tips of weapons just below the skin. They step aside for us, like the jaws of a dark machine.

Beyond the door is a room.

In the room is a painting.

The painting is old. Cracks spiderweb over an amber patina. Within the frame, a woman stands beside a small, round table, white skin as luminous as my Europa against her black evening dress and thin gold straps. Her head, on a long, graceful neck, tilts away: cold, powerful, proud—vulnerable. The portrait breathes. Below, a plate reads, "Madame X, John Singer Sargent, 1884." The painting is over six hundred years old.

"Jordis Ansari, how nice to meet you." The voice flows from within the portrait, timbre an uncanny mix of synthesized and human. It spreads moist velvet across my arms, and this time I no longer have the threads to spare to keep myself from scratching the phantom sensation.

I should be ashamed of myself for giving in to the gesture. But, despite the Nursery's best efforts, I'm really not. And that, I suppose, is the heart of my problem.

Are these the last hours of my life? The last minutes? Seconds? Will someone torture me first? For how long? My pulse is of panicked birds' wings.

I draw in breath and square my shoulders. If I must go down, I will clearly be going down with pride.

A honey-chuckle rolls from the painting, just like I remember. X, the eldritch. "Please, sit. I've ordered us a tea."

I lower onto a cherry wood chair behind a cherry wood table, facing the painting, gasping as the weight comes off my damaged limbs.

A man appears and prepares a cup—just one—for me. It smells of Da Hon Pao; expensive.

"I've been watching you grow," X exhales. "I was watching you today. You are quite the balm for my boredom."

The cup clatters into the saucer as my hands shake, but I can't tell if it's from fear or adrenal overload or slipping motor control. I hope she thinks it's fear. It's normal to be afraid. Normal like I'll never be.

And then, of all things, I feel the hobbles that prevent me from accessing informationspace dissolve and a second Madame X steps from the painting in augreal and walks through the airwaves to join me in the dark room of my mind, as though she were a fellow Operator. "Oh come now, Jordis, you're not truly afraid." Her voice echoes in both worlds at once. "You who stared down every assumption about your genetic type and said, 'fuck you, I will be who I was meant to be.'"

But she is wrong, and I am small and might die right here of my heart beating too fast. Because all I've ever done is try to be something I'm not: normal. If I have ever felt shame, for some wild, unfathomable reason, it is for that—for the trying, not for the failing.

On another thread, I process: What is she? Her presentation is too stiff and limited to be an Operator's. But too fleshed out to be a normal's, and her reaction time too quick to be transmitting through the mediation of an external interface or device. She is uncanny.

But then, so am I, from the other side. I read as normal—but not quite. Never quite. Because I'm not and never will be.

I manifest my own presentation in my mind, a duplicate of myself in black and white. In the physical world, I keep up appearances: sit proper in the cherry wood chair, sip tea with shaking hands and propriety. The tea is indeed Da Hon Pao, and of exceptional quality. In informationspace, I say, "You're wrong. I would trade everything but my birthright to be normal." But no, that's no longer true. If it ever was.

X repeats that laugh of age and earth and delicate knives. "If you were normal, you'd have been dead the moment you landed on Luna."

I will not drop her gaze. I am Jordis-Fucking-Ansari.

"Do you think your father's choice of Nursery was arbitrary? One on Ganymede would have been closer, one on Earth less expensive. Any outside the Sol-system would afford a better chance of sponsorship. But no, he sent you here so I would dispatch with you. He sent you here because he was too much of a coward to shoot you himself when he shot your mother for having you."

"And now you'll kill me so that I won't bring your secrets home. Preferably after squeezing me for everything I can tell you about the Galilean Black. And everyone is happy."

"If that's your choice."

Now I laugh. "I don't have choices. I have the k-syndrome defect. The only choice I've ever had is servitude or death, and servitude didn't seem to want me."

"Oh, you don't believe that. Those are an unimaginative person's words. Come behind the painting, Jordis. Then choose your path."

I set off the proper motor sequences to stand. To bend hips and knees and feet and walk myself with a normal gait on torn muscles and sprained ankles to the wall behind the work of art. I expect it to be a wall—and a laugh at my expense. Or a fatal trap. But no, the wall is a high-res hologram, and I step through to the other side.

Into a hospital room. Top-technology, clean and discrete, but a medclinic. I am alone. Automatic defense turrets, dense enough to leave nothing to chance, focus their barrels on me. Behind the painting is a tank.

"I grew up on Luna before grav generators."

That's history, deep Luna history. Back when some children lost the rigidity in their bones. I've no doubt now the same person has run the Luna Black for over two-hundred and fifty years. But she's much older than that.

"It's all illegal medtech," X laughs, as though illegal brain-tanking was the most notable thing about this situation. "Have you figured out yet why I always beat your father?"

"You were established first?"

"You're better than that."

I think anew, adding context just revealed. "Because you don't fear Operators."

"Just so. I've found a bridge into your world. I think I'm the only normal who has. I wear informationspace as a body because mine melted long ago, but I will never have an Operator's ability to smell logic. To feel the colors of numbers as fine fur on my tongue. I envy you the richness of your mind."

"And I envy you your empire." My voice is cold as Europa's ice.

She breathes a defiant: HA! "Ours is the power of resistance, Jordis. The strength made from years of minutes of constant push-back. We win empires because no one expects us to be the ones who try."

Could I make it to her tank before the turrets took me down?

If I have any adrenaline left, it would be, at least, a draw. Or, better yet, in my freshly unhobbled state I could take control of the turrets themselves and shut them down.

I could kill her now. I could destroy this rival to my house and go home to Europa triumphant. No matter how much he hates Operators, and even if I had to use my Operator abilities to do it, my father would have to take me back if I took down X. We are alone in this room, me and the tank. There are heavy objects a-plenty, or I could just unscrew the nutrient tap. I could even kill her and become her.

I look at the floor, making myself small and approachable, like they trained me in the Nursery. I move in closer. Much closer. "Will the Empire of the Moon sponsor me?"

A sound of wind and wrath screams out of the speakers. "Do you think me so crass?" Then the wrath-wind ebbs and X sighs. "No one should ever make you feel like a piece of exchangeable property. They should have taught you to take pride in who you are instead."

"I—" But lack of pride has never been my problem, it's been lack of shame for my defects. And those "defects" of k-syndrome, of not being normal enough, have never been my problem either. No, my problem, just coming into acute focus now, is that I have spent too much time trying to wear someone else's skin. My shame is trying to be something I'm not. "You're wrong," I say to the Enemy of my House. "I have plenty of pride in who I am. The problem is that other people are uncomfortable with that fact."

X smiles an enigmatic semi-smile. "Tell me, Jordis, how did you feel when you were escaping today? When you switched places with Liu-li? When you took down my people? What was it like?"

It was amazing. "It wasn't normal."

"But how did it feel?"

"Amazing. Freeing. Being at home inside of my skin."

"Would you like a new challenge?"

"One that lets me be who I am?" If she hadn't shown me behind the painting, I wouldn't believe the choice she's offering me right now. But then, canny Queen she is, I'm quite sure she knew that. Until now I never thought I'd meet anyone who was even a little bit like me. And, I suspect, she feels the same.

"I would not have you any other way," X says.

I'll get back home eventually. I'll have my empire eventually.

But for now, I kneel on the floor before all that is powerful and uncanny and *like me* and let go of the millions of millions of programs I run to appease the buyers, the Nursery staff, the world, and my father. I've never needed any of it. And I've known it all along. "I swear you my Devotion." I touch my forehead to her ground in proper ritual. "Teach me everything."

**[sarah] Cavar**

# *: Master Doc*

Dear Uncle Max,

I've got to thank you. I can never repay you. How to begin to repay something like an education, something so precious? But I will try. Even though, as you might notice, I am at a loss for words. When I get a good job from this good degree and learn how to write good things I will prove to you that I was not just an investment, but, yes, a good one.

I'm all moved-in now, just waiting for classes to start. I'm sure you've guessed, but The University is different today than it was when you were here. That's what I learned at our beginning-of-year Family Meeting last night: they said so explicitly, as though they were speaking just to me. They have enacted *Numerous Exciting Developments* for the *Next Generation of Lifelong Learners.* Dr. Headmaster is brand-new this year and fresh like a cotton sheet, pale, no spots. He requires rigor.

It seemed like everyone in attendance was just as excited as me. Excited to learn how to be rigorous. I'm sure you've already heard about the expedited three-year undergraduate degree—while it's been available for a decade, this is the first year that they've made it compulsory. Mr. Headmaster laughed lightly at what he called the Thinning Of The Ranks resulting from that decision. He called it a weed-out. He said congrats on being flowers.

Considering the whole expedited degree thing, you won't have to worry about me "doing all the drugs" like you did "back in the stone age." I did appreciate your other tips, though, and promise not to leave my popcorn unattended in the dorm microwave. And really, who knows when I'll even have time to make popcorn. Seems I'll barely have time to breathe.

Okay, now they're rounding us up to see the library carrels. It got so dark while I was writing. By the way, I

Sorry, sent that one by accident. Saw the cubicles and then got pre-class assignments and went to bed and then it was tomorrow and the whole day just blew by. I'm back in my room now. I meant to tell you before that we all have single rooms because of the drop in enrollment. Some of them used to be doubles, a few even still have an empty bed for the roommate that isn't there. This freshman class only has 300 people in it. Wasn't yours over 3,000?

My room here is pretty nice, a double-turned single. There's a bed off in the corner, a massive desk area where the other roommate's bed used to be, a lamp, a decent-sized closet. It's easy to snag a shower any time of evening with just ten people per floor. You just have to make sure someone else isn't there listening to one of their podcasts—nothing against them, I'd just like a few minutes to shower in peace, you know?

Okay, as I'm writing this, something strange happened. My neighbor just knocked. She had forgotten how to get to the library. I was kind of mean when I told her the directions—after all, we just got our maps last night. And anyway, I hate it when people bother me while I'm trying to get things done.

Do you remember that church song, "Somebody's Knocking at Your Door"? As a kid, when Mom and Dad would bring me to church, they'd always have us kids sing that song. I know you're an atheist, but if you came back to The University today, I think you'd become a believer. All the other gods are gone, all the churches. All the landplots bought out and turned to library annexes, did you know? I've never seen the annexes, but I trust that they're there. This metaphor is going further than I thought.

What I'm trying to say is that the library is everywhere, like a deity, and you can't miss it. When I'm done my pre-class papers, I'm going to go and explore it. I'm going to see as many corners as I can. My other pre-class assignments will be waiting at my cubicle, anyway.

Best,

•

Uncle Max,

I feel ashamed for being short with my neighbor yesterday, the one who asked for directions. I call her my neighbor because I keep forgetting her name (you know how I am with names). I smiled at her in the canteen this morning and she smiled back; it's a start. We had to eat pretty quickly—ten-minute breakfast rule—so I just snagged an apple juice and went to class.

Our first class, freshman comp, was taught by this Professor who looked more like a student than a teacher. He had just gotten his PhD. from The University. And he's only twenty-five! He called himself a "true believer" when it came to expedited undergrad programs. He did his at a little school up in the mountains that I'm pretty sure just closed, and then came here for graduate school. He gave us some advice at the beginning of class, spoke it so fast it was hard to keep up. That was the point, he said, because a good student knows how to take notes no matter how fast someone's talking. I probably failed, since we all start out as failures until we can prove otherwise. Professor told us that, too.

Failure or not, I took some notes on his advice. I've attached a picture of them to this email.

*Advice: we cant control how time passes. we CAN cntrl how we make use of it … staying ahead when time is in control means that you should be looking to get the most valu for your minutes. 20min? can [forgot] 10min? COULD go 2 vending machine with friends, etc but COULD also do problem sets; readings. five min*

Sorry it randomly stops like that. We were all so excited to listen to him that it was hard to keep up with notes. It felt like we were all moving inside of something big and wonderful, but also a little scary, like a love boat tunnel where you're not sure where it'll spit you.

I think I have a crush on Professor but I'm not sure. Maybe just on his work ethic.

•

Dear Uncle Max,

Sorry I haven't written in a bit. I wish I could remember what I've already told you and what I haven't, but everything disappears so easily here.

One new update: I now officially hate my floormates. One of them was yelling until after two in the morning last night, not responding to anyone banging on their walls or door. They only opened up after I finally started yelling back. Their hair was a mess. They were wearing glasses. They were wearing very little clothing, just a thin t-shirt and underwear. I was like, what the fuck? And they were like:

They just opened their mouth and a big blank came out.

I asked again, what? And this time they made words: I feel like I'm going crazy here.

Why, I asked.

I just went to the library like normal today—well, I didn't eat before, because yesterday I stayed too long and now have to learn my lesson—and it started fine. I got to the big gate doors and went inside, but then, everything shifted a little. It was like I had been tipped on my side.

I convinced myself I was just dizzy, and drank some water. Thought I was fine. But when I walked through the door to the Reading Room, I ended up someplace I'd never seen before. I don't know how to describe it. It was like I had entered an old, dry fountain. I walked and walked and nothing changed, like a dream. Afterward, I fainted, and when I woke up I was laying on the grass outside the building. Campus police were there shaking me. Or maybe the shaking was just me.

My floormate was shaking while they told me this. They
had removed their facial jewelry—a lip ring, a nose stud, a
philtrum—because it was uselesswasteful, so now their face
was dotted with tiny holes.

Okay, but why are you yelling about it in the middle of
the night? I demanded. You think *I* want to miss breakfast
tomorrow?

They picked at a patch of dry skin on their bare thigh. I
watched it turn red, until I couldn't watch anymore, so I was
like *whatever* and went back to my room.

•

Uncle Max

I'm losing my pinky. My useless pinky finger. Luckily, everyone else is, too. At first we were a little freaked out, since
it's not like anyone necessarily *wants* to have their pinky
amputated. But the headmaster called a Family Meeting (as-
sembly) and explained that no one was going to amputate
anybody here, that wasn't what this was at all. We were just
losing our pinkies because eventually all meaningless things
would go away. He looked so sad and continued. "I'm so sorry about the confusion. I can assure you we just don't do
violence here. We're a college. We're a family."

Everyone dispersed so quickly after that. Off to the library, silent as if in preparation. I was busy wondering if
they'd make my appendix disappear next, and if they did,
how would I know? On my way to the library, although I'd
assumed everyone else was going there, too, I got lost. But
then I turned and oh, it was behind me all along. On my

way, I mean, I had passed it. Here I was thinking everyone else was stupid and worthless for getting lost when I'm just the same.

•

Dear Uncle Max,

I've been wondering why, if the library is that hard to find, we don't just sleep there too. I finally tried it last night, and it was pretty good. I did that thing where you sleep in two different shifts and get things done in between. I went to bed at seven-thirty, got up at twelve-thirty, then went back to bed around two-thirty for another three hours.

I guess you could say I've been taking Professor's advice to heart. On the way to the canteen today I was looking at my notes for next week's test. I'd have looked at them in the canteen, too, but I never made it, and then breakfast was over. I met a campus policeman where the canteen used to be, or where I thought it was. Where my stupid fucking head thought it was. STUPIDFUCKSTUPID

Sorry, I think I sent the first part of that email by accident. I can't find it in my sent folder, so I'm going to try to remember where I left off. The policeman asked me what was wrong with me, and I told him I was just trying to find the canteen. He looked at me like I was a monster. I told him I was sure it was here. He gave me a six-ounce bottle of water and a Nutrigrain bar, but didn't say a word.

My other fingers are getting loose, so the bar was a little hard to open. But when I got it, it tasted like childhood.

They just make you feel so cared-for here, you know? I am full of strawberries.

●

Dear Uncle Max,

I promise you, I *am* signing my name to every message. I know how to be polite. I'm also sorry my emails have been less frequent lately. I'm a little jumbled because I can't find much. My room, the canteen. Everything is a little bit of a jungle, so I'm moving to the library permanently.

The police walk around in here with water and Nutri-grains. We get three of each every day! One just made his rounds, and I admit, it was a little weird. I said, hi officer. He rolled his eyes and told me to get back to my problem sets. These were my extras, I explained; I was ahead of schedule. These were optional. He said, so now you're going to sit around doing nothing when you could be doing your extra problem sets? Sorry, I said, just making conversation. But I don't think he heard me

●

Uncle,

I sent you an email last week, but you never replied. Sorry for the impersonal address; I'm bad with names. There's so much in my head it's hard to keep them straight!

What else. Winter is turning to spring. I can't wait for the nice weather, so I can take all my books and things outside. Headmaster said he'd start unlocking the library doors again April 1. I hope it's not just a prank!

I'm looking forward to my Nutrigrain today. They give us a Nutrigrain and a bottle of water every day, isn't that great? Wait—I need to STOP thinking about it because once you start a distracted train of thought, it's hard to stop. STOP. STOP. It's not even noon yet.

This is exactly why the police have started hanging out with us when we eat the Nutrigrain bars. They have timers, but it's a no-pressure sort of thing. When I asked why they had timers if it was a no-pressure thing, they were all, what timers?

They're so funny.

Had to go to class. I'm back now and need to finish this even though I want to WANT TO fucking DIE. Professor gave me back an essay today and sort of shook his head, so personally disappointed. It was the lowest grade I had ever FUCKING DIE gotten in his class. This girl who I think used to be my neighbor got the best grade. The one who asked me for directions to the library. He wouldn't stop talking about her.

But there's also some good news: I heard Headmaster say he was giving extra-extra credit to the person with the most cubicle discipline. It could apply to any class we wanted. The winner would also get a free pair of compression socks to fight clotting. We all yelled THANK YOU into our microphones. We don't have Family Meeting anymore; Headmaster now speaks through a P.A. system and we can speak back and he hears. It feels like having a father.

I have to win so I can get back in Mr. ———'s good graces. The only other way would be to kill my old neighbor to get her and her grades out of my way. I don't have the time to plan something like that.

My eyes hurt so I'll write again another time. Probably after spring exams. We're going to get new emails around then, too, so keep an eye out for mine.

●

AUTO-GENERATED: Exams are just around the corner! QuikSend helps YOU keep your family close while studying the most!

Dear

Love you. Can't wait for summer sun and fun!

Your favorite student,

[[[Delivered with QuikSend, donotreply@quiksend. com]]]

●

AUTO-GENERATED: Exams are just around the corner! QuikSend helps YOU keep your family close while studying the most!

Dear

DON'TKNOW WHO YOU ARE BUT YOU NEED TO LEAVE ME BE.

Seriously, I shouldn't even be writing because I'm going to fail my bio final tomorrow and writing this just makes it more real that I'm going to fail

Today I walked out of the library for the first time in a

little while to clear my head because the doors were open but then it wouldn't budge? What I asked myself today is April 11. When I got outside I closed my eyes for a moment before remembering that they were gone, as were my eyelashes. I think that now that I have exhausted the possibilities attached to my eyelashes I will begin with my extra skin.

And then I looked around and realized silly me I was inside. I was in the green fountain, and there was no water, and everything was very dry especially my lidlost eyes.

Sorry to be weird, but I also have to ask: how did you know about my fingers and toes? Why do you care? If you're really my benefactor, you should know there are many things worth losing to get a good education. Maybe you never got a good education. Maybe you're even dumber than me. Well, dumber than I'm trying to be. DUMBER THAN I WILL BE WHEN I JUSTGETMYSHIT TOGETHER im trying to get my B.A. in two years, after all. im iam halfway to salvationSo just let me win

**Anastasia Jill**

# Mrs. Sardonicus

*Act I.*

Mrs. Sardonicus
killed her husband
to steal back her
gold star lottery ticket—

a fortune taken in trade
from her black pearl
of grace;
she now wears those pearls
on her neck,

each night,
she takes a female lover
while her husband rots
in his grave—
and she smiles.

the show must go on,
though the show has only
just begun.

•

*Act II.*

Mrs. Sardonicus
has a smile

like a lottery winner
it's a Botox filled show tune,
the glimmer in her teeth,
but all she can do
is smile;
smile dearie, smile,
for the lover
waiting in pearls and swine meat—
she waits just for a femme pulp.

Mrs. Sardonicus
paints her nails in leeches
and eyes in gutter gold,
drinking vodka from a mug that reads
*DONT FUCK WITH ME FELLAS*
in black letters.

Her lover sits upon a bed
framed in the chiffon of a widow;
black, holding two glow in the dark
cards in pallid hands
while spectators watch.

Mrs. Sardonicus
knows her fate hangs
like a woman by her thumbs
from the ceiling, by which card
is brought to light.

Mrs. Sardonicus
has a horrifying grin—
her lover is tortured
while

Mrs. Sardonicus
smiles;
there is no cure for
this lesbian's stiff affliction.

●

*Act III.*

The physical self:
a woman in blonde
living a life free of muscle movement
lips fold into a grinning skull;
a guest of honor in any woman's bed.

The mental self:
soil black eyes traumatized by the grin
of a man in brown, killed for his money.
her face is mutated to match his own;
she cannot abscond her husband's shadow.

●

*Act IV.*

You'll see to the end of this punishment poll;
softness between legs marinated in plant extract.

"Mercy? No mercy?"
Has Mrs. Sardonicus suffered enough?
Mrs. Sardonicus seeks further punishment.
She is a sadist, a submissive writer.

"Mercy? No mercy?"
Her lover overcomes a climax to find a body
staining like dirt under fingernails—
telltale and psychosomatic.

She decides.
"No mercy?"
So be it.

●


*The End.*

The sentence is carried out backstage,
a poisoned ladle of spotlight

to sweeten the soup of deprivation
and syringe of the starved;

the needle has a say
in how the story ends.

The queen is poisoned.
Like this.
Not like this.

No, fellas.
Like this.

**Nick Mamatas**

# A Moment of Silence Before the Action Begins

It's not in any handbook on the theory and practice of executive protection; the technique is only whispered about, passed down from generation to generation. They say it started up at Harvard, after McKinley was assassinated by the anarchist Leon Czolgosz, and the Secret Service was charged with Presidential protection duties. Members of Porcellian, the famous eating club that began with a pig roast in 1791, passed on the secret they had held for more than a century to the feds in order to guarantee the safety of their member, and the new President, Theodore Roosevelt.

It is called the Pearled Diamond.

After the briefing, after the huddle, but before positions are taken up, four men gather together, forming an equilateral quadrilateral. Each one slides their erect penis from their pants with their right hand. The man on their right takes hold of it with their left hand. Then, when everyone has another man's penis in hand, they begin to jerk in time to a certain song popular in the late eighteenth century. You know the tune, but perhaps not the lyrics the men sing:

*Arnold is as brave a man as ever dealt in horses*
*And now commands a num'rous clan*
*of New England jackasses*

*With sword and spear he vows and swears*
*that Quebec shall be taken,*
*But if he'd be advised by me,*
*he'd fly to save his bacon.*

*But t'other day he did assay*
*to do some execution,*
*But he thought fit to run away*
*for want of resolution.*

*They gave him a commission straight*
*and bid him not abuse it,*
*Told him his rusty sword to whet*
*and sent him here to use it.*

*'Tis thus, my friends, we are beset*
*by all those damn'd invaders,*
*No greater villains ever met*
*than are those Yankee traitors.*

With frequent practice, the men will always reach their climax in unison, and spill seed onto the floor, where it is not to be cleaned up or trod upon. These men will find that their somatic and vegetative nervous systems have been synchronized for twenty-four hours, and that they will be able to instantly understand the behaviors and movements of their fellows, creating a nigh-perfect bodyguard force that can intercept and defeat attackers in all four directions.

*Nigh* perfect.

The Pearled Diamond has failed utterly only once, on a day so infamous I need not go into detail. There have been other close calls—Presidents fired upon without result, others wounded thanks to the slightest disconnect between masturbators during the Pearled Diamond ritual. Not every man has the courage to be masturbated and masturbate a colleague on command. Some suppose it unmanly or homosexual, though it is a ritual that has served this nation since near its founding.

I had to fuck a lot of guys to find out the secret. I didn't even know at first I was on the hunt to understand the Pearled Diamond. I was at a private party in a restaurant, being spanked while sucking another stranger's cock, when I noticed that my ass was being smacked to the famous tune. I was doing my undergrad at Tufts—it was sort of a thing to throw myself at the richer, preppier, Harvard guys who came to such events. Some of them were pure doms, or 99.44% pure anyway. Others liked to wear lacy panties or command a sub to penetrate their anuses. Still others wanted me to step on their necks and tell them that they should suck my toes like they were five little cocks, nice and slurpy. The parties were fun. There were ciswomen too and an array of gender-fun sorts, but despite my sexual extravagances I preferred to play with cismales, especially the ones with hard bodies and sheepish schoolboy smiles. I kept my recently installed cunt shut and my eyes open. The events had everything I liked about sex—the musk and flesh of heavy mammals, giggling and sudden shocks, sensations that embedded pleasure in the pain, but without the complications of emotionality beyond fellow-feeling and cooperation. These group sessions were like everyone helping a neighbor push their car out of the February snows, but with orgasms.

So this night, I was being spanked; when I recognized the tune I started to laugh and almost circumcised the fellow I was sucking off. We had to take a break, proffer apologies, and almost even exchanged names. They were both cute, and blushing, and kept semi-hard erections even during our triple embarrassment. My nipples were huge.

When I saw one of them, the spanker, at the other end of my coach on the T three days later, I decided to follow him surreptitiously. I wore no domino mask, and my hair was loose rather than in the simple braid I twisted it into for parties. Also I wore my usual uniform of an enormous sweatshirt and leggings, not lacy boy shorts and glitter, so he certainly didn't recognize me.

Everyone in the Boston metroplex knows of the Harvard eating clubs and other secret societies. It's especially true of us who go to the local still-exceptional-no-really-very-good-indeed-schools that aren't either Harvard or MIT. I spent a week following him, then decided to make him my boyfriend by stumbling onto his lap as I raced for the door at a stop that wasn't my stop. His name was Aiden, of course, as every white male his age was named Aiden.

It would be gauche to say that Aiden passed me around to his friends in Porcellian; he probably remembers it as a fling with me that went well and ended well, and by then I was a member in good standing of his broader social circle and was able to get another boyfriend from that crowd, then another, then a couple that overlapped for a few weeks. The other girls and non-club boys involved all did the same. It takes about three semesters for a close group of twenty or so students/drinkers/hiking enthusiasts/RPG gamers/bitcoin traders/whatever to achieve panmixia.

Slowly but surely, without even realizing it at first, I tumbled from bed to bed and collected the elements of the Pearled Diamond. Some boys hummed the song while they jackrabbited atop me, others were right-handed in all respect but jerked themselves off southpaw. One had no direct sexual tells, but he was writing a major paper on Roosevelt, and like a dutiful girlfriend from a lower-tier university in *gawd* Medford four miles away of all places, I proofread both his sloppy 3am drafts while he snoozed and my vagina leaked with his semen.

Despite its pedigree, Porcellian itself is a dump. There's a small bar and a pool table and a mirrored wall—the sort of thing a stoner high schooler would set up in his parents' garage in Michigan's Upper Peninsula in order to introduce 14-year-old girls to pot and fingerbangs. It's for club members only, except if you fuck enough of them.

And if you fuck enough of them and get to go to the clubhouse, and if you're an easily bored Tufts undergrad who'd read the side of a toothpaste tube were it in arm's reach, you may find yourself on a lark snagging the oldest-seeming book from a shelf just to see what's in it, and be delighted by the long s's and the generations of marginal notes—the dead critiquing the dead for the sake of the living—and come across the notes for a "ritual of conviviality, solidarity, and somatic chronosymmetry," the Pearled Diamond.

Since those days, I've monitored the television and social media, watching Presidents come and go, speak and stump. My gaze was on the Secret Service agents around them. Which at this meeting with a foreign head of state were the four with empty balls and crosswired nerves? I got a job in the industry town of Washington DC pushing paper and proofreading for a think tank you'd recognize if you watch PBS and pay attention to the talking heads, and from that vantage point got to observe both the President and their protectors much more closely.

Aiden had become a Secret Service agent.

A terrible terrible man had become president.

CAMAB, I know a thing or two about both blending in and oppression. I'm in student and medical debt that I can never pay off. My identity has historically been a free pass to murder me in a sexual panic. Under the terrible terrible man, the tentative gains folk like me experienced were being rolled back. Camps on the borders were built for migrants, then camps in the heartland for the *other othered*, as we used to say in school and on blogs. His increasingly unhinged public pronouncements, often made off-the-cuff, became law and neither the judiciary nor the legislature could stop him.

But I can. I can stop him because I know the secret of the Pearled Diamond. Because I work for a certain think tank and thus I have a badge that got me green room access to the latest interminable rally. Because through a vent against which I had placed by ear I heard the off-key tenors of a familiar tune with unusual lyrics. Because the semen stains in the hall carry a familiar scent. Because I understand how the four men surrounding the President will act and react. Because I know that Aiden will pause for a second when he sees my face, my winning smile, my subtle wink. And so too will the other three, reflexively, unwillingly. They'll smile for me as I complete my mission in the moment before they regain their senses.

Don't you love it when a lover smiles, right as they see you for the first time, or the first time in a long time?

Don't you love it when a lover smiles, right before they come—right after they come? There will be many a smile tonight. I'm smiling now, just like I do when I see a lover for the first time in a long time. Just like I do right before I come.

Because

toNIGHT

my BITCHES and BITCHOS

I PULL OUT A GUN

AND

I

EXECUTE THE MOTHERFUCKING PRESIDENT

OF THESE UNITED STATES!

**Julie Sondra Decker**

# Her Experiment

The bracelet is made from a hardy yellow string—the stuff my father once used to make his yo-yos. Its single adornment is a piece of flexible white metal, about half a centimeter across, folded over the string like a fat staple. I've never known what the metal is. Maybe that's part of the reason its magic worked for me; I couldn't place its origin in my head the way I could the yo-yo string. Therefore, maybe it was otherworldly and powerful.

The metal's firm bite upon the string inspired me to rely on its strength; I never worried that it would let a monster through. I'd trusted little else besides the bracelet in my life, and that remained true until I met Melody.

●

"So are you ever gonna tell me?" she asks.

"I don't really wanna talk about it."

She exhales and rolls back onto her side of the bed, watching with one eye as I put the bracelet on and get back under the covers.

I don't comment and hope she'll drop it, but when I try to put my arm around her she catches my wrist and pinches the bracelet.

"Tell me," she says, and she's using her *kidding* voice, so I blow her bangs off her face and tickle her neck instead of answering.

It backfires. Instead of giving up, she flips into serious mode. "How come you won't tell me this stupid secret?" She rocks up onto an elbow, now looking down on me in the partial darkness. "I'm about to be your wife. Why can't you tell me why you *have* to put this thing on before you go to bed?"

"It's nothing. My dad gave it to me when I was a kid. It helps me remember him."

Now I'm getting her narrowed eyes, easily seen as the hallway nightlight glints off them. "That's not the whole story. Why would you need a trinket from your father only at night? It's some kind of compulsion. Don't I deserve to know the story?"

I love Melody. This intense curiosity, this burning need to know the truth, this passion she has for discovery and the lengths she's willing to go to for its satisfaction—it's all so attractive, and it's the central reason why I was drawn to her. It's made her a star in her research career. It's made her the queen of our board game nights whenever there's a strategy game. But when she turns it on me like this, like my right to privacy is an insult so personal I might as well have slapped her face and killed her dog, because how dare I keep *the truth* from her to preserve my own safety, well . . . when she does this, it's the only thing I don't love about her.

"I'm not unwilling to tell you," I say, and there's sand crackling off the words and dusting down my throat. I cough. "And one day, if you still *need* to know—"

"Of course I need to know," she says, brightening just a little. "You know me."

". . . I'll find some way to say it. But I know you'll ask questions, and I don't know how I'll handle what you'll ask. It'll just keep going and going and—"

"You won't tell me because I'll annoy you to death with questions? That's what you're so afraid of?"

"No, I—"

"How about instead of avoiding them, you just answered them?"

"Because you'll keep cutting me off when I try to tell you, just like the last three things I tried to say."

Two responses fight for dominance on her face. My statement has made her realize she's doing that thing—she's pursuing her curiosity so aggressively that the subject's experience being questioned is completely ignored in the face of her truth quest. She doesn't want to do that to me, and she's lost people in her life over this before. But at the same time, she wants to tell me off. She wants to tell me I'm impossible, I'm the problem, I'm making her feel bad for making me feel bad. She wants to be sorry about being like this and wants to defend her right to keep being like this at the same time.

Annoyed Melody wins tonight. "Fine," she grunts, dropping back onto the pillows and executing impressive acrobatics to spin herself facing away from me without disrupting the covers. "I'll just *die* without ever knowing what it's for, with a husband who keeps secrets from me for no reason."

"There is a reason," I say in a low voice. "If you expect me to tell you, I need to know you'll be . . . respectful about it, and right now it seems like you won't."

"Okay fine!" she calls out in a remarkably loud voice for so late at night. The pitch of her voice catches the metal clothes hanging rod in the closet and sets it ringing. It's spooky, then funny. I chuckle despite myself.

"As long as you'll tell me one day," she says, "I guess I'll just wait 'til you're ready. Whatever."

"And I get to decide when that is," I say—both cautiously and as a warning.

She sighs darkly into the covers, still not looking at me. "Yeah."

Then she's silent and I look at her back, watching as she drifts off without turning back to me, without reconciling.

It's an almost perfect reprise of the first time we had this conversation.

•

We'd only met twice before we agreed to start dating exclusively. And on the night of our second date there we were in bed together, both giddily assuring the other that this was unusual for us, unusual to care about someone this fast, unusual to take this step so soon, unusual to feel comfortable enough with another person that we wanted to jump through the hoops required to be safe in a physical relationship. We were both gobsmacked by our good fortune in finding each other, and still in disbelief that the other person was *so good*.

We slept together and then we were planning to *sleep* together, but Melody objected when I needed to go get my bracelet before settling down.

"No, stay here!" she murmured.

"I'll be right back."

"I hereby forbid it!" She held me in the bed and repeatedly restricted any limb I tried to move, playing a weird game of whack-a-mole with my body.

"Just a second! I gotta—" I trailed off. She wouldn't understand.

"What, need the bathroom or something?"

I should have just said yes.

Instead, I told Melody that I needed to grab something I wanted to wear to bed, and I vaguely referred to it as "jewelry," and she was so dismissive about the idea of needing to *don a bracelet* before I could sleep that I started to feel really stupid and couldn't find the words to explain it to her. I caved, left my bracelet unworn until I drifted off, and didn't offer any more explanation.

And the monsters came for me.

It had been so long that I'd almost forgotten what it was like to be taken away so utterly, to be so helplessly at their mercy in my sleep.

Monsters came to me through my dreams and did things to me that were so awful I could barely make sense of it when I woke. What would a monster get out of taking a person's body apart in gruesome ways by turning parts of it inside out, or forcing a person to eat until their body broke, or burying a person in an impossible dirt maze with air bubbles that could only be breathed if a person clawed their way to the goal in time? How could my brain invent these torture fantasies and subject me to them while I tried to rest, and make them feel so eternal and hopeless that waking felt like a hundred years later?

I woke up sobbing for the first time since I'd been a child, grateful that this time it was over, and without care for whether I was waking Melody, I got up and plucked the bracelet from my dresser. Melody saw me put it on.

She asked me about it, about whether this was the mysterious jewelry, and though I agreed it was, I didn't want to share any details when the inevitable questioning started. I was so relieved to have survived another meeting with the monsters and simultaneously so devastated that they were indeed just waiting there to pounce on me if I ever forgot to wear this little piece of string and metal. And I was exhausted. I begged her to just let me sleep.

Normal sleep returned to me that night, and I haven't failed to wear the bracelet since.

I fell in love with Melody not long after, and we officially said the L-word only a few weeks into our relationship. And I found that more and more I was able to write off her initial dismissiveness as a speed bump on the road of getting to know her. She wasn't trying to be cruel, and had no reason to know I would suffer if I didn't wear the bracelet. She'd wanted to keep me in her arms, in the bed, not prevent me from having restful sleep and peace of mind. But I couldn't share the details of my problem with her because her way of *being a scientist* about these things had thrown up red flags about danger I might face if I became her experiment.

•

No one could explain why the dreams started or how to make them stop.

I was six years old and had recently started kindergarten. Several weeks into the school year, I had a dream of floating on a raft by myself in the ocean. A monster surfaced, looked me in the eye, and said, "I'll be back for you."

"What do you want?" I asked it.

The monsters never spoke again, but they did indeed come back for me.

When the monsters did unspeakable things to me for weeks on end, my parents became very concerned. They tried letting me sleep with a radio on. With the lights on. With them in their bed. Covered in stuffed animals. Under the influence of cough syrup. After staying up as late as I wanted. Dosed with warm milk. To the soothing sounds of whale songs. Nothing made the monsters leave me alone, and my parents tried having my head scanned for brain tumors, investigating my teachers, and putting me in counseling. No one could explain the origin of these monsters or why I couldn't escape them, and my health took a nosedive because I couldn't sleep.

And then one day my father took me out into the tinkering shack he called his workshop, sat me down, and closed the door.

"I need to know what these monsters look like," he said.

I hesitated.

"Don't be scared," he continued. "They can't get you here, all right, Lucas?"

"I know, Dad. I just don't really know, they all look different."

"Tell me about some of them."

As I described some of my more recent torturers, my father's eyes got a strange knowing look. "Aha," he said after I'd given him my third account of claws and teeth. "Well, it's time to tell you something important."

"What?"

"I know who those monsters are. I think they must be trying to get to me through you. But we can stop them."

Suddenly the world felt different, sitting there in that shack with my dad, the sunlight coming through the poorly matched strips of wooden wall, the mustiness in the air, the comforting warmth that says winter isn't here yet. Dad had come into my world. He knew what to do, maybe.

"They're after me because I'm secretly a powerful wizard," my father said. "Looks like you're going to grow up to be one, too. But not if these guys suck away all your magic first. Let's get to work."

Star-struck and speechless, I watched my father the wizard go to his shop table and measure out a length of yellow string—much shorter than he typically used for yo-yos—and he cut the twine with a knife I'd never seen before. Then he rooted around in a toolbox and brought out another knife and something small and shiny.

"Time to make you a charm, boy," he said. Then he sat right down on the workshop floor and gestured for me to do the same.

My father swung his strange curved knife around in a vague circle with one hand, while holding the twine and the scrap of metal in the other. He seemed to be muttering something under his breath, but I couldn't catch whether they were words. Then he told me to hold out my arm.

"Here we go," he said, looping the string around my skinny wrist and tying a sliding knot to secure it. And then he clamped this white wisp of metal around the twine and bent it over itself, joining it to the fiber soundly. He tapped it once with his knife and released my hand.

"That's it," he said, patting my shoulder and grinning down into my face. "You're under protection."

I stared at the bracelet. "Do I have to wear this forever?" I asked, mouth dry.

"Just wear it until tomorrow morning—let it get used to you. Then you can take it off when you wake up tomorrow. Just wear it to bed and they'll never get you again."

And then my father the wizard did some simple operation to free us from the magical space he'd created, put his tools away, and gave me a wink before sending me back to the house.

The next morning I confirmed to him that I'd had a dreamless, restful sleep, and I asked him about his wizardry—what had he done, and why did the monsters want us? What should I be doing for my wizard career? What else could he do with his magic?

He blew me off with excuses about the wizard code and future lessons for when I was older.

And then I never got those lessons because he died when I was seven.

It would have been an understandable time for the monsters to come back, but they did not.

•

"I couldn't sleep," Melody says. "I kept waking up thinking about your damn bracelet."

The coffee freezes on my tongue as I look at her over the table in the bustling café. "You want to talk about this *here*?"

"Oh, I wasn't going to say anything," she murmurs. "That just came out. But honey." She grabs my hands and guides my coffee cup back to the saucer. "I can't help it. My brain is doing the thing."

"That's what I was afraid of," I say. I scratch my fingers through the front of my hair, trying to think of how to approach this with her and coming up blank.

"It's not even just that I want to know *why*," she says, and suddenly her eyes are enormous. "It's that—you don't trust me. You won't tell me something that's part of your everyday life, and I *know* it's something important. It means I don't have the whole story of you, even though I really thought I did."

"If your brain is 'doing the thing' now, trust me when I say it'll 'do the thing' ten times harder if I give you the details. Nobody wants that. So I think we should leave it."

"Well, you can't leave me with *that*, Luke."

"I just did."

"This is cruel and unusual." Her eyes finally fade back to a more familiar expression—fooling around, not so deadly serious. "I can't investigate the why unless I excavate in your brain, and you won't let me dig."

"All you need to know is that the bracelet helps me sleep. That's it."

"But if you say that's all I need to know, that means there's more in there to know, and now that I *know* that, how can I stop asking?"

"Simple," I say. "When you think about asking, don't."

"What if I ask your mother?" she teases.

"Go ahead. She doesn't know anything more than you do."

She gawps at me. "Really?"

That is kind of a lie. My mother knows my father made the bracelet for me to keep bad dreams away, but she doesn't know that I saw my father make it as part of a magic spell.

"Okay, listen." I see our breakfast on its way to our table and nod at the server as he sets down our omelets. We unroll our silverware. Melody is listening. "If it bothers you so much that there's something about me you don't know, I can give you what you want to know. But we have to do it my way."

"What's your way?"

"You let me tell you the story without interrupting, without drilling into everything I say with your analysis, and without acting like this is stupid. You need to listen as my fiancée, not as a scientist."

Her eyes are gleaming. She knows she's going to get what she wants. She nods and takes a mouthful of cheesy egg. "Okay, go."

To her credit, Melody doesn't interrupt me. I take my time with the story, choosing words for it carefully, chewing on them in between bites of my actual breakfast. It feels weird saying them out loud; this story has always been part of my life, but it's also been something I leave behind when I get out of bed, and it's strange both to speak it aloud and to speak of it in the daytime. But before we're finished with our coffee, I've told Melody all the basics: I had unexplained bad dreams when I was a kid; my father seemed to recognize them from a mysterious wizard life he'd never spoken of before or since; my father forged a talisman that keeps the monsters away; and I have to wear it when I'm sleeping or the monsters will return.

"You look relieved," I say after I've come to the end.

"I guess I'm . . . just glad that it isn't something you're hiding from me for a dealbreaker reason." She smiles weakly. "But I've got to ask you . . ."

"I thought we agreed you aren't interrogating me."

"Oh no. I didn't agree not to interrogate you. I agreed not to *interrupt* you."

"That is *not* what I said. I said I would tell you if you wouldn't analyze me or act like it was stupid."

"You said you had to be allowed to tell it your way," she counters, eyes innocent, "and you got to do that. You didn't say I couldn't ask questions after."

"I don't want to answer questions. I was serious."

"Just one thing," she pleads, crunching a napkin with the hand that carries her engagement ring. "I need to know. Do you believe in all this?"

"Believe in what?"

"Do you believe your dad did magic spells and you've been wearing a magic bracelet? Do you believe in magic?" She cracks a smile. "Because . . . Luke, we've been through this. You agreed with me every time we talked about reasoning and critical thinking. So I think I really deserve to know whether I'm marrying a guy who's participating in a magic ritual every night while he lies beside me in bed."

I rub my hair again. "I don't know if I believe in it, Melody. My dad never gave me any evidence that there was a wizard world he was part of. He was a weird guy who made yo-yos and wooden toys in a shed. But I do know the bad dreams come back like clockwork if I don't put the bracelet on at night, and okay, sure, it could have been some psychological thing my dad did that stuck with me. But having those dreams even once isn't worth testing it."

"You have nightmares that are kept at bay by a delusion and you don't think the natural next step would be to see a mental health professional?"

I sigh loudly into the remains of my breakfast. "I knew you would do this."

"Don't you want *real* help? Don't you want to know what's at the root of your nightmares so you don't have to fake yourself out with a piece of string? It's like taking aspirin for a headache every day when it might be cancer that needs to be cut out. I can't believe you've been content to let this lie this whole time."

"I feel like a broken record, but all of this is why I didn't tell you."

"This is important to me, Lucas. I want you to see some-one. Will you think about it?"

I sigh again. "Okay. I'll think about it."

•

*See a therapist*, they always say. *Get help!* Easier said than done. Despite the fact that I was actively trying to access counseling—in between the early stages of planning my wedding—finding someone who was taking new clients, was in my budget, and fulfilled Melody's standards of appropriateness based on online reviews turned out to be nearly impossible. It was two months before I finally had the opportunity to go to my first session.

And when I get there, it's definitely not what I expected to hear.

Shellie, the counselor who wants me to call her by her first name, explains that we're just trying each other out for this session and deciding whether we want to work together. She wants some clarification on why I'm here—to address bad dreams?—and to discuss why I said I didn't really think I needed counseling but agreed to come as a concession to my fiancée.

"I will say, Lucas, that people who enter therapy without really wanting to be in therapy might not make progress, or at least will make slower progress," she says. "You do have to want to change. And we can work on that."

"It was my wife's idea. Well, wife-to-be. And it's not really that I don't want to be here. I've kind of thought the world might be a better place if everyone had a therapist." Shellie's expression brightens when I say that. "But if I'm honest, I don't feel like my dream problem is a problem. Or at least, I had it solved, in a way that was working for me. But I care about my wife, and *she* thinks something deep and dark must be wrong with me, so I have to consider what she thinks."

"Does your wife tell you that your differences of opinion mean something is wrong with you often?"

I laugh. "Well, kind of. Yes."

"But you are a compromising soul who wants to keep the peace, so you do what she wants you to do?"

"Not quite. I know she's really smart, and she knows me really well, and she cares about me more than anyone. So if she says something, it's usually reasonable, and so I'm always open to thinking maybe I'm the unreasonable one."

"Right. I wonder if your wife is equally open to thinking that about herself, though."

I rub my hands on my pant legs. "Well, we sure got into it quickly."

Shellie clears her throat. "So why don't we discuss the issue you're here about—can you summarize for me what's going on with your dreams and why your wife doesn't like how you handle it?"

An hour of someone's time is really short when you're paying for it, so I condense my explanation. Shellie seems very interested when I say that I'm not particularly concerned about whether the magic bracelet is "really" magic so long as it works to keep my dreams pleasant, and that I'm willing to dig into why I have bad dreams if that will also work to get rid of them.

"But you said you tried medical intervention and counseling as a child and no one was able to figure out a cause behind the dreams, right?" she asks.

"That's right."

"And no other disordered mental events or symptoms appeared after your father's bracelet stopped the nightmares, right?"

"Right again."

"Well, I'll tell you, Lucas," says Shellie, "I can't give you specifics, but many of my clients would do anything for a solution as effective as the one you've found. Sometimes a symptom like pervasive bad dreams is part of a much larger dysfunction or trauma that will manifest in other ways, but for you, at least so far, it's been just this. The mind isn't a jigsaw puzzle where we can find 'a cause' for a certain problem and then 'find it' for sure, fix it, and solve a psychological issue. Your brain decided to give you nightmares, and it decided equally to stop them if you wear a bracelet. That seems surprisingly simple."

"I always kinda thought so. And the dreams are gruesome enough that I don't really wanna do experiments that bring them back. But I think that's what Melody wants. She wants me to find out a root cause of the dreams and 'solve' it by addressing whatever is causing it, even though I don't know what that could be."

"Right. Well, Lucas, I understand your wife's fixation on getting to the bottom of mysteries, but if the goal is stopping you from having nightmares, her approach is just as irrational."

I laugh. "Hoo, boy, how she'd hate hearing that!"

"It's true. And I'll tell you something. Therapy—it isn't about 'fixing' people, or putting labels on their disorders so we can medicate them. It's about making you able to live your life."

"Huh. Really?"

"Yes. Now, if it was really bothering you on a deep level that you never found out what caused these dreams, and you personally needed to know why, you could keep digging and trying to pin it on something for the rest of your life. But maybe there isn't an answer. Maybe it's just how your mind works and will always work, and somehow your father found the loophole. A lot of therapy is about managing—about finding loopholes exactly like this—especially when the costs of not addressing them are really high."

"Yeah. I mean obviously I've wondered why the monsters wouldn't leave me alone but I'm way more concerned with not having to go through that when I'm trying to rest."

"Exactly. One case study I learned about was this person who had paranoia that mostly manifested as specific worries about the security of their home. They would suffer from this debilitating fear that they forgot to lock their door, even though they always locked their door when they went to work. They'd be late to work all the time because of having to turn around and check again, or they'd have a meltdown and have to leave before lunch because they'd be obsessed with the idea that they'd forgotten. When their therapist suggested they could set up a video feed pointed at their door to show it in the locked position, something they could check on their phone . . . it worked. It gave the person relief."

"Whoa, really? It was that simple? Give them a way to check and then they can go back to a normal life?"

"Well, usually with people who experience those kind of intrusive thoughts, they'll have a pattern of believing they forgot something important and there aren't always ways to help with certain fears. But some of them are manageable. And while we look for other ways to reduce paranoia, these practical ways can also help. The person gets some relief. And they also get more confidence—like 'oh, well of course it's still locked, because I always remember. I'm not forgetful. I'm not that person who leaves the door unlocked. Maybe I also didn't leave the stove on or leave the water running.' That sort of thing."

"Hmm. Oh."

"The point is that mental health professionals aren't necessarily able to work miracles. It's not realistic to think we could just find the right pill or provide the right catharsis and suddenly the person's fixed. That clear-cut kind of cure is very rare. Mostly it's just about managing." Shellie smiles. "And you already are."

"I have some stuff to think about, I guess."

•

When I give Melody my thoughts on counseling, she loses it.

"No, you shouldn't just stop here. You need to at least try a few more sessions."

"I don't think I can justify the cost if the therapist basically agrees I don't need therapy."

"Well of course she says that if you're not there willingly. She told you what you wanted to hear, not what you actually needed to hear."

"Okay, so you told me to get help, and the professional opinion I got is I don't need help. What, you just want me to keep going to different therapists until one of them tells me what *you* want to hear?"

She stares at me with glassy eyes. She isn't used to me getting confrontational about anything.

"I am *worried* about you," she says finally. She walks closer and grasps the sides of my open flannel overshirt. "Something must be causing the bad dreams. It's going to find some other way to manifest in your life. It'll hurt you."

"Mel, to be honest, the only thing hurting me about it right now is that you won't leave me alone about it. Your 'treatment' is way worse than the cure."

"I'm not treating you!" She drops my lapels and turns away. "Just . . . listen, can you do a few more sessions? Actually, can we talk to her together?"

I have a sneaking suspicion that this is a bad idea. But I agree to look into it.

•

After some negotiation with Shellie, we determine that she cannot help us as a couple, though she can refer us to couples' therapy. Melody hates this idea because she doesn't think we have relationship issues. She wants to use a therapist to push her opinion on me more aggressively, and as I watch the woman I love continue her obsession with fixing what isn't broken, I realize I'm looking at her a little differently.

Then when she does something even more awful, I wonder if we need that couples' therapy after all.

I wake up from a nightmare in which monsters were slowly pulling my tongue out of my body. I'm aghast, baffled, because I hadn't forgotten the bracelet. Had it stopped working?

No. I'm not wearing it.

Melody is comforting me, seeming concerned. "I had a nightmare," I sputter. "Why did I have a nightmare? Did you—did you take my bracelet off while I was sleeping?"

Instead of acting confused or lying to me, she just says yes.

"I was hoping to prove to you that this is psychological," she says, her words halting. "Maybe you still noticed me taking it off in your sleep . . ."

"Give it back," I say through clenched teeth.

"It was a good experiment," she argues as she brings the bracelet out from under her pillow. "If you had slept through the rest of the night with no nightmares, that would have proved you're dependent on the act of putting it on, not the bracelet itself."

"But it didn't work, did it?" I say, slipping it back on my wrist.

"That's not how experiments work," she scolds. "I wanted to see what would happen, and I saw what happened. So now we know it's not the act of putting it on before you sleep that keeps the nightmares away. It's something else . . ."

"Do you know I just dreamed that a demon spent several hours extracting my tongue from my throat, millimeter by millimeter? Do you know I had to go through that because you won't leave this alone?"

"You didn't go through it, Lucas. You're talking to me with that tongue. Maybe it's something about the presence of something on your wrist? We could try with a different bracelet—"

"I can't believe you're dismissing it like this. You have no idea how exhausting these dreams are. Why is your hypothesis more important than my sanity?"

"Because *your* hypothesis is that your wizard father gave you a magic bracelet that protects you from dream monsters!" she bursts, sitting up in bed.

I sigh and get up. "I can't sleep next to you right now."

Melody buzzes with annoyance. "Oh, come on, Luke, don't."

"I'll be on the couch. Hopefully sleeping through the night."

"Fine." She relaxes, looking defeated. "Look, I'll talk to you in the morning. We'll figure out something that can— that can make both of us happy here."

"That sounds nice," I say, taking my pillow and a blanket. I flee to the couch and fall asleep in no time.

Little did I know Melody's idea of making us both happy turned out to be her stealing my bracelet again—casually swiping it between her alarm clock and her coffee—and flushing it down the toilet.

And now the nightmare monsters seemed less scary than the fact that I was living with one.

●

"Oh, Lucas? Why are you calling from a different number?"

"It's a hotel number, Mom. I'm—"

"Don't you have your cell?"

I sigh, walking back and forth in the unfamiliar room, clutching the cordless telephone. "I turned my phone off. I don't wanna turn it on in case I have messages—if I see I do, I'll be tempted to—Mom, just hang on a second so I can tell you what's going on."

"What's happening?"

"I think I might need to leave Melody."

After a short silence, my mother gently supports me through saying all these words for the first time. I tell her how unnaturally obsessed Melody got with the real story of my bracelet; how she replaced a professional's opinion with her agenda; how she experimented on me against my will; and how she destroyed my only protection *after* she already saw what sleeping without it did to me. Now I have to face that my fiancée may have ruined my life on purpose on top of the fact that I don't know if I'll ever sleep again.

"And the worst part is, she thinks she's doing this in the name of science," I say, "but destroying an essential part of an experiment isn't even good science. If she actually flushed the bracelet down the toilet, she can't do any more tests that depend on it. That's rash, that's impulsive, that's stupid, that's—that's illogical. As soon as I figured that out, I realized . . . I think she enjoys being cruel." I sit down on the bed, tired from pacing. "She resented me fighting her on this even though I just want to be able to sleep, and so she wanted to punish me. She's as bad as one of the monsters."

"This is so bizarre," my mother's voice says from far away. "Has she—have you ever known Melody to do something like this before?" I had always known about her intense drive for knowledge—and I knew it was usually helpful in her career that she would not rest until she found the answer. But I knew about the time she'd had to revise proposed research because the ethics committee told her she'd be subjecting human subjects to inhumane treatment—not only had she not thought about what the participants would feel, but she was furious that their comfort mattered more than her experiment. And in her personal life . . .

With new acquaintances or even strangers, I'd seen her cite her burning curiosity as a reason she just couldn't be expected to stop asking hurtful, personal, or prying questions just to spare someone's feelings. *Her* need for the knowledge was more important; what was she supposed to do, just *wonder forever*? If a person *minded* being asked invasive and triggering questions, it was way worse that they didn't just put their feelings aside for science, because her hunger for answers outranked everything! What about her?

I'd written this off as a quirk, but now that I'd become a casualty of her curiosity, easily destroyed as she plowed a path to satisfaction, I realized this was a defining trait of her morality, not a quirk that was usually charming. Why had I made excuses for it or overlooked what it meant about her? How had I even fallen in love with someone like this, admiring how driven she was without questioning what she was driving toward or why she drove?

"Yes, Melody's always been like this," I say to my mother. "I've just never been on the other side of it about anything important."

"I see. Honey, I'm so sorry."

"I wanted to tell you first," I say, "but I also need to ask you something really important and try to deal with it and then I can . . . talk about my marriage later. I need to figure out what to do about the bracelet."

"What about it?"

"I still have nightmares if I go without it, so I have to figure out how to get another one. So I . . . need to ask you something kind of weird about Dad."

"Okay," she says softly.

"I didn't tell you the whole story about the bracelet. The day he made it for me, he told me it was magic and he was a wizard."

My mother doesn't say anything.

"Did you know anything about him . . . thinking he was a wizard, or something?"

"Well, he was a whiz at some things, that was for sure," she manages to say, "but I never heard him claim to be a 'wizard.'"

"Okay, so he wasn't in any . . . secret societies or anything, that you know of."

"No, Lucas."

"I guess telling me the bracelet was magic was a good strategy for something that wasn't logical in the first place. At least it was good enough to satisfy my six-year-old brain."

"He has some journals that I kept," my mother volunteers. "They're full of words I can't read. I didn't know about them when he was still with us, so I couldn't ask what they meant."

I rub my hair. He never told me about any codes either,

so I doubt seeing these journals would help me. But it does suggest a pretty weird side to my father—that he at least thought he had use for arcane scripts, even if I don't believe in magic or wizards.

But maybe the very thing that had infuriated Melody can save me. It might not make sense that my father could protect me with a bracelet, but I have proof that it *did* work for the overwhelming majority of my life. So maybe before I dismiss all of this, I should try leaning into it first.

"I guess I'm going to try to make my own bracelet and see if it works tonight."

"I'll look through his stuff for you," my mother volunteers, far away on the other end of the line. "Maybe he had other bracelets."

"That would be great, if what I make doesn't work," I say, brightening. "I need to go to the craft store and get supplies."

"Good luck, dear," says Mom. "Call me later."

•

Armed with coarse yellow string from the craft store and a sheet of metallic-looking stiff card stock, I make myself a bracelet to keep the nightmares away. I know it isn't exactly the same—the string isn't the right color or texture, the bangle isn't even actual metal—but my father said I was a wizard too, so a bracelet made by me, for this purpose, should be good enough. Right? I tie it on my wrist with the familiar sealing knot and get into the hotel room's double bed.

Predictably I have trouble falling asleep. I chalk it up to feeling weird sleeping alone, in a strange bed, but I know most of it is anxiety about whether I might have nightmares. My thoughts turn to sentiment: I miss the original bracelet, even though I'm much more worried about what will happen to me without it. It hurts to think an item I treasured, an item that touched my skin every night of my life since I received it, is now in a city sewer system somewhere.

Unless Melody lied and didn't really flush the bracelet. Which actually seems way more likely now that I think about it.

But it doesn't change my feelings about what she's doing. Even if she's faking me out and this is all part of her experiment, she is a cruel person for doing it.

I wonder as I fall asleep whether she would be proud of me if she knew I'm doing my own series of experiments.

I wake up choking, fresh nightmares sliding down the sides of my brain. I can't remember what they tried to do to me this time for more than two seconds—I'm suddenly blocking out the horribleness. Terror descends. *They can still get me. My new bracelet doesn't work.*

I'm definitely going to have to call out of work tomorrow. It's the middle of the night but I decide I'm going to need to text my boss and get a sick day. Which means turning my phone back on.

As expected, my texts are full of Melody saying I'm being irrational, pleading with me to come back while mocking me for getting mad about "jewelry" and finally imploring me to use this time apart to get the help I clearly really need.

*You're not going to call off our wedding over a BRACELET, are you?* her message taunts me before I squint the tears back and force myself to scroll to my boss's name. But then I see my mother has texted me too.

*I looked through your father's things*, the message says. *The journals are just nonsense but do you want pictures? Also there was a how-to witchcraft book in with the journals. Here's the title.*

I pull up the title on my phone and find it's a book still in print. Staring at it on the screen fills me with wonder. It never occurred to me that someone besides my father might offer a peek into whatever world he inhabited. A plain old mainstream book on modern witchcraft seemed like a strange place to start this journey, but it must have been something my father trusted. Maybe this book can teach me how to do what he did . . . and maybe it can help me reconnect with the man I never really knew.

●

At the bookstore, groggy from lack of sleep, I find myself face to face with multiple four-foot sections of books on occultism, Paganism, witchcraft, and folklore. The title my mother recommended has three copies in stock—I grab one—but I'm amazed that so much information exists on this topic I never took seriously. Another book with multiple copies available jumps out at me, so I grab that one too and check out.

"Great choices," says the cashier, looking up at me with a knowing glint in her eye. I notice she's wearing a necklace with a pendant featuring a star in a circle—similar to the art on the spine of one of my new books.

"They're good?" I ask.

"If you're just getting started, these two are classics," she says. "If you need to come back for more, visit again and ask for me. I'm Cathy."

I nod and let Cathy give me a bag. I walk out feeling dazed from more than just lack of sleep. My father's claim that he'd done magic in front of me had always seemed so weird it would have had to be a dream except for the undeniable existence of the bracelet, but now modern witches are popping up in my everyday life, writing books and standing at checkout counters to wish me luck. Confidence, hope, and wonder begin to replace my despair as I head back to the hotel.

•

After an afternoon of reading, some vending machine chips, and an early evening full of corroboration of the first book's basics with the second book, I understand several things: One, that witchcraft in various forms has been performed (sometimes as a society's accepted science) since the dawn of human history; two, that it's sometimes paired with religious beliefs but doesn't necessarily have to be; and three, that special tools for the craft exist, but they aren't necessary as long as the most important tool is there: the mind.

I recognize several references to special knives and protected space from the one magical deed I witnessed. What I don't recognize is his self-proclaimed title of "wizard." The books don't seem to be using it. Practitioners are referred to as "witches" in both books, and one even specifies that gender doesn't matter—male witches are not "warlocks" on basis of gender. "Wizard" isn't mentioned. Am I barking up the wrong tree?

*Mom said he had this book, though,* I remind myself, smoothing its cover. *Well, at this point I have nothing to lose by taking its advice.*

My father called the bracelet a charm, and the impromptu ritual in which he created it fit some of the descriptions in the books. What mattered most was personal meaning—my father didn't tell me what the string or the metal represented, but what seemed most relevant was figuring out what those items *meant* and inventing that meaning for myself.

Acting on a whim, I go home to get some materials. There's a possibility that Melody will be home by now unless she went out for drinks after work or went shopping or something, but I'm not afraid of confronting her. I've been avoiding her texts but dealing with her no longer seems impossible. I park and head inside to get some meaningful charm pieces.

I start with the easiest. I carefully unbox some special items I keep under the bed and lift out one of my father's yo-yos. I kept a collection of them after he died, first as mementos and then with the intent of giving them to my own kids one day. Feeling a little sad about it, I cut a short length off one of the yo-yo strings. This is definitely the same material he used, and it represents a link to that protection and power. But I'm still a little stumped thinking about what I can use for the strip of white metal.

I end up going to the garage and opening my toolbox. It's a pretty ordinary toolbox—nothing extensive like my father had, and certainly nothing that contains ceremonial knives. I end up finding some slim metal hooks meant for hanging picture frames; they're not white and the metal isn't as flexible, but I like that I just found them in the toolbox, like Dad did. I decide to also grab some paint to paint the metal white, since the color symbolism section in one of the books did say white is a protective color, but there's no white paint out here so I head inside to get some correction fluid from my desk.

Melody has come home.

She looks at me as I come into the house from the garage. At first she doesn't say anything, and I note how she looks tired—as I'm sure I do. She's holding her keys, studying me.

"Are you . . ." She trails off and swallows, then tries again. "Are you home?"

"I just came to pick up a couple things," I say.

"You doing okay?" she says, and I stop.

"No," I answer.

"Did you stop having nightmares?"

"No," I repeat. I feel my face harden and move to walk past her.

"Luke, wait. There's something I need to tell you."

I stop again. "Okay?"

"I . . . didn't flush your bracelet."

I hear myself saying words. "I know."

"What? You know?"

I smile, a little sadly. "Of course you didn't destroy it. You're a scientist and it's a piece of the experiment." I walk past her and put my hand on the doorknob. "Just like I'm a piece of your experiment. Just a variable to you."

"Come on. I'll give it back to you if you stay and work this out."

My heart teeters on the edge of a cliff. I have an awful feeling that if I say another word, she'll threaten me—she'll say if I leave, she really will destroy it. And I do not want her to destroy my father's bracelet. But with that realization, a flood of anger and confidence comes from nowhere and fills me with the strength to turn that knob.

I will not give her the power to use the threat of torture to make me stay with her when she is the torturer. I can and will save myself.

I walk out the door.

•

I'm a little hesitant to try this after the reading I've done today. One of the books seems to take magic attempts a little more seriously than the other and implied that attempts like this not backed by full understanding can be dangerous. But both books confirm that people have used very casual folk magic for charms, superstitions, and various attempts to attract good luck since the beginning of human consciousness. Folk magicians have been blessing objects with their breath, with their rhymes, with their spices and salt, with their garden soil, for ages. My memory of my father's charm creation doesn't include any invocations or much preparation at all, though I seem to remember the ending better than the beginning. Did he create a circle of sacred space like these books mention, or had this been such a casual act that it didn't really even count as a spell? I don't know.

I'm a newbie so I decide to err on the side of caution. I sit in the circle I've cast with my book listing the instructions, and then I just look at my charm items. I mumble my intentions as I'm picking up the metal—speaking aloud helps define intent, they said—and as I'm declaring the correction fluid a symbol of protection, I'm hit with a feeling of calmness and certainty. *This is going to work*, I think, and then try to put it out of my mind so I can be in this moment. I'm doing what my father did, and suddenly it becomes more about that connection for me than it is about whether I'll sleep tonight. There's nothing inherently magical in frame hooks, office supplies, or yo-yo strings, but the idea that I'm *making* these things meaningful is suddenly so satisfying.

The quiet, sure feeling pervades my immediate space as I finish painting the metal white. And then I take up the yo-yo cord, remembering with a smile that my father touched this—in a way, the same way I'm now reaching back through time to connect to his actions. I spend a moment just holding the string as I wait for the paint to dry, letting it wash over me that I'd been letting my father protect me when I surely always had the power to protect myself. But this isn't an expression of getting rid of his influence so I can grow into my own—quite the opposite! This is a parallel path. It's mine, and I'm claiming it.

I don't have a ceremonial knife—and wasn't sure whether or where to get one when I thought about it earlier today—so I decide my pocketknife will do. The books of course recommend using a spiritually dedicated knife that isn't used to cut anything, while this is definitely a working knife, but I rationalize that it's better than a knife from a kitchen drawer. I'm applying some mixture of by-the-book advice and home-grown intuition, hoping I'm not making too many assumptions, but I can't shake how right it feels. That or I'm woozy from sleep-deprivation chemicals.

Picturing my dad's motions, I take the finished bracelet and swing the knife over it with a swish, imagining I'm channeling energy I've raised even though I don't know what that's supposed to be like. And then it's over. I've dedicated my bracelet as a protection charm, and the only thing left to do is clean up my circle and go to bed.

"Thank you," I say out loud, to I don't know who. My dad? The book authors? Any spirits or deities that might be listening?

And that night, I sleep like a baby.

●

I can do it.

I don't want to get too overconfident, so I don't tell my mom until I've had two peaceful sleeps in the hotel in a row, but it's established. I can do it.

And not only can I do this one thing: I've managed to modify the bracelet so it will still work if it's tied on the bedpost rather than my arm. All it took was a second mini-ritual and the bracelet's intention is clearly defined for the same purpose from a different place. It feels weird to know I can be protected in the ways I've cultivated and chosen, but at the same time it's invigorating.

So I call my mom and tell her.

"Well, looks like you're following in your father's footsteps in even more ways than I expected," my mom says. "It's so strange to know the man I married never shared any of this with me, though."

"I don't think he would have shared it with me either, if I hadn't turned out to need it."

"If—if you'd get some use out of them, I can mail you a box with these books and things. Would you like that?"

"No, Mom. I thought I'd come down and get them myself. Is that okay?"

"Luke, you're going to be visiting?"

"I'd like to stay with you for a little while to give Melody some time to find a place and move out of my house."

". . . Oh. So this is final, huh?"

"I guess I'll be sure pretty soon. I'm about to go see her and tell her. Wish me luck."

•

"Well I guess it's best that we don't get married if you're going to be this irrational over a bracelet."

I grimace and look away. "That's what I thought you'd say."

Melody tries to slide closer to get my attention but I won't look at her now. She takes my hand. I don't have it in me to shrug her off.

"We had a disagreement. You're ready to leave me over our first real disagreement? I still can't even process that you're not joking right now."

"Why do you even still want to marry me if I'm so irrational?"

"Because we never even had problems before this! I still love you! But now you're ending *us* for throwing your bracelet away when I didn't even actually throw it away?"

"No, I'm ending *us* because you think this is about a bracelet. How can there be an *us* if you were willing to torture me to get answers?"

"'Torture' sounds like a bit much," she protests.

"Right, and easy for you to say when you weren't living it." I sigh and look her in the eyes with sincerity for what I'm suddenly aware might be the last time. "You wanted me to explore what might be wrong and I was willing to sacrifice a lot to make that possible. But I needed to figure out if my dreams were dangerous from a place where I was safe. And you took that away from me. Without asking." I pull my hand away from her and break the eye contact. "Being together with somebody means you should be able to be vulnerable with them. But I saw what you did with it when I was. I don't like what I saw. I can't be with you."

Now she's crying—nothing too showy, nothing that makes me suspect she's trying to manipulate me—but I feel detached. As detached as she must have been from seeing me as a person when she took my bracelet away.

"What am I supposed to do now?" I hear her say. I don't get the sense she's actually addressing me, but I answer.

"I guess we go on with our lives," I say gently, standing up, "but before I leave . . . were you telling the truth about not flushing my bracelet? I want it back."

Her eyes glint strangely. "Stay one more week," she blurts, "and let me prove to you that we shouldn't break up over this.

If you still feel this way at the end of the week, I'll move out and give your bracelet back."

I turn back and stare at her. "This whole conversation, *especially* that last sentence, already proved that we definitely should break up over this. This 'experiment' is over." I go to the doorway and start putting my shoes on.

"Luke! It's not an experiment. I just don't want you to make a rash decision here. At least sleep on it." She gets that weird glint again. "Which I thought you can't do without the bracelet protecting you from monsters."

I'm suddenly so angry I can't even see straight. But I say one more thing.

"I'm handling that the best way I can, because you gave me no choice." My jaw is tight and my teeth are clenched, so it's hard to get the words out. "Now I guess you'll never know how it turned out. Hey, maybe the unknown will torment you the way you tried to torment me." I yank the door open and grab my keys. "Maybe it'll be unresolved *forever*. That'd really be too bad. You'll just have to find a solution that doesn't come at someone else's expense."

•

My boss grants me a vacation and I hang out with my mom for a couple of weeks. Melody doesn't try to call or text me during that time, and after the first couple of days of being preemptively angry over what I think she'll say, I finally have room to grieve. I know I loved her, and thought she loved me. I consider using my new charm-making skills to make a trinket to banish my sorrow, but I decide this is something I want to process and feel. I'm in a safe place where I can do that.

My mother lets me claim my father's "wizard" things, and I'm undecided as to whether I want to use his knife in the future, but what I'm very interested in are his journals. My mother's description was accurate: they're all in code. The formatting makes them look like there were a lot of lists or poems. I conclude this was probably something the intro books called a book of shadows. It's actually a thing. I wonder if I'm supposed to start one.

I still have no clues as to why my father called himself a wizard or why he seemed to recognize the monsters from my dreams, but weirdly, I find that mystery charming. It's comforting to know my father got to take his secrets with him, and that no one—not even his son—could claim knowledge he didn't intentionally leave to his descendants. It's a kind of respect that Melody wouldn't have let him have. I'm glad that he married someone like my mom, and not someone like my . . . my ex, I have to call her.

When I finally do get a text from Melody, it's all business, saying she'll be staying with a friend until the apartment she wants becomes available. I can come back and go back to work.

She wants me to know she left the bracelet on my nightstand.

And she expresses the hope that one day I'll tell her how I tamed my nightmares.

I wonder how much she'd hate to hear that I beat them with magic.

**Cirrus Wood**

# Lawn Moving

When I was eighteen I had a summer job moving lawns. My mother had made it clear that my intended way of passing the months—which is to say, in indolence, drifting from book to book—was insufficient for someone on the cusp of independence, and I would need some form of income before the fall semester, my first at university.

She had agreed to cover tuition, but I would cover supplies. And because I had chosen a school more than an hour away, I would also pay half of room and board. In exchange, she would foot occasional bus tickets home.

As it happened, she had a connection to someone with a lawn moving business. This was through one of her online groups, so a friend of a friend of a friend. They didn't know one another otherwise. Though as it turned out, Vince, the man who became my boss, graduated the same year as my uncle—my mother's brother—and my mother had gone to high school with his wife.

Vince had posted about needing someone for the season. One of his regular members, a third-year university student, had landed an internship and wouldn't be back this year. My mother sent Vince my contact information, a bit about me, and the name of the school I was to attend—a respectable, decent enough state school, but a name that didn't mean very much outside of neighboring counties. Vince called the next day.

Now, I was a very average suburban teenager. Bored, lacking in ambition. More-or-less a housecat in adolescent form. Not much in the way of money, though only because I was so accustomed to spending other peoples'. So laboring for wages was a bit of a wakeup for me.

Although I would never have gotten the job on my own, I quite enjoyed it. Even more surprising, I was good at it, in spite of a complete lack of experience. But then I had no experience in anything really. And when you come right down to it, your work history must begin somewhere.

For the first three weeks on the job Vince worked with me directly. He wanted all workers trained identically, and every lawn uniform. But for most of the summer I worked with a variety of other movers, none more than twice.

We would show up at the client's house a few days beforehand, usually after the furniture was out but before the new residents moved in. Not always though, which sometimes led to confrontations. New homeowners weren't always aware that the lawn hadn't been included in the bill of sale. When that happened, we just left. Our contract did not require us to play mediator, and it wasn't worth it to stop everything when we could be moving other lawns.

Most clients had all the legalities sorted though, and we could just get on with the work. First we gave the lawn a go over to remove any stones or debris, which could really destroy the tools, not to mention be a hazard for anyone standing nearby. Then we would give it a mowing, quite short, like golf course sod. Then a thorough soak, unless the forecast called for rain and then we wouldn't bother. The trick was to give enough water that the lawn held together—this reduced transplant shock—but not so much the whole piece flopped like over-stretched dough and was impossible to load in the truck.

After watering and mowing, we edged the lawn with bill hooks, to cut it from neighboring property. Then we took a tool a bit like a spatula, though heavy set and with fine sharpened teeth, and slid it all around the freshly cut edge. This loosened the lawn and gave it a bit of a lap that made it easier to pull up. Finally, we went at the lawn with a darooter, a tool shaped like an over-large vegetable peeler crossed with a two-man saw. You and your partner each grab an end, slip the blade just beneath the cut edge, and then the two of you rock forward and back while taking small steps to the side until the blade slices down to the far edge of the turf, cutting and lifting the lawn in one long sheet.

The darooter—or what Vince just called a 'daroo'—was I think a misspelling of 'de-root-er' because it cut the roots. Though if customers asked  since we did often get clients who liked to watch—we told them the darooter was an old Dutch tool, long used in the Netherlands to cut patches of sod off higher ground and move it into low as that country built dikes and expanded out to sea.

We—or rather, I—told customers that several times in history, while under threat, the Dutch had also done the reverse; using darooters to cut lowland fields of wheat and tulips and then, as though lifting a tablecloth, dropping them onto hillsides, barn lofts, windmills, anywhere higher than sea level. And, as a final defense, breaking the dikes and flooding their country, frustrating would-be invaders. From high above the waters, those industrious Dutch grew crops and grazed sheep, as church bells rang beneath meadows of blooming daffodils. Much later, during the Second World War, they revived the technique as camouflage from Allied and Nazi air raids. Whole towns and even small cities disappearing under grassy cloaks of flowers.

"Fascinating," clients would say, and we would nod.

All made up, of course. Not a bit of it true. Vince had bought the tool from a nursery with a Dutch name, so guessed that it was probably Dutch in origin, and the rest I just ran with. So long as we did the work and did it well, Vince cared little about the stories we told. The result was all that mattered. Clean, straight lines of green. Precision, and predictability.

Most lawns though were too large to get in a single swipe of the daroo and had to be cut into swatches. Three was the general limit, on account of the length of the blade and the size of the truck bed. But there were a few larger jobs that we sometimes needed to do in chapters of four or even five. Once cut, we'd roll the lawn like carpet, move it to the truck, and drive to the new site, leaving behind a flayed square of bare earth. The next owner's responsibility to fill.

If, at the new site, the old lawn was still there, we'd cut it out, though not so delicately as we did the first lawn. Then we'd give the bare earth a good watering. Dirty work, but quite important so the sod could make contact with water as soon as it was off the truck. Finally, we would unroll the lawn, trim it to fit, and then barefoot and on hands and knees, stitch it in place with sisal twine.

Now, it sometimes happened that a lawn was too small for the footprint of the new property. Those times we would just fill in the blank space with scrap from other projects or else with the old lawn, so long as the sod was of the same quality and comparable design. But when it was the other way, and the lawn was much larger than the footprint, we cut the excess and brought it back to the warehouse, then sorted the scrap by size and type. The pile—what we called 'stash' or 'odd sod'—was like a pot of bottomless soup stock, continuously drained even as it refilled.

I got quite strong from the work. Not buff exactly, but capable, a body shaped by labor. My forearms had never looked so defined—before or since. Lawn moving, you see, is a hard yet delicate business. Not just because of all the lifting, but really the control. Especially because we did it all by hand. We even tried to limit the number of steps we took, choreographing our motions to leave the least possible number of footprints upon the sod.

Clients appreciated that level of care, most of whom were quite wealthy, as I'm sure you will be unsurprised to hear. And I don't remember moving a single off-the-rack lawn. It was all designer. Takaki, Malovski, that sort of thing. Quite chic stuff. So customers wanted a level of service that matched the quality of lawn. Handwork only. No mechanized tools. Of course, that made our service quite expensive, but the price too was part of the allure.

It did look good to do all the work by hand. I don't just mean the final result, which was quite sharp—there really is nothing like a freshly tailored lawn—but seeing a pair of bespoke lawn movers at work, with their tools and blades, the bareness of their feet on an early summer morning, the synchrony of their careful step upon the grass. I speak of the sight of craftsmanship in action. (Of course now that I am no longer in the business I can say honestly that, whether you move a lawn by hand or with a rental machine, it really doesn't make a difference. The technology has vastly improved in the time since I was a mover, and—unless you are handling vintage lawn—really, most turf does just fine either way.)

Looking back on it now, it wasn't a particularly eventful summer. No wild experimentation, never anything harder than aspirin. September came and I was still a virgin. It was personally significant only because it was the summer of the first job I ever had, the beginning of a curriculum vitae.

I made enough through wages, and tips especially, to cover expenses for the upcoming year. I didn't get work study—which was more a disappointment to my mother than myself—but as a concession for this shortfall, I agreed to pay my own bus fare home on breaks.

Through both fall and spring semester, I found myself daydreaming of being out there, cutting turf, fitting it in place. When I thought of those months, they came to me as an extended meditation. The work required focus, but I wouldn't exactly say that it required thought. It was, to me, a season of simplicity, and of defined and measurable purpose.

So when I didn't get an internship I had applied for, nor a second backup internship, my disappointment was only slight, and it was with some relief I went back to work as a lawn mover the following summer.

Vince took me out on the first job to make sure I remembered how to do the work and scrape off the winter's rust. Once he was satisfied that I hadn't lost the touch—and my body recovered from the million little aches of flexing joints long left in storage—he had me work thereafter with Joon.

Joon had already worked for Vince for several seasons. He had been there the previous summer as well, but I still had yet to meet him. There was a just large enough crew of us that even with rotation, we still didn't all know each other. Like morning and evening shifts at a restaurant, I imagine, though I've never worked at one myself.

Joon was slightly older than me, so probably around twenty-two or twenty-three at the time. Certainly old enough to buy beer, as he usually kept a few in the truck for when we were finished for the day. He dressed the same as any lawn mover—jeans, work boots, grass-stained tee shirt—but he wore his hair long, which was different from most of us with our crew cuts and short-back-and-sides, and he kept it tied back in a ponytail. That and a slight mustache gave him a sort of Dread Pirate Roberts appeal to women of a certain age, and also to some men.

Now, in case you are getting ideas by this description, the answer is, no, I don't believe he ever slept with any of the customers. Though you could tell the ones who wanted to with him. Leaning a little too far over, answering the door in a robe, toying with a button on their shirt. Pretty cliché stuff. They'd probably already traumatized the paper boy and were moving on to the landscapers. Mail carriers would be next, I supposed. Joon didn't seem to mind. Relished it even, and sure to stay just outside the circle as he might that of a chained and pacing dog.

Working with Joon was like dancing with a really excellent partner. One who let you believe you had each been the leader, yet also the follower, and there soon developed a real and genuine affection of professional respect between us. We liked the work, and liked other people who liked the work, and so we liked each other.

It was the third or fourth time that we were on a job together that a client came out to watch. It was a quite hot day, very humid, and the client held a drink in his hand while watching us swing the daroo back and forth and peel down his lawn. Not quite the heaviest part of the work—that was the loading at the end—but certainly the most arduous for the level of mental and physical focus it required to sustain. He commented on the humidity, how it must be hard working in this heat, yet never offered anything in the way of relief. This was not uncommon. Some customers, I think, just could not pass up the chance to oversee another's toil.

Most clients were curious and appreciative of our work, so it's not particularly that I minded being watched. It was just this one watched us like a warden, with a clear expectation of disappointment and disgust. I hoped he might get the hint in our silence that we neither needed nor wanted him there, but we couldn't very well ask him to get off his own lawn. So I started talking to fill the silence, though really more to distract myself and get back to the task at hand.

I described the process of lawn moving—edging, peeling, installation—most of which he would have already known from the brochure. But when I got to the daroo I laid it on real thick. I told the story again, the origins, about the Dutch furling and unfurling their country. Then added details about families picnicking on suspended meadows, and nobility hunting game—horns, hounds, horses—in pursuit across the rooftops. And then, of course, the Nazis.

Most clients especially liked this last part. The plucky Dutch hiding entire towns from the Luftwaffe, beating the Third Reich back with flowers. (I left Allied bombings out of this telling. Kept it simple. Uncomplicated villainy, blameless heroes.) The clients liked it, I think, not only because it made despots look silly, but because it tied their own dreary existence to something greater. Something noble. They identified with the triumph of a clever underdog and came away feeling virtuous, as though there was something heroic about the continued business of moving lawns.

"Fascinating," the man said. Something most clients said. Something most people say when they don't know what else to say.

And so this was why, I continued, in many towns in the Netherlands today there are weathervanes on nearly every rooftop displaying pastoral scenes—shepherds and hunters, farmers and monarchs—wheeling and whirling, as remembrance of when much of the country lay under water and the rest of it hidden under turf. (I should be clear, however, that just because there was now more story did not make any of it now more true.)

Joon and I finished, got the lawn in the back of the truck and pounded a bottle of water each. (That client never did offer us anything.) As we were leaving, Joon asked just how much of that story really happened. I answered it was true there is a place called the Netherlands, and that the people who live there call themselves Dutch. Also tulips are real, and so, I believe, were Nazis. All the rest was filler.

I had never been to the Netherlands. (And still have not.) At that point in my life I had only twice left the state. So I may as well have been describing a storybook kingdom. But it wouldn't have worked if I had done it that way. 'Once upon a time in a land far far away...' You needed a bit of truth as a jumping off point. Even just the smallest bit.

After we finished that particular job—trucking the lawn to the new house, installing it, stitching it in place—Joon asked me to join him on something separate.

I've said already how lawn moving generates quite a lot of scrap, and how we sorted this into odd sod. That summer we seemed to be accumulating much more than we were using on patch jobs. Joon was concerned that if we didn't do something with it soon the whole pile might go bad. So he had an idea. When we got back to the warehouse, we loaded the entire stash into the truck. We should have asked Vince about it first, since we were using his scrap and his vehicle, but we decided to instead ask forgiveness, if it came to that, and drove into the city.

I am embarrassed to say that despite growing up just outside of one of the more exciting and picturesque of metropoles, I hardly ever went into it. At that point in my life I'd only ever gone in before on grade school field trips, and my experience was confined to museums, matinees, and anywhere else regarded by chaperones as sufficiently scrubbed and safe.

So when we arrived at our destination I thought we must be somewhere on the outskirts, but in looking at a map we were well within city limits. No more on the outskirts of the city than say, the liver is on the outskirts of the body simply because it isn't the heart. This, rather, was a separate heart, a smaller, more fitful one, an enclave that pulsed with life within the greater whole.

Joon drove us to a market, and parked the truck between two similar vehicles, with the engine facing the street while the bay faced back into a lot. In the middle of the lot were tables where people sold second and third hand goods of, it seemed, every decade previous. Blenders, record players, juicers, electric carving knives—the kinds of things you really only needed one of, if you needed one at all—while to either side of us, drivers hawked clothing out the backs of open trucks. Flashy, bold textured garments. Luxury knock offs, really. The labels read 'Guicci'.

I didn't understand what we were doing there. I mean, yes, I got that Joon intended to sell off the odd sod but I could not figure who does their lawn shopping at a neighborhood flea market.

"Take a look around," Joon said and gestured at the jumble of brick and concrete slumped together, barely a foot of space between the buildings. "Not a living bit of green in sight, farm boy, and us come in off the prairie with the motherlode."

"But who would even buy odd sod when there's nowhere to fit a lawn?"

"Flip the thinking," he said. "The obstacle is the advantage. Who would buy odd sod *because* they can't fit a lawn?"

We dragged a table out the back and unloaded the stash. We had good stock to work with. Top shelf, luxury lawn. Takaki, Malovski. *That* kind of quality. Really first-rate material, as well as some respectable, if not quite so cutting, second tier product. Tattinger, mostly, which, for my money, is honestly the better buy. Takaki is a nuanced lawn, and nothing says lavish like Malovksi, but you could get nervous just walking on those, even barefoot, as though you might break it on accident. I never had that worry with Tattinger. You could spill something on a Tattinger, and it would usually wash out. You didn't have to hold your breath while handling it.

Just what exactly Joon had planned made still less sense to me, considering that while our neighbors advertised clothing from 'Parda' and 'Louise Vittoun', what we had was genuine. When you hold a piece of Takaki, feel the spring of the turf, examine the blade and root count per square and cubic inch, observe all the different shades of green—more than you thought the world could hold—there is no possible way to mistake it for anything but the very best.

"It's not that it is the best that matters," said Joon. "What matters is making people believe that it's the best. Make people believe that there is something special about it."

"But there is something special about it," I said.

"That's the ticket."

We didn't make that much on our first visit to the market. Enough to fill up the gas tank on the truck, with around fifty dollars left over for each of us. Word would first have to spread. The grapevine needed time to buzz. Which it did, and much faster than I would have imagined. No one else in lawncare had even thought of selling to apartment dwellers. The market was untapped, cramped, hungry for turf of its own. We had a line on our second visit. And after the third we were regularly selling out.

Most people would never be able to afford an entire designer lawn. So our overstock was a very affordable option for those who wanted the cachet of a recognized name. Even if only accessory, it still conveyed the glamour of brand.

Still there was a trick in presentation. You couldn't just jumble everything together as though they'd tumbled from a sack and then let the customers pick through. Each swatch needed to look irresistible. They needed stands and pedestals to distinguish themselves as deserved.

In this regard, Joon displayed the same craftsmanship he had when moving lawn, though dilated down to the miniscule. He wove net and bamboo cradles, each custom made to pair with a specific swatch of turf, and in shapes besides the usual rectangles. He made ellipses, hexagons, and curves. When he finished a stand, Joon positioned the sod on top, trimmed off any excess with bonsai scissors, then misted the resting turf. Sometimes he would position contrasting swatches together, something Vince would never have even considered.

Joon's handiwork still created scrap. Albeit, scrap of scrap. Ever smaller bits of odd sod. It was then he came up with his next innovation, which was to stitch these bits together. Remixing lawn. Tattinger and Takaki, Takaki and Malovski, and all of it with the occasional bit of homespun turf from smaller, independent designers. Where others saw refuse, he saw unrealized perfection.

The created patchworks were stunning, but also too new. There was nothing else like them, which made them simultaneously both deeply appealing and also somewhat alienating. I found them breathtaking. And while not exactly fraudulent, neither were they wholly honest. We needed a veneer of respectability, a name to cloak our daring. Like the fiction of the daroo, we needed a founder. So we invented Lindorff.

'Lindorff', we decided, because we liked how it sounded with both 'lawn' and 'turf'. He would have to be German, because of the name, and also fairly recent as we wanted to exploit some prejudices—the favorable ones—and then avoid all the others. Make him too old and you raise suspicions of goose steps and swastikas. So middle-aged at the time the Wall came down, we decided.

We also made him a banker. Bored, boring, and living in Frankfurt, but who had survived the bombing of Dresden as a child. I had suggested that because of how much artwork was destroyed in the raid. It seemed poetic. An artist from the ashes.

Though this did create the problem of geography, since Dresden had been in East Germany while Frankfurt is in the west. So Lindorff must have defected as a teenager and, practical Teuton, become a banker. Lawn design was a hobby, a creative outlet done in secret. Whenever on vacation, Ernst Lindorff (he needed a first name as well) would bring home plugs he had obtained from yards and parks he admired. At home he combined them in collage wherever he, an urbanite, could find a bit of open earth. His works were all personal, his genius undiscovered until his death, when the living mosaics he had created for backyards, gardens, and windowboxes came to light, a top rate example of which can be yours for the bargain price of...

Well, you see how we did it.

The story was good, or at least good enough, containing innocence, experience, transformation, destruction, and creation. At its center a lone artist, toiling in solitude, unappreciated in his own lifetime. Like Van Gogh. But unlike Van Gogh, a Lindorff was still new enough to seem charming rather than elitist or bourgeois (which was worse), though with the promise of appreciation. A Lindorff was an investment.

People ate it up. But we had to be careful, protective of the brand. So we manufactured occasional shortages. Declined customers. Said we were out when we weren't, started getting very particular of how much we would sell—which is to say, just how many of those harlequins Joon would stitch together—and got very choosy about which kinds of customers we sold to.

I had some sense of our success when, trying to placate a customer, I said while we didn't have Lindorff we did still have some very nice Takaki, and the customer shot back, "I don't *want* Takaki, I *came* here for *Lindorff*." I should have felt indignant as they walked off empty handed. Instead I felt ridiculously, irrepressibly giddy.

Joon took a slightly different tack. Less manufactured shortage, more strategic denial. A tall woman, all in pink, was housebreaking a terrier and asked for some practice lawn to start. Joon shooed her off with a scolding, that "Lindorff is too damn good for dogs to piss on."

Later, on the drive home we entertained one another with our best impression of the scowl she gave as she walked off. A flamingo whose pride has been violated. A very angry bottle of Pepto-Bismol.

I am embarrassed now when I think of how crude we were. How gleefully we contrived to convince people to desire something they both could and could not have. How merciless our mockery for their credulity and shallow taste.

The confirmation of our masterwork came nearly at the end of summer. There were only two weeks left before classes, so this would be one of my final moving jobs. Divorce settlement, we learned. He got the house, she got the lawn. We came a few days beforehand for the usual preparations.

I was quite surprised at the job. The house was a knockout, a three-story, clinker brick, neo-colonial. Two fireplaces, one at each end, the doorway flanked by persimmon trees, fruits showing slyly through shadowed leaves. The lawn, however, was a catalog order. A TufTurf. What we called a 'tuffy.' Pennies on the square foot. It's cheaper by far to buy a new tuffy than to bother moving an old one. That's rather the point of them. We'd burn more in gas moving it than the thing was even worth.

The contrast of that elegant house against such tacky, disposable lawn struck me as bizarre. Not to mention, just what woman would agree that a TufTurf was of equal and acceptable value to a home like that?

One too glad to be out of the marriage, I supposed. Or maybe it held sentimental value? Anyway, none of my business to ask, only my business to move.

We treated it well, of course. Just because it wasn't Malovski doesn't mean we treated it like trash. So after mowing and watering, then edging and cutting, we rolled and loaded it, then drove it all to the new address.

The wife was waiting for us. Or rather, the ex-wife, I should say. She apologized. Said she would have met us at the old site, but well, too many bad memories. It was fine, we said. No problem at all. Having been over-scrutinized for most of the summer, Joon and I had enjoyed the respite of a job left to ourselves.

Her new house was a small, beach-type bungalow. Modest but perfect for someone just starting their life, or starting a new one. But there wasn't much of a footprint to put the lawn. I've sat at larger restaurant tables. So it puzzled me why she had paid for a lawn moving service to begin with. Punishment, maybe? Getting in one final jab before the door could shut for good?

She brought out some cans of sparkling water and we drank it as we talked over the particulars. Joon pointed out that there was no way to fit even a third of the lawn in the footprint. And given there was also no sort of irrigation system, he advised that she might do better to consider some other kind of landscaping, like a rock garden or drought resistant shrubs.

But no, she wanted the lawn. We could trim whatever wouldn't fit, as long as what would fit went in.

"It's Lindorff, you see," she said.

Joon and I locked eyes. Of course, we knew that the lawn wasn't Lindorff. That it couldn't be Lindorff because there never was a Lindorff, and that we had invented both Lindorff and Lindorff lawn. But clearly someone believed there had been such a person and there was such a lawn. Or, if nothing else, that the name had power. That Lindorff meant something.

Did she know? Was she in on the game? Or did she have the kind of faith that fills the gaps? Just how much of the emperor's new clothes could she see? I had no idea how to respond, still less how to ask for provenance. (Just how had her "Lindorff" been acquired??) It felt cheap to pretend her tuffy was priceless, but we could see no way to come clean without cheapening ourselves. I chose silence. I decided to defend the brand.

"Oh," said Joon. That 'oh' filled a century as I waited for what he would say next. "We hadn't realized."

"Something the matter?"

"No, no," said Joon. "This is just a first for us. We never installed a Lindorff before. At least, not one of this size." That at least was a partial truth. The largest of Joon's creations would only have covered a card table.

"Yes, well," she said and gave a gentle smile, or was it a knowing smirk? "Please be gentle, boys."

"Don't worry. We will," Joon said and gave one of those winning smiles of his. A fifty-dollar tip smile. A smile that said, 'now now, not yet. Let's just get the lawn in first and then we can fuck.' The goddamn Adonis.

In the end we took only around half the dollar amount that we had originally agreed to. Joon insisted on renegotiating the terms, seeing as we couldn't install the whole piece. And yet, neither of us felt cheated. We installed that lawn like laying carpet at Buckingham Palace. Did it all choreographed and barefoot, more delicately than most jobs. We even gave it an oiling and a massage, which is something we almost never did. Only the vintage lawns got that kind of treatment.

When we finished we sat on the curb, wiping the lawn oil off our hands and feet. It's good smelling stuff, highly moisturizing, but it doesn't come out too easy when it's thick on the skin and we were looking to leave. Joon doused an old tee shirt in solvent, then soaked another and handed it to me so we could slip our shoes back on and head out.

She came out of the house then and started walking around the grass barefoot. It's best to let a new oiled lawn set for at least five hours before walking on it to give the oil a chance to soak in. It won't damage the lawn to walk on it early, and it doesn't harm the skin—your skin comes out baby soft and smelling like fresh cut grass—but you want to be careful if you're going straight indoors after since it can seriously stain carpet and hardwood.

I thought to tell her as much, but she just looked so peaceful as she walked, cuffs rolled up, barefoot on the lawn, her lawn, a look upon her that was almost beatific in its grace, her movements like the steps of a dance upon the grass.

I don't mean to sound voyeur, but I think she liked being watched, turning the heads of landscapers more than a decade each her junior. I think she wanted us to see her, specifically to see her in possession. There was a smile on her still as she stepped off the lawn and onto the concrete walk, though Joon stopped her before she could take a second step, almost shooing her back onto the grass. He pointed down at the oiled shadow of a footprint pressed upon the concrete.

"Easy," he said. "Easy." Like she were a calf about to spook.

He guided her towards the stoop, squatted on his heels and cradled her feet one at a time on his knees. He took a squeeze bottle of solvent and dribbled liquid on her soles. The solvent made your skin feel cool for the quickness of evaporating alcohol, and she gave a bit of a start at the shock.

Then Joon took the tee shirt he'd used on his own skin and dragged it from ankle up the instep to her toes, rubbing each one in turn. He set the one clean foot on the concrete, then did the same for the other. She looked directly at him as he worked, a look on her like a famished caterpillar after a long climb on a bare branch, and Joon the final leaf. He gave a last, slow, swipe at her foot, being real thorough about it—overmore than I felt he needed to, frankly—then guided it down. His hands stayed by her ankles, and his thumbs stroked at her heels. I wondered if he might kiss them, and if I could bear to see the press of them against his lips. Then they both got up and went inside together, and their two pairs of shoes stayed sitting by the door.

Here we go, I thought. I wasn't going to stand around listening. I went to the passenger side of the truck and got in. There were two beers in the glove compartment. Warm, but what the hell. I popped the top of one, the snap hiss sound of aluminum breaking along the seams and of $CO_2$ come spitting out. I took a long pull when Joon opened the driver side and swung himself in behind the wheel, dropping two hundred dollars down in the space between us on the seat. You could have lit a match off his grin.

I was confused and indignant. He hadn't slept with her. He had done—what exactly? A pedicure? Highly unusual, certainly not within contract, but I don't think it crossed a company line. But because it seemed clear that she would have slept with him, I kept thinking that he had, even though he hadn't been gone so much as a minute. What I'm getting at is that it took a while for me to come down off my high horse, to stop thinking about what he'd done and to realize what *we'd* done. Just what we had gotten away with.

We stopped at a corner store to celebrate, got some more beers and a flat and flask-like bottle of bourbon. There was a taco truck across from the store, so we split the two hundred dollars and Joon got the booze while I bought the food. Lawn moving can work up a hell of an appetite, so I bought us three tacos each of prawn, chicken, carnitas, and lengua. The place used shredded red cabbage and boxed the tacos with lime wedges and cilantro. I'd asked for mild and hot salsa on the side, so we could mix to taste, since I wasn't sure which Joon preferred. Then we drove the truck up into the hills and parked between a pair of tennis courts. It was getting dark, and the city was there below us, lights winking on with the first of the stars. There was still about three quarters of the lawn in the back. We unrolled a section and spread ourselves out on it. The tortillas were still warm from the grill.

Joon started with the lengua, squeezed a lime wedge over it, then picked up one of the cups of hot salsa, dumped it in with the mild, and stirred it with the edge of his taco. Sauce dripped out the end as he bit into it, glops of blue-black pico de gallo spilling out in the dark of the newborn night and splashing onto grass.

"That's a Lindorff you're dribbling on," I said.

Joon snorted, choking back the bite midswallow, which sent hot sauce up his nose.

"Ahfuck!"

He waved at his face, then pinched his nose and snorted it down. He chugged a beer to cut the spice while I fell over laughing.

When we'd both gotten over it, I asked Joon just how much he thought she knew.

"Either she was real with us and believed she had some fancy item," he said. "Or she knew that it wasn't but wanted to look like the kind of person who would have one that was."

"Which do you think?"

"I think she believed it," he said. "I think she thought she was coming away with something good." He took another pull of beer, then pulled together the rest of the lengua and bit it, chewing it around from side to side.

"Of course one doesn't cancel out the other," he said. "It might also be important to her that other people see her as a certain kind of person. She wouldn't have told us the lawn was Lindorff if the name didn't mean something. And whatever that something is she wants that same something also applied to herself." He finished the lengua and went on to the prawn.

"Even when it's all made up?" I asked.

"It is all made up," Joon said. "All of it. It's just make-believe. Takaki. Malovksi. Tattinger." Joon swept his hands, one side to the other. "Make. Believe."

I couldn't follow what he was saying. No one who handled Malovski could.

"Bullshit," I said.

"*Exactly.*"

He finished the taco, then licked at his fingers and pulled his wallet from his pocket. He took out two items, one from each side. In one hand he held a square of paper. In the other, he held a razor blade, the hard glint of it a slash at the dark. The coolness of it unsettled me. Its clean lines, the slim menace of something that could slide along my contours and unseam me. He moved the blade between the knuckles of his right hand and gripped it so the edge pointed out, towards me, and then took the paper in a pinch between finger and thumb of the same hand. He smiled, and the flash of his squarish teeth completed the image, an expression midglow between paper and blade.

He lay the bottle of bourbon on the flat of the lawn, and scraped at the label with the razor, working it up from the edge, peeling it off in a slow shuck. Then he put down the paper and rolled a blunt on the back of the bottle. He had brought a dime bag with him, and ground out some of the bud into the paper, then brought it to his mouth and swiped it against his tongue to lick it shut. Somehow I'd lost track of the razor. It had vanished somewhere within the arc of motion.

Joon lit up the blunt, took a drag, and passed it to me. I did the same. Then he told me to close my eyes before he pulled the stopper out of the bourbon and held the cork beneath my nose.

"What do you smell?"

I smelled oak barrel, vanilla, caramel, smoke, the slight sting of alcohol at the back of my sinuses. Also cedar and tea tree—lawn oil, I guessed, in the cracks of Joon's fingers— and lime and cilantro and corn tortilla just burned at the edge and lengua and seared prawn and grass and grass and cut grass and grass stains and sweat gone dry in the cool of the night and Joon. I smelled Joon.

"Is it high end?" he said, and I felt the heat of his breath in my ear. "Or low end? Or is it only the experience that pegs it high or low? Makes you believe it's one and not the other?"

"Which?" I said. "Which?" My eyes opened. Joon was above me, twirling the stopper in his fingers.

"Shhh," he said. "I'm not telling. You get to choose." He pressed the cork against my lips and dragged it just along then below the edge of my mouth.

We didn't go back but stayed out on the grass. The night rolled on over us, and the fog came in with it. We did not rise from the spot even well into the grey of an oncoming day.

I had the bladder dream, the one where you can't find a toilet. Then in the final few minutes of the dream, you let it all out, then wake up feeling somewhat relieved, but also panicked, in case it hadn't been imagined. Last thing I wanted was to soil myself while still next to Joon, his chin at my neck, lips against my ear, the breath coming out of him at the softened pace of sleep. I reached my waistline and undid the button on my fly, easing the pressure so I wouldn't have to rise from his arms just yet.

All around us were beer cans, paper trays from the taqueria, the butts of cannabis blunts, a half empty bottle of bourbon, and Joon and I in the middle of it all as though in the center of an impact crater. Players were already out on the courts. Trainers scuffing clay, rackets swatting balls with sound like a suction come undone. I twitched awake with the slap-grunt of game, sore in each joint, stiff from sleeping rough. My mouth tasted of turf and old tacos and of every part of Joon.

From somewhere close by came the hiss of liquid hitting grass. I stirred some, craning for a look. A dog was walking around the sod. Bitty thing, some vanity breed about the size of a toaster, sniffing at the wreckage of the night before.

Behind, and at the street edge of the grass, was a pinkish marshmallow thing, the source of spatter. My eyes had yet to focus, so I couldn't quite tell what it was. Then the marshmallow stood up, took the shape first of a bell, then of a woman, who shook out her skirt and I recognized the flamingo from the flea market. She stepped to one side, smirking at the two of us and shaking her head, letting what she'd just done sink in to the slowness of the morning. Steam rose off the spot where she'd just been.

I grabbed a beer can and threw it. It was empty, and I missed her by a wide margin, but just the act was enough to knock the grin out of her. It clattered off into the road behind her, bouncing with the sound of aluminum that's had all the hope crushed out.

"Get off our lawn!" I yelled, stumbling up to my knees, grabbing at my pants. I picked up another can and thew it, missing her again, but by less this time. I reached for another.

Joon stirred awake, took a look at me, at her, then lay right back down.

I lobbed the can, knocking the dog on the nose, better than I ever could have aimed it. (Which, in truth, I hadn't.) The blow sent the creature yelping down the hill, and the woman trailing after, calling us all manner of assholes and sons of bitches as she went.

"Guess the housebreaking's going well," Joon said, still flat on his back. "I just hadn't realized it was for herself." He groped the turf till his fingers found a blunt that still had some bud in it and stuck it in his mouth. Then he pulled out a lighter and struck the end into flame. He took a deep breath and let out the smoke like a sigh.

I stumbled back towards him, off balance, having never fully gotten myself to my feet, and something bit me hard in the flesh of my left hand, just below where finger meets thumb. Even though it was my hand that was hurt, the cut seemed to slice all the way to my tongue. My mouth swarmed with electrons. I tasted steel, having come down hard on the cutting edge of Joon's razor as I had tried to catch myself. I snatched up napkins, smudgy with hot sauce and grease, and gripped them in a fist of wadded blood. I bellowed out a great loud curse, bold, underlined, and all in caps.

You could feel, even if you couldn't hear, the sound of tennis games in suspension and of cell phones coming out. Joon came to. His eyes moved from me, to my hand, then to the bloody razor in the grass. He picked the razor up, turned it blade side down, and with his thumb pushed it straight into the turf.

"We ought to be going," he said. He still had a joint tucked in the corner of his mouth. "The Money doesn't like it when the riffraff comes out of the flats and into the hills," he said.

"You know why? You know why?" he goaded.

I said nothing.

"Because they don't keep off the grass."

He bounced the words, slinking down into the final consonant like a snake, grinning at his own joke, falling back, and laughing at himself till he choked. I waited. When he finished he passed me another grease stained napkin and watched as I repacked the wound myself.

We shook off our idleness and climbed into the truck. Didn't pick anything up. Not the cans, the bottles, the wrappers, or the lawn. Just left it all lying there like a car we'd stolen and driven till the gas ran out. Joon turned the engine

and threw it in reverse, the beep of backwards motion puls-
ing over tennis courts as he backed the truck over all that
mess, then out into the street and down the hill.

Vince fired us pretty much as soon as we got back. He'd
been wondering for some time where the scrap was going,
and why the fuel gauge on the truck always read full yet there
were never any gas station receipts left on his desk. Not to
mention whatever bacchanal we'd gotten up to with the
company vehicle.

He was about as embarrassed to do it as we were to get
it. It didn't matter that we filled the truck back up after each
trip to the market, the market where we sold stolen lawn,
lawn we'd stolen from Vince. There was no coming back
from it for either of us. Should've asked permission after all.

Joon gave me a ride home in his pickup. I spent that ride
in silence, watching suburbia slide past, cubes of houses,
trapezoidal roofs, tidy squares of lawn, again and again, the
scenery set on loop, until we got to the cube on the square
where I lived. The geometry of my own rectilinear, predict-
able, and well-margined life. Joon hadn't even stopped all
the way before I opened the passenger side and bolted from
the door.

"Hey," he called. "Be seeing you."

"Yeah," I said. "See you around."

My mother was inside, playing a round of solitaire on the
computer. I walked right past and into the shower. There
were still stains all over my skin and clothes and grass in
my hair. It filled up the shower drain like a bird's nest as I
washed. A neat cup of grass leaves dimpled in the middle.

I wrapped the cut on my hand in a bandage, toweled off and went to my old bedroom to dress, then started up some laundry. The cut wasn't so bad as it had first appeared—not even so wide as the finger above it. It had seemed larger in the moment, having bled out of proportion to its size. I wondered if it would scar at all. And if it did, would I even remember the how of it, or only that it had been something that happened once, among a thousand other onces.

My mother asked where I'd been. I told her that a job ran late the day before and I'd spent the night out with a colleague. I also told her that I'd gotten the rest of the day off, and that there might not be any more work for the rest of the season, of which there were only two weeks left anyway. I said Vince would call if he needed me.

She didn't press for the truth. There was enough of it there to placate if not satisfy entirely, and she didn't squeeze me for the rest. I was home and alive, and I was paying for most things myself—I'd already written the check for the fall semester—and would be gone again soon. My intention for those remaining weeks was to regress into the summer of two years before. Just me and the books—reading in bed, on the couch, on the lawn  and wondering when or if Joon would ever call.

Two days later he texted.

I picked up at the first vibration, watching the wave pulse of ellipses as he thumbed his lines, and waiting for the tremor as the words came through.

*got a job*

then

*interested?*

Joon picked me up the next day, the back of his pickup loaded with sod.

"Hey."

"Hey."

We drove off.

I recognized the site immediately. The persimmon trees, the handsome clinker brick, the flayed and drying earth where the TufTurf lawn had been.

"Jesus," I said.

"Yeah," said Joon.

The man was already standing in the driveway as we pulled up. Overfed, under-exercised, a boiled potato in dockers. The watching type, I pegged him for. We parked and got out.

The guy explained his situation, as though we didn't already know it. Then it occurred to me that he actually might think we didn't. He wasn't the one who hired us to take the old lawn out, after all. And he hadn't been here when we did. So he probably thought we were seeing the place for the first time.

"You should've seen the old one," he said. "The one she took. It was a beautiful thing. Lindorff, you know. Cost me about as much as the house. Top of the line turf. Just, the best. But she wanted to give me a kick in the balls on the way out. A real hard kick to the balls, and she took it with her. I had the Lindorff insured, you know, so I could get a new one. A brand new one, top shelf, market price, and she's just got to settle for the old one. So I'm like, let her have it. I'm coming out ahead!"

We nodded. It was clear he knew nothing about how to treat lawns, women, or the institution of marriage. I understood then that he knew that his old sod was trash, but wanted her to believe it was something special. Wanted us to think that too, and by extension, wanted us to see him the way he saw himself. Except we didn't. We already knew what was there before, and thought just as much of him as we did his old lawn: which is to say, if men came out of vending machines, for a quarter you could buy a better one than him. You'd burn up more in gas just driving away than the man was ever worth.

We stood at the back of the pickup. We hadn't unloaded anything yet, and Joon walked him through the process. We'd measure, moisten, then plot out the segments on a to-scale graph, then lay out and stitch in the swatches. ("Good. Real good.") It was starting to get humid, not as bad as when we'd taken the old lawn out, but bad enough to chase him out of our faces and into the AC. He watched us from the window as we wetted the bare earth and then unloaded the truck, but soon got bored of watching us and left off to do whatever it is blowhards do without anyone to witness.

Joon took out the first long sheet of turf and dropped it to the ground.

I stared. "You've got to be shitting me," I said.

Joon was giving me a devil smile, that tip-me-fuck-me grin of his that then shifted into a quieting shhhhh. He kept his hands down low on the sod where anyone could see them. A TufTurf. A leftover section from but a few days prior. We were going to sell this man his own lawn back.

Joon had gone back to the warehouse to grab his last paycheck and his personal tools, and seen the remainder of the tuffy in pieces in the dumpster. So he pulled it out and stashed it in his pickup. There wasn't as much as we'd removed from the property just a few days before, since some of it was now proper lawn at the bungalow, and some of it we'd abandoned in the hills. What we had there onsite made up just about half the footprint. All the same, just to make sure the tuffy didn't look exactly the way it used to, we rotated each piece ninety degrees, leaving a big gap between the sections and a wide border at the edge.

We filled it in piecemeal. Joon had a network of contacts, other lawn movers he could hit up for scrap, so he had brought a collection of odd sod. All the usual kinds and then some. Joon plotted how we would piece the lawn together. Then we took off our shoes, trimmed the swatches and stitched them all in place. We even oiled it at the end, though purely for our own pride.

Maybe it was seeing the same lawn in a new way. Maybe it was how Joon accessorized the cheap TufTurf sod with quality accents that made it all seem rich. But it really did look quite striking. The contrast of colors and textures made every shadowed blade appear more perfect than the one before, such that no matter where one looked the grass was always greenest, even as the eye returned to the selfsame spot from which its wandering had begun. It was an all-original. A one of a kind. The first, complete, authentic Lindorff lawn that ever there was.

By the time we'd finished it was late in the day, and late enough in the summer that it was already getting on towards dark, and our tools not yet even back in the truck. Joon and I just walked around out there, barefoot in the grass, turning circles round each other in the quieting of the day, the newly oiled lawn swishing by beneath our feet. Hiding our grins. Then not. Me, watching Joon, watching me, as my highs and lows all mixed together, and a feeling like a kind of love came over me, the bearing of which was yet also a sadness, and me not knowing, not able, to sort out which was which was which.

**Mark A. Nobles**

# *Amber Hue*

The jackrabbit hopped willy-nilly across the West Texas dirt like a pinball swatted by flappers and bumpers, stopping only occasionally and briefly to nibble on a nipple beehive cactus or the fruit of a Christmas Chola.

Vladimir shifted slightly on the bench.

The night was clear, cool, still, and moonless, a welcome respite from the hot August sun. The Milky Way tracked across the sky northwest to southeast like a glistening ribbon of smoke and light. A longhorn beetle snacking on a fallen mesquite branch was moments away from becoming dinner for the approaching striped bark scorpion, who was himself seconds away from becoming a midnight snack for the diving burrowing owl. The tarantula hawk wasp purposefully scurried across the brown tarantula's web sending vibrations into the spider's burrow, drawing her out. The unsuspecting female advanced out the dirt expecting to be the predator but instead became the prey. The struggle appeared epic, but the outcome was never in doubt. In minutes, the tarantula hawk wasp was dragging the brown tarantula back to her own burrow to become food for her larvae. The nine banded armadillo carcass rotted in the east bound lane of 1008, food for flies, beetles, and turkey vultures. The dirt and skies of West Texas are a constant theater of death.

Vladimir pulled a canteen from his brown paper sack and drank water on the bench.

A large flock of altocumulus clouds ambled over and past seven parallel and stationary nimbostratus clouds. The nimbostratus had been welching on their promise of an early fall thunderstorm all morning when the Post Office truck from the Sectional Facility in Lubbock barreled down County Road 54, kicking up dust and bustling Vladimir's black pants, jacket, and wide brim hat. The truck driver must have been lost as the route from Lubbock to Muleshoe did not run through the intersection of County Roads 54 and 1008.

Vladimir relieved himself and returned to his seat on the bench.

A molting red star pullet came from the direction of the setting sun and crossed the road.

Vladimir ate a cucumber sandwich from his brown paper sack on the bench.

The Blue Norther galloped through more fierce and brutal than the four horsemen of the apocalypse. The gale force wind shook the metal sign for County Road 1008 and threatened to shake it out of the dirt. The sign for County Road 54 stood true and straight, horizontal to the gale, but frost from the sudden drop in temperature coated the length of the sign. Vladimir's black wide brimmed hat gusted by the storm was later found and eaten by Jacob Housegow's billy goat all the way down in Pep.

Vladimir rubbed his eyes and scratched his nose while sitting on the bench.

The spring air was crystal and dry. The sun climbed the horizon, bathing the cacti, mesquite, and sage in gentle yellow. A cock crowed in the east. A Texas spiny lizard ate a katydid before she had the chance to lay her eggs in the hard packed dirt.

Vladimir napped on the bench.

A solitary figure approached on foot from the east on County Road 1008. Three hours and twenty-four minutes elapsed from the time the figure appeared as a speck on the horizon before reaching Vladimir's bench.

"I came as fast as I could, Vladimir."

"That's as fast as you can go?"

"It is."

Vladimir crumpled the empty brown paper sack and looked around. "There should be a trash basket out here."

"One would think."

"Are you ready to continue, Estragon, or would you like a repose?"

Estragon stretched his arms, twisted his torso, and looked around.

Vladimir tossed his lunch sack on the ground and the moderate breeze blew it in the general direction of Farwell, a nervous little town on the edge of death and the border of New Mexico ten miles to the northeast of the bench at the crossroads of County Roads 1008 and 54.

Estragon dropped his arms to his side. "I can continue to mosey."

Vladimir stood from the bench, turned to the north, grabbed Estragon's frail hand, and the two stepped off, and continued their journey north along County Road 54.

A ringtail cat came from the southwest, hopped on the bench, still warm from Vladimir's posterior, and watched the figures slowly shrink on the horizon.

# About the Authors

**J. S. Allen**, PhD, is a neurodivergent writer in Fort Worth, Texas. Psycholinguist, anthropologist, microbiologist, data scientist are all words that fail to describe him. Hypergraphia is a clinical term that does not adequately describe his compulsion, since early childhood, to write a hectology of interconnected tales set in an imaginary world.

**Alicia K. Anderson** is a PhD Candidate in Mythological Studies and Depth Psychology. Her stories have appeared in anthologies by World Weaver Press and Improbable Press. She tweets about everything from mythology and storytelling to her experiences as a late diagnosed autistic at @A_K_Anderson.

**[sarah] Cavar** is a PhD student, writer, and critically Mad transgender-about-town. They are Editor-in-Chief at Stone of Madness and swallow::tale literary presses, and have had work in *Bitch Magazine*, *Disability Studies Quarterly*, *Electric Literature*, *The Offing*, and elsewhere. Their third chapbook, *Out of Mind & Into Body* (2022) is available now from Ethel Press. Cavar lives online at www.cavar.club and tweets @cavarsarah.

**Luigi Coppola** is a teacher, poet, first generation immigrant and avid rum and coke drinker. Shortlisted for Bridport Prizes, longlisted for the Ledbury and National Poetry Competitions, publications include Worple Press' anthology

*The Tree Line, Acumen, Ink, Sweat and Tears, Iota, Magma, Rattle*, and *Rialto* (LuigiCoppolaPoetry.blogspot.co.uk).

**Julie Sondra Decker** is a Floridian author who writes fantasy, science fiction, contemporary fiction, and nonfiction in both short and long forms. She is the author of *The Invisible Orientation* (Skyhorse/Carrel, 2014, a Lambda Award finalist). She is a passionate activist, hobbyist musician, amateur baker, jellybean eater, prolific doodler, cartoon enthusiast, and collector of thingies. Her other short work can be found in *Kaleidotrope, James Gunn's Ad Astra, Timeless Tales, After Dinner Conversation, Psychology Today, Good Vibrations, Everyday Feminism, Drunk Monkeys*, and *The Toast.*

**CB Droege** is an author and voice actor from the Queen City living in the Millionendorf. His latest book is *Quantum Age Adventures*. Short fiction publications include work in *Nature Futures, Science Fiction Daily*, and dozens of other magazines and anthologies. Learn more at cbdroege.com.

**Dean Gloster** is a writer of young adult and middle grade fiction in Berkeley, California. His YA novel *Dessert First* is out now from Simon & Schuster. This is his second story for *Spoon Knife.*

**Anastasia Jill** (she/they) is a queer writer living in the Central Florida. She has been nominated for Best American Short Stories, Best of the Net, and several other honors. Her work has been featured with *Poets.org, Pithead Chapel, Contemporary Verse 2, OxMag, Broken Pencil*, and more.

**Nikoline Kaiser** is the author of several poems and short stories, including "ode to an asexual" published with *Strange Horizons* and "The Dawn Was Gray" with *Underland Arcana*. Their work focuses on family, feminism and queer themes. They live in Denmark and have a Masters degree in Comparative Literature from Aarhus University. When not writing they work on a project communicating knowledge about women authors around the world.

**Nick Mamatas** is the author of several novels, including *I Am Providence* and *The Second Shooter*. His short fiction has appeared in *Best American Mystery Stories*, *Asimov's Science Fiction*, and many other venues. Much of his short fiction was recently collected in *The People's Republic of Everything*. Nick is also an anthologist, most recently of *Wonder and Glory Forever: Awe-Inspiring Lovecraftian Fiction*. Nick's editorial work and writing have been variously nominated for the Hugo, World Fantasy, Bram Stoker, Shirley Jackson, and Locus awards.

**Mark A. Nobles** is a sixth-generation Texan. Born on Fort Worth's infamous Jacksboro Highway, Mark proudly claims blood and kinship with Thunder Road's gamblers, outlaws, and wastrels. He is a Pushcart nominee and his work has appeared in various publications and anthologies. He is the author of *Fort Worth's Rock & Roll Roots* and his historical novel, *We're for Smoke* was published by TCU Press in 2021. Mark lives in Fort Worth but hopes to die in the desert.

**Carmen Peters** (she/they) is a writer and student living in Portland, Oregon. As a lover of horror and speculative fiction they aren't afraid to dive into the deep end, and as a sapphic trans woman she strives to express the magic of queerness. In their spare time they enjoy tarot, exploring strange nooks and crannies, and recalling nightmare fuel from her childhood. Their latest fiction can be read in *Prismatic Dreams: An Anthology of Queer Speculative Fiction*. She can be found on Instagram@Carmen_Dreams_Ghosts.

**Taylor Rae** is a professional mountain troll who holds her bachelor's degrees in psychology and English literature from the University of Idaho. She writes about lost gods, spaceships, and lost gods in spaceships. Her work appears/is forthcoming in *Pseudopod*, *Flash Fiction Online*, and *Fit for the Gods* from Vintage Books.

**Dora M Raymaker**, PhD, is an Autistic/queer/genderqueer scientist/author/multi-media artist and troublemaker whose work across disciplines focuses on social justice, systems thinking, and the dance between hope and fear. Dora is author of the novels *Hoshi and the Red City Circuit* and *Resonance* (in which a much older Jordis Ansari appears), and short works in various *Spoon Knife* anthologies.

**Dani Alexis Ryskamp** is a freelance writer and the editor of *Spoon Knife 2: Test Chamber* (with Sam Harvey). Dani is not the same person as when these poems were written and will be an entirely different person again by the time they are published. Let's hope that person is better than this one.

**Holly Schofield** travels through time at the rate of one second per second, oscillating between the alternate realities of city and country life. Her short stories have appeared in *Lightspeed*, *Analog*, *Escape Pod*, and many other publications throughout the world. Find her at hollyschofield.wordpress.com.

**Emily Jon Tobias** is an American author and poet raised in the Midwest who lives and works on the coast of Southern California. Her work has appeared in literary journals such as *Santa Clara Review*, *Talking River Review*, *Flying South Literary Journal*, *Furrow Literary Journal*, *The Opiate Magazine*, *The Ocotillo Review*, and *Jerry Jazz Musician* with work nominated for the Pushcart Prize, *Typehouse Literary Magazine*, and upcoming in *Tahoma Literary Review* and *Big Muddy*, among others. She holds an MFA in Writing from Pacific University Oregon and a bachelor's degree in creative writing from the University of Wisconsin Milwaukee.

**Heather Truett** is an MFA candidate and an autistic author. Her debut novel, *Kiss and Repeat*, was released in 2021. She has published poetry and short fiction with *Drunk Monkeys*, *Split Rock Review*, and *Hunger Mountain*, and she serves on staff for *The Pinch*.

**Cirrus Wood** is a writer, photographer, bicyclist, journalist, polyglot, and general *bon vivant* who lives and works in Berkeley, California. Though trained as a food writer, he dabbles in fiction on the side. Aside from *Spoon Knife*, his writing has appeared in *The Sun*, *The San Jose Mercury*, *Taste*, and *Alta*, as well as on postcards, on grocery lists, and in the missed connections section of Craigslist, where he writes personalized messages to all the drivers who cut him off in traffic. "Lawn Moving" is his first piece of published fiction.

# About the Editors

**Mike Jung** is the author of *Geeks, Girls, and Secret Identities, Unidentified Suburban Object,* and *The Boys in the Back Row,* and has contributed to the anthologies *Spoon Knife 3: Incursions, (Don't) Call Me Crazy, The Hero Next Door,* and *You Are Here: Connecting Flights.* His books have been honored by the Bank Street College of Education, Children's Book Council Reading Beyond List, Cooperative Children's Book Center, Georgia State Book Awards, Iowa Children's Choice Awards, Kansas State Reading Circle, National Parenting Publications Awards, Parents Choice Foundation, and Texas Bluebonnet Awards. He's proud to be a founding member of the #WeNeedDiverseBooks team, and lives in Oakland, California, with his family.

**Nick Walker** is an author of neuroqueer speculative fiction and equally speculative nonfiction, including the essay collection *Neuroqueer Heresies,* a handful of stories in previous volumes of *Spoon Knife,* and the ongoing urban fantasy webcomic *Weird Luck* (in collaboration with co-author Andrew M. Reichart and artist Mike Bennewitz). She's previously served as co-editor of *Spoon Knife 3: Incursions* and *Spoon Knife 5: Liminal.* Some of her essays, interviews, and academic-type work can be found at neuroqueer.com, and *Weird Luck* can be found at weirdluck.net.